Born in South Yorkshire, Wendy is the youngest daughter of John and Connie Moxon. She had her first book published at the age of 70. She enjoys embroidery and loves art. Liverpool is one of her favourite places to visit and she loves visiting The Walker Art Gallery and the Lady Lever Art Gallery on the Wirral.

All the best
Wendy Gill
30/05/2023

To my husband, Kevin Gill, for his continued support and encouragement.

To the ladies that lunch: June Pickles, Pat Roe and June Ogley.

Wendy Gill

CHESTER'S FAULT

AUSTIN MACAULEY PUBLISHERS™

LONDON · CAMBRIDGE · NEW YORK · SHARJAH

A CIP catalogue record for this title is available from the British Library.

ISBN 9781528946490 (Paperback)
ISBN 9781528971799 (ePub e-book)

www.austinmacauley.com

First Published (2020)
Austin Macauley Publishers Ltd
25 Canada Square
Canary Wharf
London
E14 5LQ

To my son, Spencer Gill, daughter, Deborah Hotchkiss, and sisters, Valerie Owen and Carol Wood, for being supportive and giving me confidence to continue having my stories published.

Chapter One

Clara ran up the steps leading to an impressive oak door and pulled the bell. She heard footsteps heading towards her, and the door was opened by a butler dressed in dark blue livery.

He looked taken aback upon seeing a young woman dressed in the modern trend of slim fitting long dress, the height of fashion.

"Can I help you?" he asked, looking down his nose at her.

In the year 1829, it was not the correct behaviour for a lady of quality and her young years to be knocking on the door of a wealthy bachelor without being accompanied by a chaperone.

"I have come to see Lord Hunter," the young woman said.

"Is he expecting you, Miss?" the butler wanted to know.

"No. I am the last person he will be expecting to see, but nevertheless, I must insist on seeing him."

"In that case, I am sorry, Miss. I cannot let you in unless you have an appointment."

Ignoring the butler, Clara pushed past him. Walking across the hall, she opened the first door she came to and looked inside. It was a library, but alas, empty.

Clara went to the next door and flung it open, and this time she was rewarded by the sight of an elegant gentleman dressed in a tailcoat, tight trousers and shinning top boots.

Ignoring his startled expression, Clara advanced into the room.

The butler followed close on her heels and said, "I am sorry, my lord, this young lady burst in when I told her I could not allow her admittance unless she had an appointment."

"No matter, Wilson, if the young lady is so determined to see me, I am most interested to find out why."

"Very well, my lord," replied the butler.

"May I at least know your name?" asked Lord Hunter.

"Miss Clara Lander."

"Am I supposed to know that name?" he asked.

"You may be able to fool those silly young girls who inhabit the ballrooms of Frithwood with that innocent look, but you cannot fool me."

"So, it would seem," was his reply.

"Do you deny refusing to give your permission for your sister to marry my brother?"

"My sister is above the age of one and twenty. She does not need my permission to marry if she so wishes."

"She may be of marriageable age, but if you told her not to marry, I am reliably informed, she would do as you bid," she flashed at him.

"If you have met my sister, you would know how far off the mark you are," he countered.

A low, constant growl came from a black Labrador that was sitting by the fireplace eyeing Clara with distrust.

"Oh, for heaven's sake, shut up," she snapped at it.

The Labrador lay down on his stomach and placed his head between his front paws and gave Clara, a soulful look.

"Now look what you've done," Clara accused the gentleman and went over to the dog, crouched down and started stroking it on the head.

"I am sorry for shouting at you, but it's very rude to make that noise while I am trying to talk. I know it is not your fault. You do not know any better, living with him." Clara shot his lordship a quick glance from her crouched position.

The dog, going from being shouted at to being patted, jumped up and placed his front paws on the stranger's shoulders and proceeded to lick her face. At the same time, Clara overbalanced, gave a delighted laugh and tried to push the dog off.

The door was flung open once more. Two youths of about eleven years of age rushed in, each holding a pistol in front of him with both hands and they both said in unison, "Stick um up."

The youths were wearing the same cut of clothes and sporting the same face.

Wilson appeared behind the youths in the doorway and told his lordship, "I am sorry, my lord, these two boys are much quicker than I am."

"Never mind, Wilson, it would seem it is an open house here this morning. Go and have a cup of tea and calm yourself," Lord Hunter told the old retainer.

"Thank you, my lord." Wilson closed the door before his lordship could change his mind.

Clara, still sitting on the floor was shaking her head at the two boys.

The dog sat next to her, wagging its tail at all this unexpected commotion.

His lordship, instead of being angry at this turn of events was beginning to enjoy himself.

Addressing the two youths who stood in the doorway, he demanded, "Are those pistols loaded?"

"Loaded, of course, they are not loaded. What do you take us for, flats?" the youth looked insulted that the gentleman should even have to ask. "If we went about carrying loaded pistols, Oscar would cut off our allowance."

The gentleman strode over to the door and took the pistols from them, and he checked to make sure both pistols weren't loaded. Satisfied, he put the pistols on the table where he perched on the edge with his ankles crossed.

The young lady was still sitting on the floor next to the dog completely unself-conscious.

Turning to the two boys his lordship asked, "You two are twins I take it?"

One of the youths who had walked across the room to look out of the window remarked, "Of course we are, it doesn't take a genius to work that out," the youth by the window said.

As he looked out of the window at the spacious back garden, his twin said, "I say, Lee, look at him, he's a beauty."

The twins threw themselves on the floor, one at either side of the dog and put their arms around his neck.

"These two urchins are related to you I suppose?" the gentleman addressed Clara.

Before Clara had time to reply the door opened and a young woman in her early twenties came into the room and stopped short.

"Oh, I am sorry, I did not know you had visitors," her bright blue eyes took in the scene, and they danced with delight.

"As I understand it, you know their brother," Lord Hunter told her.

"Do I? How interesting, may I enquire of this gentleman's name?" the young lady asked.

Finding herself the object of two bright blue eyes, Clara lifted up her chin and said, "Oscar Lander," keeping her eyes on the young lady.

"Oscar Lander. I'm sorry, but I do not seem to recollect the name," the young lady replied.

"He told you to say that," Clara said indicating the gentleman with a nod of her head.

Before the young lady had time to reply the door opened behind her and this time a gentleman about the same age and height as Lord Hunter came striding into the room. He glanced around the room and saw the twins, each with an arm around the neck of a dog and his sister sitting on the floor beside them.

"What are you doing sitting on the floor?" he asked.

"He did it," Clara told him, indicating Lord Hunter.

"Really, Edwin," the second young lady addressed her brother, "I am surprised at you."

The newcomer smiled over at her and said, "Before you start accusing anyone, I think it might be a good idea to find out the full fact's first."

He walked over to the young woman sitting on the floor and held out his hands to help her stand.

Once on her feet, still holding her hands, the second gentleman only had to look down at his sister with an unspoken question in his eyes.

The young lady had to admit, "Well, he didn't actually push me, his dog did."

"At least that clears that up," said the second gentleman.

The young man turned and held out his hand to the gentleman sitting on the edge of the table and introduced himself, "Oscar Lander, and I think you must be, Lord Hunter."

"I am, and this," Lord Hunter indicated to the other young lady in the room, "Is my sister, Effie."

"I am pleased to make your acquaintance, Miss Hunter," Oscar gave her a slight bow.

"And I you," and Effie gave him a small curtsey.

"This pack of ruffians, belong to me as you might have already guessed. My sister, Clara, and the twins, Tom and Lee," explained Oscar.

"I understand you have asked my sister to marry you?" questioned Lord Hunter.

"Has he? I know nothing about this Edwin," Effie accused.

"I didn't know myself until five minutes ago. I thought you must have refused this gentleman's hand and these three are after my blood because of it," said his lordship.

The door burst open and in strode a young man wearing gleaming brown boots with a black turnover top, tight-fitting tan coloured trousers, red waistcoat, white shirt, blue cravat and a bright yellow tailcoat.

He burst out, "I say, Clara, I hope you haven't dropped me in it."

"What do you mean by that?" demanded his sister.

"You read the letter I sent to you about Lord Hunter refusing to give Oscar his sister's hand. I never meant it to go any further. Although I know it is something he would do, I was only winding you up. You fly to Oscar's defence at the least little thing so I thought it might be a good lark to see what you would do if I told you he had been refused the hand of the notorious Lord Hunter's sister. I didn't expect you to come around here stirring things up. I have just arrived home, and Trueman told me you had all gone to see Lord Hunter so I came to stop you making a cake of yourself."

"Too late for that," said his elder brother Oscar, "What are you doing home from boarding school, I thought there were another two weeks to go before the holidays?"

"I have been rusticated, but it is most unfair. There was this travelling circus and they had a dancing bear. Poor thing…"

He was stopped mid-sentence by his brother who said, "The mention of a dancing bear is explanation enough, thank you. This, Lord Hunter, is my younger brother Harvey. I think you both owe Lord Hunter an apology," Oscar said looking from Clara to Harvey.

"I do not. It is Harvey that owes the apology, not me," said his defiant sister.

Lord Hunter and Oscar exchanged glances, and Lord Hunter said, "You have my sympathy."

This did not go down very well with Oscar, and he replied, "You are mistaken, Sir, I would have her no other way."

Oscar turned back to Clara with just the slightest of raised eyebrows.

Clara said ungraciously, "I apologise. I may have been mistaken."

Lord Hunter made a small bow and said with only a trace of a tremor in his voice, "Apology accepted."

All eyes turned to Harvey who had no such inhibitions as his sister.

He held out his hand and pumped Lord Hunter's hand while he said, "Lord yes, my apologies, Sir. I cannot wait to get back to school and tell them all I have met you. They will be green with envy."

"This is all very well, but I think it is me that needs the apology. After all, I have not had the chance to refuse the proposal of marriage, and at my age, they are getting less and less frequent," the offended Miss Hunter said.

"I shouldn't worry about not being offered for again. I think you are very beautiful for your age and after all, you are loaded," Harvey added.

"Why, thank you, young man," replied the lady with a polite nod of her head.

"What does Harvey mean when he says Effie is loaded?" asked Lee.

"It means she has big you-know-whats," replied his brother Tom and they both fell about laughing.

Clara looked over at Lord Hunter with a mischievous sparkle in her eye and was rewarded with a smile from the gentleman that matched her own humour.

"I can only apologise for my brothers, Miss Hunter, but at least, Harvey got one statement right, you are beautiful. As for the twins, they will be dealt with when I get them home," Oscar looked over at Effie.

"Please, Mr Lander, don't apologise. To be truthful, I prefer the twin's version of being loaded to Harvey's inference. Do not chastise them on my account; it is something children find amusing at that age, I would not want to spoil their fun," Miss Hunter smiled.

"You are very gracious. I will remove them all now and take them home before they get into any more trouble. It has been a pleasure meeting you both," Oscar kissed Miss Hunter's hand and shook Lord Hunter's.

"It has also been a pleasure to meet all of you. I can assure you this meeting has certainly livened up my morning. Feel free to call whenever you like," Lord Hunter told them.

"Thank you, I return the invitation. I have rented number one hundred and thirteen for a few weeks, so we are just down the road. We have only been in the city for three weeks, mostly sightseeing, and have not met many people as yet.

"You might rue handing out such a generous invitation. My brother Harvey seems to have heard of you and stands in awe. You will have to forgive his attire; he is very young." Oscar smiled at his new friend.

"These are the height of fashion I will have you know, all the young bucks are wearing them," said the indignant young man.

Clara flew to her brother's defence and said, "I think he looks very dashing."

Miss Hunter nodded in agreement and said, "I agree. You look very smart, Harvey."

This comment, coming from the enemy, made Effie instantly Clara's best friend and she sent the young woman a dazzling smile to which Effie responded by sending Clara one back. Their friendship was sealed.

A gentle tap came to the door, and Wilson announced, "Mr Elmer Wolf."

Clara saw Lord Hunters face turn to stone and turning to Effie she saw Effie's face drain of colour and she was gripping her hands in front of her so tight her knuckles turned white.

A gentleman of small stature appeared in the doorway then made his way into the room. His dress, compared to that of Lord Hunter and Oscar's, could easily be described as, very well worn.

"Good morning to you all. Wilson told me you had visitors, but as it is so early in the morning, I was curious to meet them. This is a pleasant little party indeed. I told Wilson I was sure you would not mind me joining you," the new visitor looked at Lord Hunter and waited to be introduced.

"If my butler told you I had visitors, Mr Wolf, in polite society, it would have been better if you had left your card and come back at a later date or time. But as you are here, let me introduce you to our friends, this is the Lander family," said Lord Hunter who then added in a cold clipped tone, "They have been invited. What brings you here, may I ask?"

"I know you only jest with me, my lord," he held out his hand to Oscar then shook hands with the others.

"Elmer Wolf, Effie's fiancé, at your service. Effie, my love, I have come to take you for a walk in the park. It is such a lovely morning."

Clara went over to her new friend, tucked her hand through Effie's arm and said, "You are too late, Sir, Effie has offered to take my twin brothers and I to the fair. We are not as yet very streetwise of our surroundings, and Effie has been so kind as to offer to be our guide. Come along boys, time to go."

Lee and Tom jumped up and asked in unison, "Can we take the dog?"

Lord Hunter walked over to a desk by the window and took a leash from the bottom drawer and threw it over to them.

"I want to hold him," said Tom as he caught the leash.

"That's not fair; I want to hold him. Why should you have the first turn?" Lee wanted to know.

"I'll tell you what," said Lord Hunter, "I will toss a coin and whichever twin wins the toss may hold him on the way there, and the other on the way back, then you have both had a turn."

Lord Hunter took a coin out of his pocket and tossed it in the air, deftly catching it on its way down. He placed the coin on the back of his other hand and looked at Lee and asked, "Which one are you?"

"Tom," replied Lee.

There was a discreet cough from his left, and he had the grace to blush before amending, "Lee, I am Lee, he is Tom."

"Well, Lee, what is it to be, heads or tails?"

"Heads," called Lee.

Lord Hunter removed his hand and offered the coin for them to see. "Tails," shouted a delighted Tom, "I'm holding him first."

"We will be on our way now," said Effie grabbing Clara's hand and practically dragging her to the door.

Once outside Clara said to Effie, "Is he really your fiancé?"

"I am afraid so," admitted Effie.

"But he looked like a little creep," Clara told her. "His hand was damp when we shook hands, and he has pinholes for eyes to say nothing about how he smelled. Surely you cannot be in love with him? You are so very beautiful and such an elegant lady, there is no way that you can hold that man in affection. I am sorry if I am talking out of turn, for it is none of my business, but I saw your reaction when the man was admitted, and it was not the reaction of a young woman who is madly in love."

"Yes, Elmer Wolf is a little creep and no, I do not love him, I detest him."

"Then why in heaven's name are you engaged to him?"

Effie took a deep breath and told Clara, "Some years ago when I was young and foolish, I thought I was in love with a captain of the guard, and I wrote him a very amorous letter. When I say amorous, Clara, I mean amorous. Somehow Elmer Wolf got hold of the letter, and now he is blackmailing me.

"Nobody likes him. He is desperate to gain membership to a gentleman's club called The Ravens.

To become a member of this club, an existing member has to sign them in. It is supposed to stop gentlemen, who are not considered gentlemen, gaining membership. As Edwin's brother-in-law, it looks like he will become a member.

"I cringe with shame every time I set eyes on him. It's just that I have not hit on a way to get my letter back and he is becoming more and more demanding. I agreed to become engaged to him on the condition it was kept secret. Edwin is the only person who is aware of the engagement. Elmer is pushing me to name a date for the wedding and I cannot, Clara, I just cannot marry him," Effie told Clara.

"Why don't you tell Edwin? I am sure he would think of a way to get the letter back. I saw the way Edwin's attitude changed when the Wolf was shown in. He did not like him in the least."

"Can you blame him? Oh, Clara, I would die if Edwin ever saw that letter and if the Wolf should put it in the daily paper for all the city to see, I would never be able to show my face anywhere again," Effie moaned.

"We shall have to put our heads together and think of a way to get the letter back."

"Would you, Clara, would you really help me to get the letter back? I feel much better for having told someone about the letter and although I do not know you, I feel we have been friends forever."

"I know. I knew I was going to like you as soon as you stuck up for Harvey. Let us forget about the Wolf and enjoy our day at the fair. We are nearly there, for I can hear the music and smell cooking."

Tom and Lee went on ahead with the dog happily trotting by their side. One or the other of them kept turning around to make sure they were still in sight of Clara and Effie, and when they arrived at a pie stall,

Clara fished some change out of her pocket and bought them all a pie. Even the dog was treated to one, once it had cooled down.

They had turns on the coconut shy and hoopla, then Tom spotted a hot air balloon standing in an open field and of course, they had to go and have a look.

"Sixpence a ride," shouted the balloon attendant.

"Can we have a go, Clara, please? We have to have a go, please, Clara, please," begged the twins.

"Sorry, I don't have any money left. What little money I had on me is spent, after all, I had not intended to come to the fair when I set out this morning so I did not bring much money with me," she told them.

"I have some money," Effie said. "Let me see if I have enough for us all. I would like to have a ride in the hot air balloon too. Wouldn't you, Clara?"

"I most certainly would."

Effie fished in her pocket and pulled out a pound note. Handing the note over to the attendant she said, "Four please."

"You will have to tie the dog up. No dogs allowed in the balloon," the attendant pointed to a railing. "I will get you your change. Why don't you all get in the basket and I will join you in a trice, and then we can be off."

Lee asked Effie what they called the dog, and Lee was told his name was Chester.

"I am sorry I have to tie you up, Chester, but we will be back to get you when we have had our trip in the balloon," he told the dog whilst he fastened him to the railings.

Lee ran to join the others who were already installed in the basket.

Chester, on the other hand, was having none of it. He pulled at his restraint, and without much of a tussle he was free and charging after the retreating Lee.

No sooner had Lee been helped into the basket than Chester took a flying leap and landed in the basket with such force there was a cracking sound and the balloon tipped to one side. One of the anchor ropes had snapped. The sudden pull to one side was too much for the other anchor rope and that too snapped.

The four adventurers and their dog found themselves airborne.

Chapter Two

By the time Clara and Effie had managed to pick themselves up from the basket floor, they had floated out of sight of the fairground below. Although there wasn't a strong wind, the gentle breeze carried them effortlessly along.

"Do you know how to stop this thing?" Effie asked.

"No, do you?"

"No, but we are going to have to find out before we get carried much further," said Effie.

The two boys were now on their feet and looking over the edge of the basket, neither worried about their predicament but pointing out landmarks to each other.

Chester was standing between them on his hind legs, his front paws on the edge of the basket barking his head off and wagging his tail.

Clara looked around then above her head, and she saw a chain with a handle attached so she took hold of it saying, "I wonder what this does?"

Giving the chain a yank, the basket plummeted down, and the four found themselves once more in a heap on the basket floor.

Jumping up Clara shouted, "Throw the sandbags over the edge we are descending too rapidly. We need to lose some weight."

They each took hold of one of the sandbags and heaved it over the side, and the balloon stopped descending but continued to float away.

"Right," said Clara, "At least we now know how to lose height, so I am going to gently pull this chain then release it and see what happens. Hold onto the side."

Gently pulling on the chain then releasing it, the balloon began to slowly deflate, but Clara had no control over where it was going to land, or if indeed, she could land it at all without injury or worse to them all.

"We seem to be heading for that wood, Clara. Can you make it go left or right?" Effie shouted.

"I can't make it do anything; it has a mind of its own. We are losing height, and I think, too fast, but there is nothing I can do. Better hold on real tight because as you said, Effie, I think we are destined to land in that wood," Clara shouted back.

There was a loud hissing noise, and the flame cut out. The balloon started to deflate at an alarming rate. They all held onto the side of the basket with the exception of Clara who stood in the middle trying to control their descent without any success.

They came to an abrupt halt when the basket hit the top of the trees and became lodged. The balloon canopy completely deflated and covered the basket rendering the occupants in total darkness.

"Is everyone alright?" Effie wanted to know.

"I am," shouted Lee.

"Me too," confirmed Tom. "But I think Chester is hurt, I heard him yelp."

"That is because I landed on top of him," Clara replied. "Have you got your penknife on you, Tom?"

"Of course, I have. I always carry it with me just in case we get carried away in a hot air balloon," Tom mocked.

"Well, cut one of the ropes so we can move this canopy away, then we will be able to see where we have landed," Clara told him.

Tom felt in his pocket and produced his penknife and proceeded to cut a couple of the ropes. Once the canopy was pulled to one side, Effie was the first to poke her head out.

All were unharmed, even Chester who was only winded when Clara had landed on him.

The basket was lodged between two tall trees with plenty of footholds for them all to climb down, except for Chester.

Clara told Tom to cut two long lengths of rope, then taking the ropes she tied one under Chester's stomach but behind his front legs, then did the same at his back end so he had two slings to support him while he was lowered down to the ground.

"You two boys go down first. Effie and I will lower Chester down, but if he gets stuck on any of the branches, one of you will have to climb up and rescue him. Off you both go, and take care."

When the boys were safely on the ground, Clara shouted down to them, "Are you ready to catch him?"

"Yes, send him down," Lee shouted back.

Clara took the rope that was fastened at the front of Chester and Effie the one to the back, and they lifted Chester up and over the side of the basket then began to let the rope out slowly until he too was safely on the ground with the twins making a huge fuss of him.

Chester much relieved to have his feet on firm ground once more began to bark his approval.

Effie went next, and she had no difficulty in reaching the ground.

Before Clara descended, she called to Tom to climb back up the tree, she needed his penknife.

When Tom reached the basket again, he gave Clara his penknife, and she proceeded to cut all the ropes that attached the balloon to the basket, then she dropped the ropes to the ground.

Clara pulled the balloon back into the basket and began to fold it up, and then she dropped that too, down to the ground.

The balloon landed at Effie's feet.

Tom and Clara climbed down the tree and joined the others.

Clara, who was used to climbing trees to rescue her younger brothers, was impressed with Effie and she told her so.

"You managed to climb down that tree without a scream or hysterics. I am impressed, Effie. Not even a tear or tantrum when we found ourselves alone, floating along in the hot air balloon with no idea how we were going to land."

"So, did you, Clara. In fact, you were even braver than me. You managed to get us back down to earth. I was more than happy to be up there with you all. It made a change from the humdrum my life has become. There was no way the Wolf was going to appear without warning while I was up there like he usually does, and anyway, there was no time to throw a tantrum, it all happened so quickly. To be truthful, I would not have missed it for the world," Effie grinned.

"Why have you thrown the balloon down, Clara, why not leave it up in the trees?" asked Lee.

"We do not know how long it will be before we get back home so I thought if we roll up the material and tie it off with the ropes, we could take it with us. And if we found ourselves abroad during the night, we could use it as a shelter or a blanket to keep us warm. As for the rope, you never know when it might come in handy. We have nothing to lose by taking it with us. We can take turns in carrying it," Clara told him. "Come on, let's roll it up as tight as we can and be on our way."

"I'm hungry," wailed Tom.

"Me too," agreed Lee.

Chester barked and wagged his tail.

"While we were airborne, I saw a river running to the left of the wood; we were going against the flow. If we can find that river, we can follow the flow and hope it takes us back the way we came. There might even be some fish in the river we could catch," Clara told them, and she tucked her hand through Effie's arm, and the happy little band set off.

Word had got around by now that a hot air balloon had broken free from its moorings with two women, two boys and a dog on board.

Trueman, out on an errand for Oscar, heard the whisperings. He had been the Landers' butler for nigh on twenty years, and he knew how easy it was for the children to get into a scrape. As soon as he heard the words air balloon and disaster, he knew it could only be the Landers.

Trueman set off back to the house at a brisk walk, up the front steps and into the parlour without knocking hoping to find Oscar there.

"Begging your pardon, Mr Lander, but I was in the kitchen over at the Garner's house when a maid came in saying there had been an incident at the fair. An air balloon broke free of its moorings carrying two women, two children and a dog off into the blue yonder, with no attendant."

"Devil take it, it has to be Clara, Effie and the boys. I am going down the road to number ninety-nine. Have my horse saddled for when I get back." Oscar headed down the street.

Ringing the doorbell of Lord Hunter's house, Oscar did not wait until it was answered but turned the doorknob and walked into the hall at the same time as Wilson, the butler, was heading across the hall to answer the door.

"Is his lordship in?" asked Oscar.

Wilson, recognising the visitor, said, "In the library, Sir," and indicated to a door leading off the hall.

Oscar walked over to the door and pushed it open. He found Lord Hunter sitting at a large desk with a quill in his hand, "Edwin, have you heard?"

"Heard what?" asked the surprised gentleman.

"A hot air balloon has broken free of its moorings at the fairground with two women, two children and a dog on board. It has to be our lot. This is the type of thing Clara is always getting herself into, I am sorry to say," Oscar told him.

"Yes, it has to be them, no doubt about that. It is the type of thing Effie gets into too. Do you know which way they went?" Lord Hunter asked.

"No, I came here as soon as I heard. I have left instructions for my horse to be saddled for when I get back. I am going to look for them. I just came to let you know," Oscar turned and headed back home for his horse.

Lord Hunter rang the bell, and when Wilson came into the room, Edwin asked him to have his horse saddled and brought to the front of the house. Then Edwin ran upstairs to get changed.

Chapter Three

The adventurers headed in the direction they hoped the river could be located in with the twins and Chester running off in front.

Effie said to Clara, "I don't know anything about you, Clara, where do you come from and why have I not seen you out and about in the city?"

"We come from a little village called Styleham, about three miles from a town called Meeks. We own a farm, quite a big farm and have about ten people working for us. Poor Oscar was only eighteen when our parents died, and he was left to look after Harvey, who was eight, the twins three and me eleven.

"It was not until I had grown up that I realised what an enormous task befell him. Oscar has done a brilliant job, and I know he loves us all and he would not be without us. Things have got better for Oscar as we all became older. I help as much as I can with the twins.

"Harvey is away at boarding school and only home for the school holidays, or when he is rusticated. The twins will be going to boarding school next term. They will be going to the same school that Harvey goes to. It will be Harvey's final year and the twins' first year. I know Harvey will look after the twins and make sure they settle in," Clara told her.

"Will Harvey be helping Oscar to run your farm when he leaves boarding school?" Effie asked.

"No, Harvey has inherited an estate from our father's brother, and when he leaves school, Harvey will be running that. Oscar will be able to take things a bit easier then, I hope. At the moment Oscar is running both estates with a little help from Harvey when he is home on school holiday," Clara explained.

"What made you all come to Frithwood?" asked Effie.

"Oscar said it was about time he brought me to the city to try to make a lady of me. I told him I was happy as I am and he had no need to put himself out on my behalf, but now, having met you, Effie, I can see my education is sadly lacking. You are a very elegant lady, and I shall strive to be as ladylike as you. I shall watch you very closely and try to behave like you."

Effie laughed, "I am not much more ladylike than you are. You saw for yourself I am well able to climb a tree and I am enjoying myself in this adventure. I would be very sorry to see you turned into one of these so-called ladies who look down their noses at everybody.

"You are such a refreshing change. I feel I can be myself when I am with you and not have to think about what I say or do all the time. I have never told anybody about the Wolf, and within an hour of meeting you, I confided in you that I have written a very compromising letter and that I am being blackmailed."

"We will have to get the letter back. Where does the Wolf live?" asked Clara.

"He lives at the far end of Frithwood on File Street. It is not the best of locations and although Edwin has not forbidden me to get engaged to the Wolf, he has told me not to frequent File Street. He said if he hears I have been there he will have to have words with Elmer, and if he did that, I would fear for the Wolf's wellbeing. Not that

I care a fig about that, but I would hate to see Edwin behind bars because of me," Effie told her.

"Do you know what number File Street?"

"Number seventy-five, I understand it is the last house on the left, on the edge of the city. There are rows and rows of terraced houses in that part of the city, and I have heard a rumour that only two streets away from where the Wolf lives, there is a street called Page Street and it is known as Whore Alley," Effie informed Clara.

"That sounds charming," Clara said. "I still think you should tell Edwin about it, Effie. I would tell Oscar if something like that happened to me. He may be angry and give you a scolding about it, but I bet he would sort it out in a trice."

"I am sure he would. He would go and knock the Wolf's block off, or even worse, call him out. I could not bear it if anything happened to Edwin, especially because of me. There has only been the two of us since our parents died. My mother died in childbirth when I was six years old, and my father got pneumonia when I was twelve. I love Edwin very much. Edwin has brought me up, just like Oscar brought you and your brothers up. He has looked after me and given me a good life. No, I am determined to sort this out myself somehow," said a defiant Effie.

"Well, in that case, I shall help you. I will think of something and we will do it together. Better two heads than one. Don't you agree?"

"Yes, I do, not only do I agree; it is so good to have a friend to confide in." She held out her hand, and they shook on it.

A cry from the boys reached their ears, and they saw them pointing excitedly.

Following the direction, the twins were pointing in, Clara and Effie saw the river winding its way at a leisurely pace through meadows, into the distance. They picked up their skirts and ran after the boys.

Clara looked around but could see no cover. The ground was flat, and the river ran slowly along following a few large bends. It disappeared behind a slight rise in the landscape. Clara said they would head towards the rise. She wanted to find cover for them all before nightfall. She knew there was no way they would be home that night.

On approaching the rise, the roof of a building could just be seen peeking over the top.

They discovered what was under the roof as they skirted around the base of the rise. It looked like an old stone building or barn, and Clara said, "Let us hope it is not occupied, and then we can stay here for the night."

It turned out to be a one-roomed building with nothing inside but a wooden crate tipped on its side, an empty fireplace and two lopsided shelves bearing a variety of old tin mugs, cooking utensils, plates and a few spoons.

"It looks like a shepherd's retreat. What they make their way to in bad weather while they are out looking for their lost sheep. Not used much in the summer, so I think we should be all right here. We can't be too far from civilisation, but this will have to do for tonight. Pity there is no door on," Clara added.

Lee shouted to the two young women, and Clara and Effie joined the twins at the river's edge. The twins pointed into the water, and they all stood watching the fish swimming lazily just below the surface.

Effie said, "We could use the balloon as a big net and scoop them out. What do you think, Clara?"

"I think that is an excellent suggestion," Clara replied.

Clara told the boys to see if they could find some sticks so they could make a fire. Even better, if, when they found the sticks, to set a fire going in the fireplace. Clara knew the twins were more than capable of starting a fire by rubbing two sticks together. They had done it many times when out on one of their adventures. Then they could cook the fish over the fire.

Both Clara and Effie were glad they now had a roof over their heads for the night, and hopefully, they would be on their way back home early in the morning.

The boys were more than happy to go on a twig hunt and started heading for the top of the rise.

Effie and Clara laid the balloon out and set about making it into a net using the ropes they had brought with them. They began reattaching the ropes to the balloon.

Half an hour later one of the best catches of fish either of them had been privy to see was laid out on the grass before them. Placing the fish on top of the balloon and carrying it between them, they went to join the boys and Chester.

At the stone building, the fish was laid out on the grass and covered with the balloon, with the intention of leaving it for the boys to gut and clean.

Upon further inspection of the building, there was no glass in the windows and no door in the doorframe. The roof was in good order, and apart from under the two windows and the door entrance, the rest of the single room was dry enough.

Effie turned the wooden crate over so it could be used as a makeshift table.

There was no sign of the twins or Chester, "I wonder where the boys are?" Effie commented.

"They will turn up sooner or later," Clara told her. "I am going to take a couple of these pans and wash them in the river and bring back some water. We will have to filter the water through the balloon, to take out any creepy wriggly things that might be in it, and boil it first before we drink it. We can wash the balloon in the river, to get rid of the smell of fish and lay it out to dry. It won't take long to dry in this weather then we can use it for a blanket tonight. Will you be all right on your own until either the boys or I return? I will be as quick as I can."

"Yes, of course, I will. But I think it would be best if I came with you and take these plates and cups to wash so we can eat and drink in comfort," answered Effie.

"Good idea. In that case, we had better take the fish inside and lay them on top of the crate to stop any preying animals from stealing them. If the boys come back before we return, they will see the fish, and I am sure Tom will gut them for us. It's a good job he carries that penknife with him all the time. It has certainly been put to good use on this trip," Clara grinned.

On their return to the building, they found the boys had returned, and a fire was blazing in the grate.

Chester was laid out in front of the fire, and he managed a weak wag of his tail when the girls appeared, then he went straight back to warming his tummy.

"Where have you two been?" asked Clara.

"We went to see what is at the other side of the hill and there was an orchard. Look what we have got." Lee pointed to the corner, and to Clara's delight, she saw some crab apples laid out on the floor.

"Well done you two," beamed Effie, "fish for starters and apples for dessert. What more can one want?"

"I'm not sure Chester will agree with that, but there is enough fish for him not to go hungry, at least for tonight. Let's put this pan of water on to boil and place some of the fish on one of the plates and the steam will cook the fish," Clara told them and began to busy herself while Effie set out the tin plates and mugs on the upturned crate.

Tom and Lee went outside, taking the fish with them and set about gutting them.

After they had eaten Clara said they would have to sleep on the floor tonight, but at least it was dry. They had the balloon to use to cover them all and because they would all have to sleep together their body heat would help to keep them warm.

If Tom and Lee could find more sticks to keep the fire going all night it would be a big help.

There was also Chester who would be as good as any guard to let them know if danger approached.

"When we were coming back down the hill, I noticed what looked like a door leant up against the back wall. Even if it doesn't fit properly, we could use it to cover most of the door entrance then we should be quite safe from foxes or anything else that might smell the fish and come to investigate," Tom told them.

"What are you waiting for, off you and Lee go and let us see if we can fix up a door. Well spotted young man." Clara felt her chest fill with pride at the adaptability of the twins.

The twins had also found a plank of wood by the door, and they took that inside as well. Standing the door in the doorframe and placing the plank of wood on its end with one end digging into the floor and the other pushed against the door, they could feel safe from intruders while they slept.

The balloon had soon dried and was placed on the floor, being big enough to be used as a floor covering as well as a blanket. With Clara at one end, Effie at the other and the twins in the middle they pulled the balloon up and over them all, and it was not long before they were all fast asleep.

Lord Hunter and Oscar were not having such a good time of it. They had both set off on horseback heading in the direction they were told the balloon had drifted, but separating and agreeing to meet up later in the day at, The Wayside Inn.

A full afternoon searching the countryside and forgoing their tea and neither of them had seen or heard anything about a balloon. After dining in the private parlour Edwin and Oscar went to bed agreeing they would resume their search first thing in the morning.

Chapter Four

Next morning Effie woke before Clara, but the boys were nowhere to be seen.

Effie gently nudged Clara awake and said, "The boys are gone."

"Don't worry about them; they will return shortly. We had better go and get some more water and see if we can catch some more fish for breakfast. We will save the apples and take them with us to eat on the journey home."

When the two ladies returned with the water and more fish, they found Lee and Tom had a roaring fire going in the grate.

Lee pointed to the crate with a big grin on his face.

Lying in a neat row along the top of the crate sat six large brown hens' eggs.

"Where did you get those from?" asked Clara.

"On the other side of the orchard, there's a farm with a hen coop. We sneaked in and collected these. We only borrowed them, when we get home, we will ask Oscar to come and pay the farmer for them. We have not stolen them," explained Tom.

Satisfied with this explanation, Clara put the eggs on to boil, then the fish.

Chester had two of the eggs mixed in with two fish which he devoured in a flash.

Clara said as they had no more use for the balloon and they should leave it for the next occupants to make good use of.

Clara hoped they would be home later that day. But she added, they would take the ropes with them so, Tom coiled the ropes up using one rope to make them secure, he placed them over his shoulder.

The remainder of the apples were stuffed into any pockets that would hold them and then the happy little band were once more homeward bound.

Still following the flow of the river, they became aware of rooftops in the distance, so, cutting across the fields, they headed straight for them.

On entering a little village called Pinkly, they asked how far they were from the city of Frithwood and were told to head north for about ten miles. They were also told that they could catch the mail stagecoach which came through the village at 11 o'clock and they would be in Frithwood by 1 o'clock.

"It is a pity we don't have any money to purchase some tickets on the mail coach; we could be home in a couple of hours," Effie said.

"I have an idea," Lee told them. "Tom and I will jump on the back of the mail coach when nobody is looking and jump down once; we reach Frithwood. Then we can go and find either Oscar or Lord Hunter and get them to fetch the barouche for you two and Chester."

"I must say that is a very good idea, Tom. But will you be safe? Ten miles is a long way to hang onto the back of a coach. I would never forgive myself if either of you got hurt," Clara told him.

"We'll be all right. If we take some of the rope with us and tie ourselves to the coach, then we won't have to cling on for dear life. I don't fancy having to walk another ten miles, and I am sick of fish and apples," said Lee.

"Me too," agreed Tom, and Chester barked and wagged his tail in agreement.

"Very well, but only if you are sure," Clara agreed. "Come on, let's go and ask someone the route the mail coach is to take. I think it would be a better idea if we could hide near a corner where the coach will have to slow down so you two can jump on. If you try to climb on board while it is stationary in the village, you will be seen."

Heading north, following the directions they were given, they made their way through the village to a wood where the dirt road became narrower and the light much gloomier. They were told the stagecoach went through the wood, and they spent the next ten minutes deciding on the best spot to wait for the coach to pass by.

Clara, Effie and the twins sat and waited, keeping their fingers crossed that they had the right location.

"Don't forget you two, if the coach is travelling too fast for you to jump on safely, you are not to attempt it. Do you understand?" Clara asked.

"Stop worrying, Clara. We have done it before you know. We will be alright, won't we, Lee?"

"Of course, we will. Let's cut some strips of rope before the coach arrives. These ropes are too long, but make sure they are long enough to fit 'round our bodies to help keep us close to the coach. It will help make our hands hurt less from having to cling on too tight."

And so, when the mail coach came into view, slowly making its way north through the wood at walking pace, the two young boys waited until it had passed them by, then they crept out of their hiding place and had no trouble jumping on board.

Clara and Effie were pleased to see the twins tie one end of a rope to the big spring at either side of the coach then, they passed each other the loose end of their ropes and both boys took hold of the other's rope and pulled it across their backs and fastened it to the same spring as they had tied the other end of the rope to make two strong supports across their backs to help keep them safely held to the back of the coach. They managed to tie off the ropes before the mail started to increase its speed as it reached the end of the wood and disappeared out of sight.

Effie looked at Clara and asked, "Will they be alright?"

"I am sure they will. They look on it as an adventure and don't see any danger to themselves. They are very capable boys. It will not be long before you and I will be bouncing along in our very own transport." Clara tucked her hand through Effie's arm, and they proceeded to walk north. Heading in the direction the mail had taken.

Chester was happily bounding along beside them.

They walked in silence for a while then Clara said to Effie, "I have been thinking about your problem, Effie. The only way I can see for us to get the letter back from the Wolf is to burgle his house."

"Burgle his house! How on earth are we going to do that?" Effie gasped.

"You said he wanted to join this silly man's club, well, Lord Hunter is going to have to take him there for the night so we can break into his house and search for the letter," Clara told her.

"Edwin will never take him to his club, not in a million years. Anyway, I do not want Edwin to know about it. I am determined to get this letter back on my own without involving him."

"I do not see how it can be avoided. Let me tell you my plan before you reject it altogether. First, I will climb into Lord Hunter's bedroom and tell him he has to take the Wolf to his club for the night. I will tell him it is important that he keeps Elmer out of his house for as long as possible. I will not tell him why, just that if he doesn't want the Wolf for a brother-in-law, he has to play his part.

"I won't tell him you know anything about it. I will not even mention your name. Then, when Lord Hunter has agreed to it, he has to let me know when it is to take place, and I will tell you. I will borrow some of Harvey's clothes, and you and I will get dressed up as two gentlemen and go and search the Wolf's house. Find the letter and burn it, then you can throw the ring back in his face and be rid of him."

"It sounds all right apart from the bit where you have Edwin taking the Wolf to his club. Edwin will never agree to it, I know he won't," Effie replied adding, "but there is no ring, Clara, so I cannot throw it back in the Wolf's face although it is a very nice thought."

"If that is all that is worrying you, not wanting to ask Edwin to take the Wolf to the club. I will think of something to suggest to Lord Hunter, to get Elmer into the club without anyone knowing anything about it. I thought you might throw a tantrum at the thought of getting dressed up as a boy and refuse to do it," said a pleased Clara.

"Nothing of the kind, it is my silly mistake, and I am willing to do anything to get the letter back. It is Edwin that I am worried about. He has done so much for me, Clara. I would hate myself if he was made to sign the Wolf into his club. Once they have signed the register, they will be allowed into the club for life. I would not wish that on Edwin for anything; he loves his club. I could not do it, Clara, I really couldn't."

"I shall also think up a way so that he will not have to sign the register. There is always a way, Effie, and I am determined to figure it out. If I can work something out are you willing to have a go? A bit of burglary I mean?" Clara asked.

"The sooner, the better; I hate the man. I want him out of my life as soon as possible. I prefer burglary to this horrendous engagement."

"That is settled then. We should be home before tea with a bit of luck. I shall get some of Harvey's clothes and bring them to your house. Then you can show me which bedroom Lord Hunter sleeps in. Are there any ladders we could use for me to get up to his bedroom window?"

"Even better than that, there is a tree growing right outside his window. We used to climb down it when we were youngsters, before our father died, so he would not know we had left our bedrooms. I don't think you will have too much trouble climbing up the tree and then back down," Effie told her.

"Excellent. So, I will see you after dinner, let us get a move on with it and get the Wolf out of your life, Effie. I will not get Lord Hunter into any trouble, I promise. Agreed?" Clara asked her.

"Agreed," confirmed Effie.

The twins were glad of the ropes as the mail travelled along. Mostly the road was flat, and the coach driver cracked the whip, and the horses went into a gallop, but then they had to slow down when they hit rough patches on the road.

The jolting began to hurt the twins' feet, and their legs began to ache, but soon, they saw the built-up area of Frithwood and began to untie the ropes and hoped the mail would slow down enough for them to jump down.

An oncoming coach was their saviour. The driver of the mail had to nearly come to a standstill on a narrow part of the road, and both Lee and Tom jumped nimbly down and watched the coach move forward with the ropes trailing behind, leaving them standing in the middle of the road.

The sound of a horn being blown made the two boys leap onto the footpath as a horse and cart went lumbering past.

"Where are we?" asked Lee.

"No idea," replied his brother.

They were about to walk on when they felt a hand grab their shoulder and turning around, they saw Harvey in his multi-coloured clothes standing behind them.

Each twin grabbed a leg and clung on for dear life.

"Are we pleased to see you?" said Tom.

"And I am glad to see you two as well. Where have you been and where are Clara and Effie?" asked Harvey trying to extract the two boys from his legs.

"We got carried away by a hot air balloon, and Clara and Effie are walking back home, but it is about ten miles away. We said we would jump the mail and come and get someone to go for them in the barouche or something. Come on, Harvey, let's go and get them. There is Chester as well. We had to leave him with the girls we could not bring him with us on the back of the mail," explained Lee.

"So, you two rogues are only concerned about Chester, are you? Why didn't you all get on the mail?" asked Harvey. "It does carry passengers you know."

"Yes, we know, but we didn't have any money left. We spent it all at the fair and anyway the girls are all right. We like Effie, she is just like Clara, she has enjoyed our little adventure too," he was told.

"Why are you in the city anyway?" Lee wanted to know.

"I came in to see if there was any gossip about the balloon, to see if anyone had seen anything of it but there was no news. I saw the mail go past and you two standing on the back, so I followed it. I was pleased to see you jump down not far in front of me. I did not want to have to chase the mail all the way through the city. Glad to see you put some of my training to good use by jumping up behind the coach," Harvey approved.

"Yes, Clara was in a bit of a panic about our jumping on the back of the coach, but I told her we had done it before. Good job she didn't ask where and when, and who had taught us to do it, or it might have got back to Oscar. We came down in a wood, high up in the trees. It was a pretty deserted place. I bet that is why nobody saw us and why there has been no news of us," Tom told him.

Walking in the direction of home they had to pass Lord Hunter's residence to get to their own. Harvey ran up the steps, rang the bell and opened the front door.

Wilson was walking across the hall when he saw the three young men, "Mr Harvey, are they found?" asked the butler.

"They are indeed, Wilson. Is Lord Hunter in?" Harvey wanted to know.

"No, Sir, he is out seeking any news of the balloon."

"In that case, the twins and I will go and collect the ladies from Pinkly. If Lord Hunter arrives back home before we do, tell him not to worry. They are found, and all are unhurt."

"I shall pass the message on with pleasure, Sir."

While Harvey went and hitched up the wagon, the twins went into the kitchen to raid Mrs Saxon's larder.

Mrs Saxon was so pleased to see the twins she said they could have anything they wanted, so Tom and Lee took advantage of the situation. They had a doorstep piece of bread, butter and jam in each hand and Tom had an old newspaper full of meat pieces for Chester tucked under his arm.

Harvey picked up the twins at the front door, and they sat up top with him eating their bread and jam while Harvey concentrated on driving through the city.

Once they were out of the city, he asked, "What have you got wrapped up in the newspaper?"

"Some meat bits for Chester," was the reply.

"What about the girls?"

"They will be all right. They understand why they are hungry. Poor Chester doesn't, he has only had a couple of fish and eggs to eat, and he has never complained once," Tom explained.

"Not like the girls eh. Have they been complaining?"

"No, but if Effie had waited for her change before getting into the balloon we would not have been in this situation," Lee told him.

Harvey, still young enough to think this was a good enough explanation, let the matter drop. It was a logical explanation. It was all Effie's fault, and he was pleased for once to be able to shift the blame onto someone else. Everything was usually his fault.

"Why are we in the wagon?" Lee wanted to know.

"I thought it would be better for Chester, he can sit in the back," Harvey replied. "Also, it was the easiest and quickest transport to hitch up."

"Good idea," the twins said in unison.

Clara and Effie saw the wagon heading their way and set off running to meet it.

The twins climbed into the back of the wagon with Chester, and the two ladies climbed up front with Harvey.

Lee and Tom opened the newspaper and started to hand feed the grateful Chester with the pieces of meat.

"Have you brought us anything to eat?" asked Clara.

"You've got some apples left, haven't you? Chester does not know why he is not being fed. Don't be so mean, Clara," Lee told her.

"Just you wait until the boot is on the other foot. I shall get my own back, then see how you like being starved. I have a good mind to go and see that farmer and tell him you stole his eggs," threatened Clara.

"We did not steal them, anyway you ate one, so you are as bad as any of us, you ate stolen food," Tom came to this brother's defence.

"I am sure Edwin will go and pay the farmer for the eggs if I ask him," Effie told them, trying to make peace.

"I shouldn't worry about some paltry eggs," said Harvey.

The twins set off laughing and Effie asked, "What are they laughing at?"

"Eggs, poultry, get it?" Harvey informed her.

"Oh yes, very clever. I can see I am going to have to keep my wits about me when you lot are around," smiled Effie.

Effie ran up the steps and into the house. She was met by Wilson who showed uncustomary emotion when he saw her.

"Miss Effie, I am so pleased to see you. Are you all right?" he asked.

"Yes, thank you, Wilson, quite unharmed," she smiled at him. "Is my brother in?"

"He is indeed, Miss Effie. He went upstairs to freshen up. He has been searching for you for the past two days."

"In that case, I will nip up and see him. Would you be so kind as to have something to eat sent up to my brother's room, enough for two? I am dying of starvation."

"It will be attended to, Miss Effie," the butler bowed and turned for the kitchen.

Effie entered her brother's bedroom without knocking and sat on his bed, "Hello, Edwin, I'm back."

Lord Hunter was sitting on the edge of his bed pulling on his socks when his sister made herself at home on the opposite side of his bed, "So I see. Is everyone all right?"

"Yes, of course, we are. Why wouldn't we be?"

"You vanished in a hot air balloon and you ask me why I am concerned for you all. You need your head examining Effie."

"Edwin, it was the best time ever. It was exciting and challenging, and I would not have missed it for the world. Please don't spoil it for me. Clara and the twins are great company. We have hit it off immediately. The twins are very funny, but they are also very bright young boys. You need to go and pay the farmer for the eggs they stole, sorry, for the eggs they borrowed without the farmer's permission. We had a breakfast of boiled eggs and fish. Chester enjoyed himself too. He had two of the eggs and all the attention he could possibly want."

"Well, if Chester enjoyed it that is all that matters. I do not begrudge riding for hours trying to pick up any reports of a hot air balloon that nobody seemed to have seen. Where have you been?"

"We were not travelling for very long. We came down on top of some trees in a wood near a little village called Pinkly. Clara landed it. It was by sheer luck rather than good management, but she landed it without anyone getting hurt."

"Something to tell the children about eh?" he smiled.

Wilson knocked on the door and walked in carrying a tray laden with a steaming steak and kidney pudding. One of the kitchen maids followed behind with a tray containing hot chocolate and meat bits for Chester.

The maid placed the hot chocolate on the bedside tables at either side of the bed and the dish of meat bits on the floor for Chester who devoured them before the door was closed behind her.

Wilson cut the steak and kidney pudding in half and handed one to each.

"It has just come out of the oven, Miss Effie, the cook says she hopes you enjoy it, it should put you on until dinner," Wilson told her.

"If it tastes half as good as it smells, Wilson, I shall be ringing for seconds," Effie told him.

Edwin and Effie sat on the bed, each with a tray on their lap and enjoyed their little repast while Effie told her brother all about her adventure.

Chester, meanwhile, had jumped up onto the bottom of the bed and waited for any tasty morsel that might come his way, but this time he was disappointed, he saw their food slowly diminish and disappear.

When Clara and the twins arrived home, Oscar was nowhere to be seen. Lee and Tom went to raid the kitchen again, so while Harvey was unhitching the wagon, Clara took advantage of the solitude and ran upstairs into Harvey's bedroom.

She worked her way along the rows of clothes hanging in Harvey's wardrobe and found two pairs of black leggings and two black jackets. Then ran quickly to her own bedroom and stashed her finds in the bottom of her own wardrobe.

Looking through her blouse drawer, Clara could find no black ones. In the end, she plumped for two blouses, one navy blue and one olive green; they were the darkest she could find.

Looking at them she decided they were still a shade too light for their trip into the rundown part of the city, so she hunted out two black woollen scarves and put them with the purloined leggings and jackets.

Oscar rode back into Frithwood. He still had no news about the direction the balloon had followed, the wind could have taken it anywhere. Nobody he had spoken to had seen it. He went straight around to the stables to give his weary horse a wipe down and a good feed. Then, after making sure the horse was comfortable, instead of going inside the house, he made his way back down the road to Lord Hunter's house.

Wilson opened the door to his ring and said, "Good news, Sir, about the return of the ladies and the twins."

Oscar went into the hall and turning to Wilson he asked, "They are back you say?"

"Yes, Sir, I thought you knew."

At that moment Effie appeared at the top of the stairs, and Oscar ran up to greet her.

Taking her hands in his, he asked, "Are you all right? I did not know you had returned. I came here to see if Edwin had any good news for me. Are Clara, Tom and Lee, all right? I can see Chester has come to no harm," he laughed and let go of her hands to give the joyful Chester a pat to try and calm him down.

"Thank you, yes, I am quite unharmed and Clara and the boys, also. It was quite an adventure, but I must admit I was most grateful to see Harvey heading towards us with the wagon. Clara and I had been walking for what seemed like hours."

"Harvey came to your rescue, did he? It would seem he is not as irresponsible as he acts."

"I like him; he makes me laugh," Effie told him.

"Well, for goodness sake, do not tell him. His head is full of nonsense as it is," Oscar laughed. "If you will excuse me, I shall be off to see my lot. I am pleased to see you in such blooming health, Miss Hunter. Elmer Wolf is a lucky man."

Effie watched Oscar's back disappear out of the front door with a heavy heart. She had to see Clara. They had to get their hands on that letter. Effie had finally met a man she was attracted to and here she was engaged to the Wolf. He had to go.

Oscar marched back to his house and ran in shouting, "Clara, Tom, Lee, Harvey."

Clara heard her name being called and ran out of her bedroom across the landing and down the stairs straight into her brother's arms and gave him a big hug.

"Oscar, I am so sorry we caused you so much trouble, but we had a brilliant time. No one was hurt, we caught fish, and Tom and Lee borrowed some eggs. Chester loved every minute of it too. Effie was great, I really like her, Oscar, and she is just like us. We have become the best of friends."

Oscar held her close for a few seconds then he let her go.

"Thank God you are all safe; I was going out of my mind with worry. I like Effie too, Clara. More than is good for me. What do you mean the boys borrowed some eggs? How can you borrow eggs?"

They walked into the library together and sat on the sofa and Clara told her tale.

Once Clara's story had been told, Oscar said he would go to the fair and inform them where to collect their basket and balloon from. "Let us hope they are still where you left them."

"They have to be. The location was isolated, and the basket was high up in the trees. But thinking about it, I am not sure about the balloon. Anybody wandering into that shepherd's retreat we slept in could easily come across it and decide to keep it."

Chapter Five

Dinner was over, and Clara went upstairs to her bedroom. Taking a small canvas carpetbag, she had placed Harvey's borrowed clothes in it together with her other bits and pieces, then she made her way up the street and rang the bell of number ninety-nine.

Wilson opened the door and admitted Clara telling her Miss Effie was waiting for her in her bedroom. He pointed up the staircase and said, "The second door on the right at the top of the landing."

Clara was making her way towards the stairs when Lord Hunter appeared in the hall.

On seeing his lordship, Clara put the carpetbag behind her back and sent him such an innocent smile he knew instantly she was up to something.

"Miss Hunter, this is a pleasant surprise," he walked towards her.

"Thank you, I was on my way to see, Effie."

"Would you like me to carry that carpetbag for you, or have Wilson put it in the sitting room until you leave?"

"What carpetbag?" she asked.

"The one you have behind your back."

"Oh, this old thing, no, it is not heavy. I will take it with me. I don't want to forget it when I leave. Thank you for offering anyway."

Clara was saved further embarrassment when Effie appeared at the top of the stairs and called down to her, "Clara, there you are, come on up."

Effie smiled at her brother and said, "Hello, Edwin, I see you have met my guest."

Effie also sent him an innocent smile, much the same as the one he had received from Clara.

Edwin watched Clara make her escape up the stairs and was whisked away by Effie. The sound of giggling reached his ears.

They are up to something, he thought, *I wonder what she has in that carpetbag.* With an amused smile on his lips, he walked back into the library. It was nice to see his sister so happy. It had been a while since he had seen her smile and it was not in his nature to see his sister unhappy. If she was happy, he was happy.

In the privacy of her bedroom, Effie and Clara were trying on Harvey's clothes.

The leggings were a trifle too long, and the jacket sleeves covered their hands, but Clara set about turning over the sleeve cuffs and turning up the leggings at the bottom.

Effie had to find a belt for each of them, to keep the leggings up because they tended to drop down around their ankles. This gave the two ladies much pleasure, and they fell about laughing.

The blouses needed no adjustment, and with the scarf tied around their necks, they looked very much the young youth.

They looked at their reflection in the mirror and were satisfied with what they saw. The only let down was their hair that hung in ringlets.

Going over to a set of drawers, Effie hunted through a couple of the drawers before she found what she was looking for and produced two black woollen bonnets.

She went back to the mirror and, giving Clara one, they tucked their hair up inside the bonnets, and the disguise was complete.

"Perfect!" said Clara.

"Nobody will recognise us dressed like this," remarked Effie.

"No, I do not think they will," agreed Clara.

"When will you come and see Edwin?" Effie wanted to know.

"I thought later tonight. I will ask Lord Hunter, if he can make some arrangements to get the Wolf out of his house. It will have to be tonight because we leave for home next week, there is not much time left to get this sorted out. Unless you prefer to wait. I am going to wear my disguise when I go to see Lord Hunter and see if he recognises me in it."

"Tonight, will be fine by me. Shall we go out into the back garden and I can show you the tree and point out Edwin's, bedroom window. When you have gone, I will sneak into his bedroom and leave the window slightly ajar.

"Before we go out back, we had better change back into our own clothes, I don't want Edwin, seeing us like this or he will instantly know we are up to something."

Outside the two ladies walked arm in arm and stood back from the house. Effie pointed to a large spreading oak tree. The tree stood in front of a window that Effie pointed out as being Edwin's bedroom window.

"Can you see that big thick branch, the one that has been cut off at the end? That is the one you need to work your way across. It practically rests on Edwin's bedroom window ledge. We keep having to have it cut back because if we don't it would be growing into his bedroom. Do you think you will be able to climb up the tree?"

"I should think so. If I can't then we will have to think of something else. I will go back home now and come back around midnight. I will leave the clothes here and get changed into my disguise when I come back. It will be easier dressed in men's clothing to climb the tree, and I shall tell Lord Hunter so if he enquires about my attire. Will you be there to let me in so I can get through the house into the back garden?"

"Of course, I will. As soon as Edwin goes to bed, and Wilson locks up, I will sneak back down and unlock the door and be ready to let you in."

They said their goodbyes, but before Clara could make it to the door, Lord Hunter appeared and asked, "Are you going home already?"

"I am," replied Clara.

"Haven't you forgotten something?" he wanted to know.

"I do not think so," she replied.

"What about your carpetbag?"

"Oh yes, my carpetbag, it does not matter, I shall pick it up another day," Clara smiled back at him forgetting she had told him previously she did not want to forget it when she left.

He let the slip slide and remarked, "In that case, may I invite you all to dinner tomorrow night? You may pick the carpetbag up then."

"Thank you, that would be nice. What time?"

"Around seven, if that is convenient for you?"

"Perfect, we will see you tomorrow then. Goodnight."

Harvey, meanwhile, was hunting through his wardrobe for his black leggings without much success. He decided to abandon the black leggings and settled for brown ones instead. He would wear the brown leggings and a black jacket. This also foiled him. He could not find his black jackets either. Thinking he must have left them back at boarding school, Harvey decided to wear his brown leggings and red jacket.

Hoping everyone was asleep, Clara let herself silently out of the house just before midnight. Effie was waiting at the door to let her in, and they crept upstairs to Effie's bedroom where Clara changed her clothes before they made their way down to the kitchen and out of the back door.

Once outside Clara asked, "What do you think about the disguises, Effie? Do you think the rigout is good enough to fool anyone that might see us?"

"I can just about make you out; I think it is a very good disguise. I don't see how anyone will be able to recognise us dressed like this, especially as we are going to be going in the dark of night," Effie replied.

Effie waited at the bottom of the oak tree and watched as Clara made her way deftly up and sit straddle-legged on the branch that had been pointed out to her earlier.

Effie, with her heart in her mouth, watched as Clara shuffled her way across the length of the branch. She watched Clara push up the window, climb onto the window ledge and disappear inside.

Lord Hunter was drifting between consciousness and sleep when he heard his window slide up. He lay very still in bed with his eyes closed; he was conscious of another person's presence in the room. His heart started to beat a little faster.

Once her eyes became accustomed to the darkness, Clara saw the dark shape of a four-poster bed.

She crept quietly forward until she was standing at the side of the bed. She could just make out Lord Hunter's profile, fast asleep against the white pillowcase. She put out her hand with the intention of placing it over Edwin's mouth to stop him from shouting out. This did not go entirely to plan, for she felt a vice-like grip on her wrist and was pulled forward, then pinned down on the bed with a forearm across her throat.

Clara started pounding on Edwin's chest with her free hand but found she was unable to speak with his arm across her throat.

Lord Hunter felt the rise of a woman's breast beneath his elbow and quickly lifted his arm away from her throat and Clara, still pounding at his chest squeaked, "What do you think you are doing? You nearly choked me to death."

To Lord Hunter's amazement, he recognised Clara's voice, even with the squeak in it.

"What am I doing? What are you doing? Why are you creeping about in the middle of the night? Even more to the point, what are you doing in my bedroom and why are you entering through the window?"

"I had to creep in through the window because I did not want anyone to know about this. We need your help."

"We, who is we?"

Damn! thought Clara, *my first slip up.* "Me, I meant me. You have confused me by nearly choking me to death."

Lord Hunter let the slip pass once again and replied, "I cannot say I was very thrilled to hear my window being raised and someone creeping across the room. I would never have guessed it was you if my life had depended on it. If I hurt you, I am sorry. You could have come in through the front door and asked for me. We would have been quite private in the library. This is very remiss of you, Clara. I would hate to think what Harvey would make of it. Not only mine, but your reputation too will be shot to threads."

Clara laughed, then she put her finger to her mouth and said, "Shush. Where would the fun have been in that?" she whispered.

"If you want fun, go find another hot air balloon," he whispered back.

"Don't be such a stuffed shirt, Lord Hunter. Nobody is going to know about this only us. Listen, do you want to get rid of the Wolf?"

"The Wolf, of course, I do. But it is Effie you need to see about him, not me."

"I have a plan. You must…I say, Lord Hunter, may I sit up? This is very uncomfortable."

Realising he was still holding her down by twisting her wrist backwards, he let her go and turned to light a candle at the side of his bed so he could see her better.

"If it involves me shooting Elmer Wolf, you can forget it. I am not going to end up at the end of a noose, not even for Effie."

Again, this made Clara laugh, and she had to put her hand over her mouth to stifle the sound, "Shush," she said again. "You have to take the Wolf to this Ravens Club he so badly wants to join."

"No, that is not going to happen."

"I told you I had a plan. There is always a way 'round something if you give it some thought. You have plenty of friends. Ask them to help you to bluff his way into the club. Get hold of a loose piece of paper and get your friends to sign it and ask the doorman at the club to push it into the signing in book. I think that is what happens, isn't it? Effie said so anyway. Then get some of your friends to spend the night with you both at the club in a private room.

"The Wolf will never know it is a loose piece of paper, and anyway he will not know any difference because he has not been there before.

"When you leave, all you have to do is take the loose piece of paper with you. Then there will be no record of the Wolf ever having been there. I am sure you can rely on your friends to keep the visit a secret. Make sure no one sees you, and you will be home and dry. Just keep him out of his house for the evening. We will be very grateful, really we will."

"There goes that we again. Who might we be?"

"Sorry, I meant me,"

"Are you going to tell me what this is all about?"

"No, I promised faithfully I would not tell you. I would have asked Oscar to help us, but he is not a member of the Club, and anyway, he does not know the Wolf, so it is no good asking him."

"I feel very gratified that you should choose me to be second best in your little caper. And if I say no?"

"Then I will never speak to you ever again, and I will find another way to get the Wolf out of his house. I think you are very chicken-hearted."

"In that case, I had better help you. I would not like to think you will never speak to me ever again. It would be my loss. If you are not afraid to creep into a gentleman's bedroom in the dead of night, there is no telling what you will think up next. I will see what I can do and let you know at dinner tonight; I think it is morning already. Now you had better go. I will come down with you and let you out of the front door and walk you home. If you would go over to the window and turn your back until I get dressed, it will save embarrassment."

"You will not, you know, I shall leave the way I came in, thank you. I do not want anyone to see me, not that anyone will recognise me if they did in this outfit. Well, Harvey would, of course, if he sees me because these are his clothes, but he does not count."

"Is Harvey in on this little charade as well?"

"Good God no, I had to pinch these clothes from his bedroom when he was out in the stables. As you know, Harvey has a problem keeping quiet," she sent him a wicked smile.

Clara jumped off the bed and was out of the window before Lord Hunter could protest.

Lord Hunter always slept with nothing on so he waited until Clara was out of sight before he threw the covers back and jumped out of bed. He was just in time to see Clara drop to the ground where Effie was waiting for her. Effie gave Clara a hug, and he watched the two of them heading for the kitchen door. Now he knew who the 'we and us' was, not that he had been in much doubt about that in the first place.

As he walked back to his bed, Edwin looked down at his crotch and the thought that entered his head was, *Interesting.*

He went back to bed with a smile on his face and slept like a log.

Elmer Wolf got the surprise of his life when he called on Effie that morning. He was shown into the library where Lord Hunter was sitting behind his desk.

"Elmer, I have been very remiss in not inviting you to join me at The Ravens Club. Some friends of mine are meeting there this evening, around 10 o'clock. If I were to find you waiting outside for me, I will be delighted to sign you in."

"Much obliged I'm sure, my lord," Elmer bowed. "I shall be there promptly at 10. You will not regret it, my lord. If I could just see Effie and tell her the good news, I am sure she will be delighted. If she knows you have accepted me as her fiancé now and are willing to sign me into the club, I am sure she will set a date for the wedding."

"I am afraid you have missed her. She has gone shopping with Miss Lander and the twins. I do not know when they will be back. I will be sure to tell her you called to see her."

"Till tonight then, my lord," Elmer bowed himself out.

Elmer was not best pleased to find his fiancé absent again. Since the arrival of the Landers, he had only seen Effie the once. Once he had been signed into The Ravens Club, there would be no putting off a wedding date any longer. Effie had had enough time to decide on a date for the wedding, and he was going to make sure a date was set the very next time he saw her. No more messing about.

The outside door was closing on Elmer as Effie was entering the library dressed in her outdoor clothes, "What do you have on today, Edwin, anything interesting?"

"I have a certain amount to do, nothing to worry your pretty little head over. If I were you, I would wait ten minutes before setting out. Elmer Wolf has just left."

"What did he want?" asked Effie.

"You. I told him you were out shopping with Clara and the twins."

"Thank you, Edwin. There is time for a cup of tea before I leave then. Would you like to join me?"

"I would not say no."

Effie went over to the fireplace and rang for Wilson.

Wilson appeared, followed by Clara and Oscar.

"Wilson, would you have some tea sent up?" Effie asked.

When Wilson had left, Lord Hunter said, "Good morning to you both. I hope you slept well, Miss Lander?"

"Very well, thank you. And you?"

"I had a lot on my mind, but I dropped off eventually."

Oscar told them, "Clara told me that the twins borrowed some eggs from a farm during their little adventure. Clara and I are on our way to reimburse the unknowing farmer. We wondered if you would both like to join us."

"How long do you think we will be?" asked Lord Hunter.

"We should be home around noon, I hope. Harvey has taken the twins to the farmers market. I think he will have had enough of them by lunchtime," Oscar replied.

"I would love to come, Clara. I was just on my way to see if you would like to have a walk to the shops, but I would much rather go for a ride in the country," Effie admitted.

"I will come too; it will be a nice change and interesting to see where your adventure led you to. So long as we are back by noon, I have things to arrange for tonight," Lord Hunter looked at Clara, and she had the grace to blush.

After they had drunk their tea, the four set off in the open carriage. Oscar was driving with Edwin sat next to him, and Clara and Effie were sitting together on the back seat.

The sun was shining, and Clara and Effie were glad to be out and about, safe in the company of their brothers.

It was an astonished farmer's wife who opened the door to find four elegantly dressed members of the gentry standing on her doorstep.

"Hello," said Clara, "We were stranded here a few days ago with no money, and my two brothers came across your farm. I am afraid they raided your hen coop. We are here to pay you for the eggs they took."

"Arnold," shouted the farmer's wife, "We have visitors."

Footsteps came from behind them and turning they saw a small, sinewy man heading their way.

Oscar held out his hand, and they shook hands and he repeated to the farmer what Clara had told his wife.

"Now that has never happened before," the old man said. "We get kids from the village raiding the hen coop. We have never been paid for the eggs they steal. Much obliged I'm sure."

"They took six eggs. Would a £1 be enough to pay for them?" Oscar asked.

"Nay lad, I don't want that much. A couple of pence will be more than enough for six eggs."

"I insist. I am grateful to you for feeding my brothers and sister, even if you did not know of it at the time. After all, they stole from you really. They insist that they only borrowed them so here we are to pay for the borrowed eggs." Oscar held out the money.

"It is much appreciated. We are getting a bit old to run this farm now; it is very hard work. There seem to be more and more things going missing these days. The wife says it is my fault because I keep forgetting where I have put things, and maybe she is right. Things I have lost turn up in the most unexpected places."

"Thank you once again for your understanding about the eggs. We will leave you to get on with your work now," Effie said.

"Would you like to come in and have a glass of milk and some homemade cake? We do not get many visitors, in fact, we don't get any visitors. It will be nice to have someone to talk to for a change," the old woman said.

"That would be very nice, thank you. That is if your husband does not mind," said Effie.

"The cake has just come out of the oven, and there is plenty of milk," said the farmer's wife. "Don't worry about Arnold; he will have forgotten you are here in five minutes."

Inside, the farmhouse was immaculately neat and tidy and filled with old rustic furniture polished to a high sheen. The farmer's wife led them through into a large, spacious kitchen again, gleaming clean and a delicious looking cake stood on a cooling tray.

"How wonderful, do you do all this upkeep yourself?" Clara asked the old woman.

"There is nothing else to do. While Arnold is out looking after the livestock, I clean. I used to make the peggy rugs you see scattered around, same with the embroidered table clothes and runners. It was something to do to while away the lonely hours. Patchwork quilts too, but I have had to pack it all in now. My eyes are not what they used to be. Just like Arnold's memory," the old woman told them.

"Oh dear, don't you have any children to help you around the farm?" asked Clara.

"We do. Two boys and a girl, but the farm was not big enough to provide a living for us all. The children left and went to find employment elsewhere. We have not seen or heard from any of them for about eight or nine years," the old woman told them.

"Do you know where they found employment?" asked Effie.

"Not really, no. I think Walter went to the city to work, but we do not know where. Fred joined the army, and Dolly went into service," the old lady sighed.

"What is your surname?" asked Clara.

"Arnold can't even remember that these days. Some days he can't remember who I am. It is a good day for him today. Our name is Pomroy," the old lady told them.

A glance passed between Oscar and Edwin. They both knew where this was leading.

"Thank you for the milk and cake Mr and Mrs Pomroy, they were delicious, but we really must be on our way now. It has been a very enjoyable hour, please accept this," Edwin pressed a five-pound note into Mrs Pomroy's hand as they left.

On their way back to Frithwood, Clara said, "Oscar."

Oscar replied, "No, Clara."

"What do you mean, no. You don't know what I was going to say."

"Yes, I do, and the answer is still no."

"What was I going to say then? Tell me that?"

"You were going to ask if we could find the Pomroy's children."

That took the wind out of Clara's sails, and she asked, "Well, why not?"

"Because we do not know the whole story, we have only heard one side of it. The children might have an entirely different story to tell. It has nothing to do with us. Let it be."

Silence reigned from the back of the carriage, and both Oscar and Edwin could feel the glance Clara and Effie exchanged, but neither of them said anything.

When Edwin and Effie alighted from the barouche, Edwin said, "That was a very enjoyable morning, thank you. We will see you tonight for dinner."

"You will indeed, but I must warn you, my brood have a healthy appetite," Oscar warned.

"I will tell the cook."

Chapter Six

Clara looked through her wardrobe. She had been rigged out by Oscar before they came to Frithwood and she was in a quandary. She did not know what to wear.

In the end, Clara decided not to overdo the occasion, and she chose a little white cotton dress with puff sleeves at the top that became tightly fitted down her arms ending in a pale pink ruff at her wrist. A pale pink ribbon was tied under her bust, and the ends of the ribbon fell to just below her waist. The skirt fell straight down to her little dainty white shoes that boasted three pink buttons to the side.

Oscar had given her a little gold locket that had once belonged to her mother which she tied at her throat. The earrings were gold, with a little pearl held in place by a cluster of gold claws.

When Clara entered the sitting room all four men in her life looked up, and Tom remarked, "Heaven's, Clara, what has got into you?"

"Take no notice of him, Clara, you look delightful," Oscar said coming towards her and taking her hand in his.

"In fact, you don't look delightful; you look beautiful. I am very impressed, Clara, you do me proud." He brought her hand up to his mouth and kissed the back of it.

"I wondered why it was taking you ages to get ready, now I know," said Lee, "You look gorgeous."

"At least you have some clothes to get changed into," complained Harvey, "My wardrobe seems to be much depleted."

"You should not spend all your money playing cards," Oscar told him, "then you might have some money to buy any amount of clothes you like. Come on, let's go. We don't want to be late for our first dinner engagement, do we?"

Effie was dressed in the same style of dress as Clara only her dress was of a pale green with darker green relief to it and her puff sleeves ended at the top, showing her bare arms. She had a gold cross at her throat and that was the extent of her jewellery.

Dinner was well on the way when Lord Hunter looked Clara in the eye and said, "I am sorry to have to inform you, but I have to go out around 9:30 this evening and will not be back until the early hours. Around 5 o'clock in the morning, that is the time I expect to be returning home. Had I known about this unexpected appointment before I invited you all over for dinner, I would have made it for a different day. My appointment cannot be avoided, I am afraid. We shall have to set another date for you all to come back."

"These things happen," remarked Oscar, "you must come and dine with us next. It will give Clara some practice at being a hostess. After all, this little excursion we are on was to give her a bit of experience into polite society. She has been running wild for far too long."

"I have never run wild, and anyway, I have not done anything different here from what I would have done back home," Clara told him.

"Exactly my point," said her brother.

"I think Clara is exactly as she should be," her friend Effie defended.

"That is because you too have been allowed to run wild for far too long," Lord Hunter said to his sister. "You are like peas in a pod."

"I would rather be like Clara than some of the lifeless young ladies I meet in the tea rooms. They have no get up and go in them. I do not want to live my life like that, never speaking unless spoken to and having to think about everything I say or do. It is no life, and I refuse to become part of it," Effie lifted her chin and challenged her brother.

"I also refuse to become one of the lifeless ladies Effie was talking about, I would much rather be like Effie. We have had a very enjoyable time since we met. She is my best friend, and I will not have you saying she has to change because I do not want her to," Clara looked from Edwin to Oscar with defiance in her eyes.

"Very well, I shall say no more on the subject. Lee told me it was your fault, Effie, that you all ended up adrift in the hot air balloon." Oscar's eyes danced at her indignation.

"My fault," said Effie, "how could it be my fault?"

"He said you should have waited until the attendant came back with your change before you got into the basket. He said if you had waited for your change, the attendant would have been in the balloon with you all, and he would have stopped Chester from jumping in therefore the anchor ropes would not have broken loose," his eyes still danced in her direction.

"Did he indeed, well, let me tell you it was Tom's fault, if he had tied Chester up correctly in the first place, things might have been very different," Effie said.

"It was not my fault," complained Tom, "it was Lee's fault, it was his turn to hold Chester, and he should have been the one to tie him up."

"It was Clara's fault because she did not take enough money with her and therefore, Effie had to change a pound note, and the attendant had to leave us all to get into the basket whilst he came back with her change," countered Lee.

"In that case, it was Oscar's fault for being tight with his money and not giving me enough to see us through," said Clara.

"The reason why I keep you short of money is because Harvey spends all my money on clothes. If I had not had to spend so much on him, there would have been more than enough spare money to go around. So, therefore, it is Harvey's fault," Oscar told them.

"MY FAULT!" exclaimed an outraged Harvey. "Why does it always end up at my door? If you were to see the state of my wardrobe you would never guess I overspend on my clothes, why, I nearly had to come to this dinner party without trousers, there seems to be none hanging in my wardrobe."

Then Harvey had a flash of inspiration and he added, "It is Lord Hunter's fault. If he had not had such a reputation, I would never have written that letter about him to Clara, and she would not have come causing trouble. Therefore, we would never have met, and the balloon incident would never have taken place. It is Lord Hunter's fault."

Lord Hunter looked around the table; there was no one else left to blame, so he looked at Chester and said, "It was Chester's fault for breaking loose and jumping into the basket and breaking the ropes."

The three who sat with their backs towards Chester, who was sitting in front of the fire keeping a vigilant eye on the table in case a tasty morsel happened to drop to the floor, turned to look at him.

The next best thing Chester likes after his food is attention, and all of a sudden, he found himself the centre of it. He eyed them all back and his tail began to wag and he gave three excited barks.

The assembled company burst out laughing, and Lord Hunter did something he had never done before, he cut a chunk of beef off the roast and threw it to Chester.

Chester's mouth opened and closed, and the chunk of beef was gone forever.

"I bet he didn't even taste it," laughed Tom.

Not long after the meal was over Oscar said, "Thank you for the invitation, Edwin, I really enjoyed tonight. We will detain you no longer for you must keep your appointment so we will take our leave of you."

As they were leaving Lord Hunter whispered to Clara, "You have while 5 o'clock in the morning. That is the longest I will be entertaining the Wolf for."

"That should be enough time, thank you," Clara said demurely.

Clara gave Lord Hunter a small curtsey and went to hug Effie whispering, "Let me in around 9:30 this evening when your brother has left for his club."

"I will," she whispered back.

As soon as they reached home, Clara told Oscar she was going to bed because she was tired, and she headed for her bedroom.

After changing her gown, Clara lay on top of the bed and watched for the hands of the clock to read 9:30 and hoped that everyone had gone to bed. Opening her bedroom door, she poked her head out and looked up and down the landing. It was clear; there was no one in sight.

She pulled the bolts back and using her house key she unlocked the door and went outside. Relocking the door before looking both ways to make sure she was not being observed, she headed up the street.

Effie was waiting to let her friend in, and they made their way upstairs and straight to her bedroom where they hastily changed into their disguises then headed out of the house.

If Lord Hunter could have seen the two young ladies, dressed all in black with black woollen caps covering their hair, the comment he had made earlier about them being like peas in a pod, would have been confirmed.

They walked arm in arm thankful for the dark of night, especially when the edge of Frithwood was reached and the district became more and more rundown.

They passed row upon row of terraced houses until they finally came to File Street and turned into it.

Making their way down the narrow, cobbled street, they passed opened doors with ladies of the night standing in doorways offering to sell their wares. More than once they were propositioned, but they kept their heads down and hurried on until the last house was reached.

The door was tried but found to be locked; they had known it would be. It was too much to ask for an unlocked door.

Clara had come prepared for this, and she put her hand in her pocket and took out a buttonhook. Bending down, she inserted the hook into the keyhole and twiddled it around until she felt it resist. Putting some pressure on the buttonhook, they heard a click.

Taking hold of the doorknob Clara tried it again, and this time, it turned, and they were in.

Effie closed the door quickly behind them, and Clara put the bag down she was carrying and took out a small lamp which had a candle enclosed in it. Clara took a piece of flint and a nail out of the bag, and after giving Effie a piece of paper to hold over the flint Clara ran the nail along the flint making a spark. The spark caught the piece of paper, and the candle was lit. Placing the glass cover back over the candle so it would not blow out, they had a dim glow to see by.

Clara whispered to Effie, "Let us start upstairs and make our way down."

The stairs creaked as they ascended and both the young ladies could feel the beating of their hearts, hoping against hope they would not be caught.

The first bedroom held nothing but a single bed frame, no mattress and no other furniture. They did not waste any time in that room and opened the door to the second bedroom.

There were only two rooms to the upper floor, and the smell of boiled cabbage and stale body odours was the strongest in the larger of the two bedrooms.

This bedroom held a small wardrobe to the right of the window, a single bed with mattress to the left and at the bottom of the bed with its back to the wall stood a roll-top desk. There was just enough room to walk between the bottom of the bed and the desk.

Stopping in front of the desk, Clara tried to roll the top up but that too was locked. Out came the buttonhook and into the lock it went and soon they were rifling through the contents of the desk.

It was Effie that found the bundle of letters. They were tied together with a piece of string. She slid the string off and started to go through them looking for her own handwriting.

Effie grabbed Clara's arm and held out the letter.

"Is that it?" whispered Clara.

"Yes," whispered Effie back.

"Well done, Effie, let's get out of here. Take all the letters in the bundle. If Elmer has been blackmailing you, he might be blackmailing somebody else. We can read them when we get home. If they are nothing to do with blackmailing, we can always post them back to him."

Effie bundled the letters up and slipped them into the bag Clara had brought with her to hold the lantern. They made their way back down the creaking stairs, blew out the candle and put the lantern back in the bag.

Clara slowly opened the door and poked her head out. It was too dark to see anything, so she felt backwards and found Effie's hand. They left the house and were back on the street.

"What about locking the door again?" Effie whispered.

"We will leave it open. We need to get away from here as soon as possible. Anyway, Elmer Wolf does not deserve such consideration as to have his door locked again. I do not like it here, the sooner we are clear of this street and this part of the city the better."

No sooner had she spoken the words when two raggedly dressed youths appeared from out of a doorway, and one said, "What have we here, Gerry, a couple of fine-looking dandies. Want to share what you've got with us?" he asked the ladies.

"Get out of our way," demanded Clara.

"Why, what's the rush? Let's see what you have in them pockets. They look big enough to hold a few silver coins," said the same ruffian.

He made a grab for Clara's coat but she took a step backwards, and they heard a ripping noise as the lapel tore away from the jacket.

To Clara's astonishment, she saw a silver pistol appear at her side and heard Effie say, "Out of our way or I will shoot."

The two ruffians were startled into stepping aside and before they had time to change their minds the two ladies set off running and did not stop until they had nearly reached home.

Clinging on to each other the first house they arrived at was Clara's. Taking out her house key she unlocked the door, and they both crept in. They made their way silently up the stairs and into Clara's bedroom.

They threw themselves on the bed and set off into a fit of laughter.

"We had better get these clothes off, Effie. I will sneak into Harvey's bedroom tomorrow and put them back. I will lend you one of my dresses to go back home in and collect it with the one I left at your house when we got changed to go and get your letter back. Do you want to burn your letter now?" Clara asked when they had changed their clothes.

"Yes, I will, before it gets into the wrong hands again." Effie took the bundle of letters out of the jacket pocket and found the one she wanted.

Opening the envelope, Effie took out the letter and began to read it, "Yes, this is mine. Let me burn it and be done with it."

Going over to the fireplace Clara took a candle and held the flame to the corner of the letter that Effie was holding and they watched it begin to burn. Effie dropped the burning letter into the grate when the flames were about to reach her fingers, and they watched the last corner of the offending letter slowly disappear.

"There it is done. Clara, I will never be able to repay you for this. Now, the Wolf can no longer blackmail me, and I will be able to throw his ring back in his face. Well, I could if I had one."

"Let's have a look at one of the other letters to see what it says and if it is of a similar nature to yours, I will put them in my writing desk, and you can come around early in the morning, and we will go through them all and decide what to do with them. I don't know about you, Effie, but I am asleep on my feet."

"I am too excited to sleep. I feel as though a dead weight has been lifted off my shoulders, and so it has. Free, free at last and you expect me to sleep? I do not think I will ever be able to sleep again I am so happy."

Opening the first letter they came to, on inspection, it was obvious it was another amorous letter which was not addressed to Elmer Wolf.

"Right then, Effie, I shall walk you halfway back home and see you safely home, then later this morning, for it is past midnight now, come back here and we will decide what is to be done with the rest of the letters. We will feel much more refreshed after we have both had a few hours' sleep."

"You don't have to walk me back home, Clara, it is only a few houses away, and I do have my pistol with me."

"Yes, I had forgotten about that. What made you bring it with you?"

"I wanted to make sure nothing happened to either of us. Edwin gave me this little pistol a couple of years ago to keep me safe. It certainly came in handy tonight."

They were at the door and Effie went silently out. Clara watched while Effie ran up the steps leading to her home then closed and locked the door before making her weary way upstairs.

Instead of going into her own bedroom Clara went further along the landing and into Oscar's bedroom. She went over to the bed and seeing him fast asleep, she shook him until he was awake.

"Clara, what time is it?"

"About 1 o'clock."

"1 o'clock in the morning?"

"Of course, it is in the morning. Oscar, will you take a note to The Ravens Club and hand it to the doorman and ask him to deliver it to Lord Hunter?"

"What have you been up to now?"

"I cannot tell you just yet. Get dressed, and I will go and write the note."

"Can't it wait until tomorrow then you can deliver it yourself?"

"No, it has to do with Lord Hunter having to go out at 9:30 last night. Please, Oscar, I would not ask you if it wasn't important."

"Very well, go write your note while I get dressed."

Clara went into her bedroom and took up her quill and wrote:

Lord Hunter, mission successful.
You may now get rid of the
Wolf and go home.
Thank you. Clara.

Clara folded the letter up, placed it in an envelope and sealed it. She wrote 'Lord Hunter' on the front of the envelope and went in search of her brother. Clara handed Oscar the letter, went back to her bedroom, got undressed and went to bed and thought no more of it.

Effie woke early after a very deep sleep, she felt refreshed and raring to go.

There was no sign of her brother at breakfast, so she ate alone then made her way to Clara's.

Clara was just finishing off her breakfast when Trueman showed Effie in, "Am I too early, Clara?"

"Your timing is perfect. I have just finished my breakfast. Let's go up to my bedroom unless you would like some breakfast first."

"Thank you, no. I have eaten before I came."

They met Oscar halfway up the stairs, "Good morning, Miss Hunter, you are up and out early."

"I came to see Clara," was all Effie could think of to say.

"How disappointing, I was hoping you had called to see me," his eyes teased her.

"Take no notice of him, Effie. Did you deliver the note last night, Oscar?"

"I left it with the doorman and came home to my bed."

Up in her bedroom, Clara asked Effie, "Did you manage to get to sleep, Effie?"

"I can't remember going to sleep, but I must have. It was one of the best night sleeps I have had for a long time."

Clara opened her desk and produced the letters. Taking them over to her bed they both pumped up the pillows and made themselves comfortable. Taking a letter each, they began to read.

"Blimey," said Clara, "Just read this." They swapped letters.

"And I thought my letter was unfit to be read by others," Effie said, "Mine was nowhere near as explicit as these."

"They are a bit rude. In fact, they are very rude. We will have to read them all. Just to make sure they are all letters to be returned to their composer, of course," Clara looked across the bed at her friend, and they both started giggling.

Oscar was heading for his own bedroom, and as he passed Clara's room, he heard the giggles. He knocked on the door, and the giggling stopped.

After a few seconds Clara called, "Come in."

Oscar opened the door and saw the two young ladies sitting on Clara's bed the pictures of innocence.

"I thought I heard a funny noise coming from your room. Are you two all right in here?"

"Funny noise, we were just having a laugh," Clara told him.

If Oscar was to be truthful, he had recognised Effie's giggle and couldn't resist the urge to lay eyes on her again. He found her very easy to look at. "In that case, I will leave you to enjoy yourselves," and he closed the door.

When the door closed on Oscar, Effie said, "Read this one. There are four people in this one."

"That's odd," said Clara after she had read the letter, "It is from Sir Roy Grey to Mrs Freda Shetland. Why on earth should it end with 'Dick can't wait until he joins with Fanny again,' maybe it is some friends of theirs that are having an affair as well."

"What are we going to do with these letters?"

"I think we have to go and see Lord Hunter."

"Edwin! Why on earth Edwin?"

"We cannot go to Oscar because he does not know any of the people these letters belong to. Lord Hunter will most likely know them all. He can go and visit them and hand them back so they can burn them then the Wolf cannot blackmail any of them again."

"But he might not be blackmailing them. We do not know that he is."

"Of course, he is. What kind of work does the Wolf do?"

"He does not work as far as I know. He has never mentioned working anyway."

"Then that is how he makes his money. Blackmails people into giving him their money. What an evil little monster he is."

"Are you going to creep into Edwin's bedroom again?"

"No, you and I will walk in the front door and tell him all about it. Show him the letters and leave the rest up to him."

"Maybe you are right. Yes, let us go and see Edwin."

Chapter Seven

Lord Hunter had just finished his breakfast when the door opened and in walked his sister and her new friend.

"Good morning. You two must be up to something to be out so early. Would you like some breakfast?"

"Thank you, Edwin, no, we have already eaten. We have come to see you, to see if you will help us," his sister told him.

"This sounds ominous. Should I be worried?" he asked.

"Of course not, but we do have a mission for you," Effie replied.

"It has to do with my having to take Elmer Wolf out of your way last night, I presume," he said.

"Don't try to act as though you are not interested, Edwin. I know you; you cannot wait to hear what we have to say," Effie scolded.

"Shall we all go into the sitting room and make ourselves comfortable then," he stood up and held the door open for them to pass through.

Clara cast a sly glance up at Lord Hunter as she passed by him and felt her colour heighten when she found him looking down at her. She averted her gaze demurely and followed Effie into the sitting room.

When they were comfortably settled, Effie said, "I have some excellent news, Edwin. I am no longer engaged to the Wolf."

"Excellent news indeed, I must admit I do not like the man. What brought this about?"

"Clara and I went on a burglary last night to find a compromising letter I had written to Captain Burton that had somehow got into Elmer Wolf's hands and he has been blackmailing me with it. Can you remember Captain Burton?" Effie asked.

"Captain Burton, he must be at least forty by now," Edwin said.

"Yes, he must be. Well, when I was seventeen, I was madly in love with him, and I wrote him a passionate letter declaring my love for him. He had just got married the previous year to a very pretty young woman, and I asked him to leave her and marry me. Needless to say, my infatuation lasted about two months, and after that, he never entered my head again.

"Six months ago, Elmer Wolf came to see me and told me he had the letter I had written to Captain Burton, and he insisted that I married him. I refused of course, and to give me time to try and get the letter back, I offered to become engaged to him providing it was kept a secret and he court me properly.

"At first, I did not believe him, but he quoted some of the foolish statements I had made in the letter. He said if I did not marry him, he would take the letter to the Daily Journal for them to publish. I could not let that happen, so that is why I agreed to get engaged to him.

"Then Clara came into my life, and things began to take a turn for the better. When we were making our way back home after the balloon incident, we made up this plan to get the letter back, and you know the rest."

"Why on earth didn't you come to me with this, Effie? I would have sorted it out, and you certainly would not have had to be engaged to that slimy creature," Edwin wanted to know.

"I know you would and that is precisely why I did not come to you. You would have ended up behind bars and anyway, I was too embarrassed to come to you. I would have died if you had read the letter," said an embarrassed Effie.

"How did you get the letter back?"

"We stole it."

"You had better tell me the whole story."

"Not much more to tell really. Clara borrowed some of Harvey's clothes, and we got dressed up as boys and went to Elmer's house. We did a search, and we found my letter along with a whole bundle of other letters, so we have brought them to you to take back to the rightful owners, then Elmer can't blackmail them anymore either."

"You went to File Street, even though I had told you not to go to that part of the city. It is full of cutthroats and thieves, or so I have heard."

"I had my pistol with me. The one you bought me years ago for protection, and it worked. I had to point it at a couple of ruffians; one had hold of Clara's lapel. He soon let go when he saw the pistol," Effie told him with pride.

"How did you get into the house?"

"Clara picked the lock. I was really impressed with her. It didn't take her two minutes to get it open."

Lord Hunter looked at Clara and asked, "Harvey taught you I suppose? How to pick locks that is."

"Yes, somebody showed him how to do it at boarding school, and he showed me when he came home. Good job too, it came in handy," Clara told him candidly. "Did you get my letter, by the way, telling you it was alright to go home?"

"I did. That was the best part of this entire caper. As soon as I read it, we left the club, and we all went our separate ways."

"Will the Wolf be able to get back into the club now?" asked Clara.

"No, your suggestion about the loose piece of paper was set in place. As soon as we left the club the loose piece of paper was removed and destroyed. There is no evidence that the Wolf had ever entered the club. The other gentlemen who made up the party will deny the event ever took place."

"Good, I am glad," Clara said with satisfaction.

"I am still annoyed with you, Effie, for not listening to me about going to File Street. It is no place for either of you. I cannot believe you had no faith in me to sort the situation out. I thought we could tell each other anything," Lord Hunter looked at his sister.

Effie hung her head and did not reply.

Clara was straight to her friend's defence, "You men think we women are incapable of sorting out anything more difficult than boiling an egg. Effie wanted to save you any embarrassment, and I think it was very noble of her.

"We have come to no harm, and there is only the three of us who know anything about this. I hope you can be trusted not to go tattling it about Frithwood. When you are told not to go somewhere, it gets your imagination going, and it is at the back of your mind all the time.

"Now we have been and seen File Street for ourselves, I can assure you, neither of us ever intend to go there again. I must admit though it was illuminating. You mentioned cutthroats and thieves inhabit File Street, well you missed out the whores. Those poor women we saw selling themselves, some of them were hardly out of the nursery," Clara informed him.

"There are some things that you are better off not to have seen and that is one of them. If, by going to File Street, your curiosity has now been dampened then I will say no more about it, the matter is closed. How many of these letters do you have?" he asked.

"Thirty-two altogether, but I burnt mine as soon as we got back to Clara's. That leaves thirty-one," Effie told him, thankful to have the subject of File Street safely behind her now.

"Thirty-one!" exclaimed Lord Hunter.

"Well," said Clara, "One of the letters has four people in it, so I guess it goes back up to thirty-two, for the other two named in that letter will have to be informed. Or at least one of them so they can tell the other."

"Four people in one letter, how do you know this?" he asked.

"Because we have read them all," Clara replied.

"You have read them all?" Lord Hunter asked in amazement.

"Of course," said Clara then added, "The letter addressed to a Mrs Freda Shetland is the one with four people in it."

Clara took the bundle of letters out of her receptacle and taking the one off the top she took the sheet of paper out of the envelope and said, "This is the one, it is written by a Sir Roy Grey to a Mrs Freda Shetland, but it ends, 'PS, Dick cannot wait until he joins Fanny again'. You will have to ask Mrs Freda Shetland to tell this Dick and Fanny that if they are being blackmailed the letter is now destroyed."

Lord Hunter was bereft of speech. He stood up and walked over to the mantelpiece to hide his embarrassment and waited until his cheeks became less inflamed.

Clara and Effie both sat and looked at Lord Hunter's back waiting for him to reply.

He took a deep breath and turning he said with his eyes downcast, "You had better give me the letters and I will see what I can do," he held out his hand.

Clara handed him the letters and asked, "Are you going to read them all?"

"Certainly not, I will have to read the names at the top of the letters to make sure they match the name on the envelopes, of course, but that is as far as it will go. They do not call me Elmer Wolf."

"They do not call us Elmer Wolf either, but we enjoyed reading them, didn't we, Effie?"

"Yes, we had a good laugh at some of them. This will go no further than us. I look at it as our reward for retrieving the letters. Look how much money and upset we are saving the victims of these letters," Effie said logically.

"That is right; it was our reward," nodded Clara.

"I can see I am not going to win this argument. Just leave the letters with me, and I will see they get returned to their rightful owners," Lord Hunter told them.

"Excellent. That is our bit done now. Shall we go shopping, Clara?" Effie asked.

"If the infamous Elmer Wolf should happen to call while you are out, what shall I tell him?" Effie's brother wanted to know.

"Anything you like," replied his sister as she closed the door.

Lord Hunter could not resist the temptation of opening the first letter and reading the contents. When he had finished, he closed his eyes and thought, *Oh My*

God, thank goodness they thought they were funny if this letter is anything to go by.

Lord Hunter folded the letter up, put it back in its envelope then spent the next ten-minute checking that all the letters corresponded with the name and address on the envelopes. He walked into the hall, took his coat off the cloak stand, put the bundle of love letters in his inside pocket and left the house.

It was three in the afternoon when Lord Hunter arrived back home, and only half the letters returned to their rightful owners. He was surprised how grateful the people being blackmailed were to get their letters back, both men and women. As soon as they had their letters back, Edwin looked on as each and every victim of blackmail threw the letters on the fire and watched them burn.

Lord Hunter had just taken off his boots to give his aching feet a rest when Wilson knocked on the door and announced Oscar.

"Come in, Oscar," Lord Hunter said, "Take off your boots and make yourself at home. Fetch a glass from the cabinet over there and have a port."

"I don't mind if I do."

Oscar went and collected a glass, poured himself a drink and slipped off his boots.

"That is a relief," Oscar said wriggling his toes.

"Actually, Edwin, I came to see if you know what is going on with Clara and Effie. They were sneaking about our house early this morning, and as I passed Clara's bedroom, I heard fits of laughter. I knocked on the door, and they fell silent. When I opened the door, they were both sitting on the bed, and they had just hidden something under the bedclothes. There was such a look of innocence on their faces; I knew they were up to something."

Lord Hunter looked across at the fair-haired, handsome young man and he had nothing but admiration for him. He knew how difficult it was bringing up one sister let alone three younger brothers as well. He thought Oscar had done a magnificent job. He liked all the family.

Edwin decided to tell Oscar the truth, "Yes, Oscar, I know what is going on, or to be exact, I know what has been going on, and I am pleased to tell you it is all over. This escapade anyway, no doubt there will be others, Effie and Clara seem to have become good friends."

"Yes, they have. Unfortunately, it will not be for much longer; we leave for home next week. We are only here for a month, and this is our third week which is nearly at an end. It was a tester to see how Clara faired in the big city, and she does not seem to have changed very much while we have been here. I was hoping she would see what it is like to act like a real lady, but it has not worked. It has all been a waste of time and money."

"On the contrary, Oscar, I think it is the best money you could have spent. If you had not come to Frithwood, then we would never have met, and that would have been a tragedy. There is nothing wrong with Clara as she is. In fact, she seems to be constantly on my mind. I have never met a woman that has made such an impression on me before.

"Please don't try to make her into something she isn't, she is just perfect as she is. I must warn you, if it carries on like this, I might end up trying to woo her into becoming my wife. I cannot believe it myself, the way I am attracted to Clara after such a short acquaintance. Would you have any objections if I did?"

Oscar felt a tight hand closing around his heart, Clara was his sister, and she had been part of him for nearly twenty years. The thought of not having her around anymore left him cold.

Lord Hunter looked across at Oscar and asked, "Is your objection anything to do with the things Harvey keep's inferring about me?"

Oscar coughed and said, "I have no objection to you paying court to Clara. In fact, I think you are the perfect man for her. I have been responsible for Clara for so long it will be like losing my right hand, it will take some getting used to. Letting her go, I mean."

"You will not be losing her, Oscar, and anyway, I know Clara would never allow that to happen, and I would not want her to. You and I would become brothers-in-law so you will be gaining a brother, not losing a sister.

"I do know what you mean though. When Effie came to me and told me she was engaged to Elmer Wolf, I was stunned. How could my little Effie be engaged to that snivelling weasel? How could she leave this home and me to go and live with that dirty, ignorant excuse of a man?

"Effie has never shown any preference for any of the men that came into her life and here she was, engaged to that man. I took it personally, thinking she wanted to escape from me; I was devastated. I had tried my best to give her as much love as I could to compensate for the lack of a mother and father.

"I decided not to question her over it. But I had noticed how she cowered away from Elmer and would never go out for a walk with him, but she still insisted she was engaged to him. It was very baffling and frustrating," Edwin told Oscar.

"I saw for myself how she cringed when he entered the room the first day we met. I did not think it was the reaction to a besotted lover," Oscar agreed.

"I waited and hoped Effie would come to me and tell me what was going on, but she did not. I would never have let her marry him; you know. I found out, sort of, via Clara," Edwin said.

"Clara?"

"Yes, Clara. Help yourself to another port; you are going to need it."

Oscar stood up and brought the decanter over and refilled both their glasses then sat back down to listen to Edwin's story.

When Edwin had told his story, he added, "God, Oscar, I was so embarrassed when Effie and Clara sat there telling me about the love letters and that they had read them all and they had had a good laugh over them.

"When they came out with the bit about there being four people in one of the letters about, 'Dick wanting to meet Fanny again,' I had to stand up and go over to the fireplace so my back was towards them. I hoped when I turned around, they would think it was the heat from the fire that had made my face bright red. It has been a long time since I have blushed like that," Edwin finished.

Their eyes met across the room, and they both burst out laughing at the same time, and they did not stop until they were both wiping the tears from their eyes.

"I must admit to feeling pleased that Effie is no longer engaged to Elmer Wolf. Does he know by the way, that he no longer has any hold over her?" Oscar asked.

"Not that I know of, but it does not matter anymore. I do not care whether he knows or not. He had better not come around here anymore, or he will leave with a black eye and busted nose, to say the least."

"Surely if the letter is gone, he would not dare come here to see her."

"If he does not know who has taken the letters, and I do not think he could possibly know, he might try bluffing. There is going to be quite a number of people that he has been blackmailing who are going to be able to tell him to go to hell. If Elmer has no other way of making a living, his easy income has gone. He will have to think of some other way to make a crust, and it had better not involve this house again."

"Have you delivered all the letters back to the rightful owners?"

"About half of them but my feet were aching and I had had enough of all the gushing gratitude I got. I did not expect that; it was too much. I had a couple of dodgy moments when the people I was returning the letters to thought I was trying to get money out of them. It got right up my nose, there I was doing them a favour and I was being accused of being a blackmailer. It did not go down very well I can tell you. I felt like taking the letters back and giving them back to Elmer Wolf."

Oscar laughed, "I can imagine. Where are the girls now by the way?"

"They have gone into the city to do some shopping. I dread to think what they are up to now. It would not surprise me if they are trying to track down one or more of the Pomroy children," Edwin said.

"I agree, it would not surprise me either," Oscar smiled. "You do know we will end up being roped in, don't you?"

"It is more than likely," Edwin replied. "Enough about Effie and Clara, we will cross that bridge when we come to it. Having said that, I had thought about having a word with Colonel Peters at the club; he might be able to find something out about Fred Pomroy. I think he was the Pomroy's son that joined the army. What do you think?"

Oscar laughed, "You are as bad as them. I am having nothing to do with it; leave me out of it."

Edwin smiled, "We will see. You said you were leaving at the end of next week?"

"We are. I have to get back to the estate. It has been a nice break, and I am pleased to have made your acquaintance, but a month away from home is long enough. Besides, there is a neighbouring farm that has come up for sale, and I have been seeing a lawyer about buying it for the twins, for when they get older.

"The house is big enough to be split into two. They can run it together. It will provide them both with an income as well as a home of their own. I have to think of their future, and there might not be another opportunity to purchase this farm, so I need to get back and confirm the sale with Mrs Hawkshaw.

"I have been to see my bank manager, and there is enough money to purchase it outright for them. Harvey is thankfully set up. I have no need to worry about him. Our father's brother died two years ago and left him his estate.

"The estate is about seven miles to the south of us, and when he leaves boarding school next summer, he will take up residence there. With a little help from me, he will be able to run the estate. He knows most of the ropes about running it already. We have spent time there when he has been on holiday from school. He knows all the house staff and farm hands. The manager there is doing a good job. He and Harvey get on well together so, for the moment, things are looking up for me.

"In twelve months, I might even have a bit of time to myself. Harvey will be off to look after his own estate, and the twins will be away at boarding school, the same school that Harvey is at now. Clara is no trouble, and she is a big help around the house. I do not think there will be any trouble finding her a suitable husband, do you?"

"No, I can honestly say I do not think you will have any difficulty in finding Clara a suitable husband. Do many estates come up for sale in your neck of the woods?" asked Edwin.

"No, not very often, but as it turns out both our neighbour's estates, to either side of us, are up for sale. The estate to the north belonged to Lord Wellford. He and Lady Wellford never had any children, and his estate has passed to his nephew, who instantly put it up for sale. It is too big and expensive for me to buy for the twins.

"The estate to the south belongs to Mrs Hawkshaw, who lived there with her husband. He has now passed away, and she is selling up and going to live with her married daughter. Before we came here, she called to see me and asked me if I would be interested in buying her estate. I told Mrs Hawkshaw I most certainly would, and as I was coming to Frithwood, I would go and see the bank manager and a lawyer to arrange it all.

"I would be obliged if you could keep it under your hat for the moment, Edwin; the twins know nothing about it. Just in case the sale falls through, you never know. I do not want to get the boys' hopes up.

"Harvey and Clara know of it, of course, I had to ask them if they had any objection to my purchasing Bluebell House because it was using the money from our estate, and they had a right to be asked. They did not object of course. They both gave their consent willingly." Oscar told him.

"You know, Oscar, I am really impressed with you, and I take my hat off to you. You make a difficult job, like bringing up four siblings, seem effortless. I would not dream of telling the twins about it. This other estate that is up for sale, do you think it would suit Effie and me? That is if you don't mind having us as neighbours. I have been thinking about buying a place in the country and have seen three or four properties, but nothing has taken my fancy.

"Effie came with me to see them, and she was not impressed either. We are both sick of living in the middle of the city, wasting our time away. I want something to do. I have enough money to buy something decent. I know nothing about running an estate, but I can learn," Oscar was told.

"I think the estate would suit you very well, Edwin. The property has been unoccupied for nearly a year now, and things are beginning to need attention. You might be able to get it for a song. I think the nephew is desperate to sell.

"Why don't you and Effie come back with us and go and have a look at it. We have plenty of spare rooms, and I am sure Chester would have the time of his life with our two sheepdogs. I have to tell you though, Edwin, I love Clara very much, and I will not force her into a marriage with someone she does not love or whom she cannot respect."

"I would not expect anything less from you. We might just do that. Come back to Styleham with you. I wonder if Wilbert Wellford is the nephew. I have heard that he has come into an estate, but he was having to sell it because of his gambling debts. I think I will go and see him. Let's have another drink."

After Oscar had left, Lord Hunter put on his boots and made for The Ravens Club. He went in search of Colonel Peters and found him nodding off in an old, wing-backed, leather armchair in front of a blazing fire, a discarded newspaper on his lap.

Edwin tapped the Colonel on his shoulder, and the old man stirred from his nap.

"Edwin, my boy, what brings you here this early? Usually a night rat," the Colonel mumbled.

"Yes, Sir, I am. I came to see you, if you can spare me a few minutes," Edwin told him.

"It's a pleasure, dear boy, pleasure. Pull up a chair, and we will have a drink," Colonel Peters peered around the side of the chair and signalled to the waiter and ordered two brandies.

"Now, my boy, what can an old fool like me do for you?" the Colonel asked.

"I think you are far from being an old fool, Colonel Peters. Do you still keep in touch with your old regiment?"

"I do like to keep my finger on the pulse."

"I don't suppose you have heard anything about a soldier called Fred Pomroy. Have you, Sir?"

"Fred Pomroy, you say, unusual name that, Pomroy. No, cannot say I have, what has he done, gone AWOL? Absent Without Leave, for a civilian like you," the Colonel chuckled.

"Not as far as I know, sir. I am trying to track him down to let him know his parents aren't in such good health. Is there any way I could find out about him, if he is alive or dead or where he is stationed?"

"There is a list of dead or missing in action I could check for you, but that isn't going to help you if he isn't dead or missing," the Colonel chuckled again.

"Very true, Sir," Edwin smiled back at him.

The waiter appeared with their drinks, and Colonel Peters asked him, "Wilks, you hear a lot of gossip in the course of a day, have you heard anything of a Fred Pomroy?"

"As a matter of fact, Colonel, the name cropped up just the other day. Sergeant Brown said he had seen Fred begging on Highbrough Street. He has lost a hand in the

94

line of duty. The army booted him out, and now he cannot find a job. Sad what becomes of these brave lads who go to war for their country and that is how they get treated for their labours."

"I could not agree with you more, Wilks. Does that answer your question, my boy?" the Colonel asked.

"It does indeed. Thank you," Edwin said to the waiter. "Let me pay for the drinks, Colonel, but if you don't mind, I will pass on mine. I must be on my way as I have a lot to do, but I appreciate your help, Sir."

"I will not argue over who is going to pay for the drinks, and don't worry about the brandy, it won't go to waste," the Colonel told him.

Leaving the club, Edwin went on to deliver the last of the love letters, apart from one. He had to admit he was glad to see the back of them and he would feel even better once the last letter had been returned to its rightful owner.

Chapter Eight

Elmer woke up in a cold sweat. His life had become a nightmare. From walking home on top of the world in the early hours of that morning, his world had turned upside down when he arrived home and found his front door wide open.

The first thing Elmer did was run up the stairs into his bedroom and dive into the drawer in his desk where his precious letters were kept. Gone! If he knew who had taken them, he would not hesitate to hunt them down and get them back, but he had no idea where to start and look for them.

First Elmer kicked the roll top desk a few times, then he went over to the bed and dragged off the bed covers, and when this did not satisfy his anger, he pulled off the mattress as well. Still not satisfied, he went over and kicked the desk some more.

Elmer then ran down the stairs and straight outside and tried asking his neighbours if they had seen anybody lurking around his house last night, but nobody had.

He went back upstairs, pulled the mattress back on the bed and lay down on top of it, not bothering to get undressed. He decided to sleep on it. But the nightmare had returned, even in his sleep.

Around 8 o'clock that evening, Elmer changed into his only decent suit and set off for The Ravens Club. At least, he thought, he was now a member of The Club, and he was going to take full advantage of it.

But even that, when he strolled up to the reception desk, was a smack in the face. There was no sign of his name on last night's entries, nor that of Lord Hunter or any of the other gentlemen he had spent a few hours within the private room.

Elmer had been duped—he had no quarrel with that—he had duped a few people in his time, it was a way of life for him, but the letters were a different matter altogether. They were his livelihood, his sole income, without them he would have to get a job and the very thought of that made him come out in another cold sweat. He headed for home.

All Elmer's troubles had started when that woman Clara had appeared on the scene. True, when Effie had agreed to get engaged to him, she had made the stipulation that for the first few months it was to be their secret. Her brother knew, of course, but nobody else, just the three of them. Another mistake he had made. With the letter gone, there was no way of proving that he and Effie were ever engaged. Effie had said she wanted to do things right and that meant him courting her from the beginning and she had said they could only be seen together in public if her brother was present.

Lord Hunter had refused to accompany them anywhere so the only time Elmer had seen Effie was at their house and always in the presence of his lordship. He hated Lord Hunter, so he had kept a low profile, only calling to see Effie once every other week until just of late, and he had started to call at their residence more and more frequently.

Lord Hunter treated him like muck stuck to the bottom of his well-polished boot. He had conned Elmer into going to The Ravens Club last night. Elmer realised now it had been done to get him out of his house. He should have been wise enough to realise that, but he had been too eager to gain membership of the club.

There would have been lots of ripe pickings there, coats left hung up for pockets to be gone through, gossip to be listened to, no end of opportunities to be had. It was too late now; the letters were gone, and Elmer was not a member of The Ravens Club.

He had no one but himself to blame for being so eager to get his foot on the ladder at the club. *Served him right, he thought he knew better.*

Maybe, just maybe, he could still work on some of his old blackmailed victims. The only trouble was he did not know which one of the victims had arranged the break-in or even if any of them had.

Elmer was ninety-five per cent sure it had something to do with Lord Hunter, that is why he had been so unexpectedly invited to the club, but, as Lord Hunter and his close friends were present at the club with him while the burglary had taken place, he could hardly accuse him or any of his friends of the crime.

Elmer lived in a cutthroat world, it could have been anyone, anyone at all, someone might, at this very moment be blackmailing the victims themselves, and he had no way of knowing.

It was now 11:45 pm. Elmer could not rest at home, so he headed back into the city.

He waited, out of sight, in a dark alleyway across the road from the club. Any lesser man would have thought twice about standing by themselves after midnight in a dark alleyway, but not Elmer; he did his best work in the dead of night, night-time was his friend.

Elmer saw Mr Moorland come out of the club and walk unsteadily in the direction of his home.

Elmer followed at a discrete distance until Mr Moorland was within twenty yards of his front door before he tapped Mr Moorland on the shoulder and said, "Payday I think, Mr Moorland, or I accompany you inside and tell your wife of your little indiscretion."

Mr Moorland, although a little unsteady on his feet, turned and looked at Elmer Wolf.

Taking his walking stick, Mr Moorland raised it above his head and said, "Payday indeed for you, Elmer Wolf."

And Mr Moorland brought his stick down along Elmer's cheek and raised it a second time to repeat the action.

"You will get no more money out of me. I have had the letter returned to me, and now the letter is destroyed, burnt to a cinder. If you ever come near me again, I will have the peelers on you. Now get out of my sight, or feel this stick on the other side of your face," Mr Moorland threatened.

Elmer turned and rubbing his cheek, he made his way home. *This is not looking good,* he thought. If Mr Moorland's letter has been returned to him, how many more of his victims had received their letter back?

While Elmer was still fast asleep, Effie joined her brother at the breakfast table, "Good morning, Effie."

"Good morning, Edwin, how is the letter delivery service going?"

"I wanted to see you about that; there is only one letter left to be delivered. Do you know Mrs Warwick?"

"I think we have met a couple of times. Why?"

"The one letter that remains belongs to Mrs Warwick, and as you are well aware her husband is an insanely jealous man, how she found time to have an affair is beyond me. He keeps her tied to his hip, so I think it would be best if you were to return the letter to her. If her husband finds out I have been seeking her out, she will be in more trouble than is good for her and me too thinking about it. I do not want him coming after me wanting to know why I wanted to see his wife."

"I do not see that being a problem. I will take Clara with me, so she can see what Mrs Warwick's face looks like. She said only yesterday I had the advantage over her because she did not know what any of the people who had written the letters looked like and it had made her curious.

"I told her they all looked like us, one face, two arms, one body and two legs. She thought it very amusing, but I know she will enjoy going to meet Mrs Warwick."

"No doubt she will, I can just imagine her saying that."

"Have all the victims of blackmail been grateful for the return of their letters?"

"A few of them thought I had taken over from Elmer Wolf, and I wanted money for their safe return. They were apologetic once they knew I was there purely to return the letters. I shall be glad to know when the last one is delivered."

Effie and Clara were shown into Mrs Warwick's sitting room, and they found her sitting on a sofa which was covered in cream silk which, in turn, was covered in pink roses.

Mrs Warwick's dress was white with tiny pink flowers adorning it, and she seemed to blend into the sofa. Mr Warwick was also in attendance, standing at the fireplace with one booted foot on the fender and an elbow resting on the mantelpiece.

Effie had warned Clara about Mr Warwick's jealousy and had told her to be careful of what she said if he was present.

"What brings you here, Miss Hunter? It is unusual, to say the least. You don't usually make social calls here during the day," Mr Warwick wanted to know.

Clara jumped in and said, "Effie, Miss Hunter has been set the task of showing me around the city and introducing me to people of consequence and she said your wife was one of the most eminent ladies of fashion in Frithwood, and she wanted me to meet her. Is that all right, sir? I do not want to intrude on your privacy, we will leave right away if our presence offends you."

"Nonsense, my dear," said the puffed-up Mr Warwick taking the bait that Clara had handed out to him. "I am delighted that dear Miss Hunter thinks my wife is a lady of consequence. Now I know why you are here; I will leave you to have a natter and catch up on all the current gossip. I know you ladies like to do that." He took his wife's hand and kissed the back of it and nodding to Effie and Clara he left the room.

"Let me introduce you to Miss Clara Lander, Mrs Warwick. She and her brothers have come to Frithwood for a few weeks, and I have the pleasure of showing her about and introducing her to people. I thought it would be a good idea to introduce her to you. I hope you don't mind?" explained Effie.

Mrs Warwick put her finger to her mouth and pointed at the door then said, "I am very flattered by such attention, Miss Hunter. This makes a very pleasant change to my daily routine. Do you mind if I go and ask my husband if it will be all right to accompany you two ladies for a walk around the park? I think it would be most advantageous to this charming young lady to be seen abroad under my chaperone."

"It is certainly a beautiful morning to take a stroll, but if it displeases your husband we had better stay indoors," Effie said. "I hope we have not inconvenienced you."

"I will just go and ask Mr Warwick if he minds. I am sure it will be all right, but he does worry about me so." Mrs Warwick stood up and glided silently to the door.

Opening the door with a sudden jerk, Mrs Warwick caught her husband with his ear to the door.

Smiling sweetly at him she asked, "Gordon, dear, there you are, I was just on my way to find you. Do you mind if I take a stroll around the park with these two ladies? I may be able to introduce Miss Lander to some of our friends."

"Certainly, my dear, you go for a nice stroll around the park. It will be nice for you to get out, but do not stop out too long; I don't want you catching a chill." He bowed to Effie and Clara once more, then turned and walked across the hall, disappearing behind a door opposite.

Mrs Warwick donned her hat and coat and walked briskly to the front door, and once they were all standing outside on the doorstep, Mrs Warwick closed the door firmly behind them, then they all crossed the road into the park opposite.

"Thank you for coming, whatever the reason is, thank you for coming. Just to get out of the house alone is so pleasant. I am beginning to feel like a prisoner in my own home. Mr Warwick watches my every move, I am slowly being suffocated to death," Mrs Warwick told them.

"He will be upstairs at this very moment watching us. I only hope we do not bump into any male acquaintance that might stop to say hello or my life will not be worth living. Mr Warwick will make it sound as if I had arranged to meet him in the park. I do not know why he has become so obsessive about me meeting people."

"Mrs Warwick, I hope we are not going to be the cause of any marital misunderstanding between you and Mr Warwick. We have come to return a compromising letter you wrote to someone, that somehow, got into the hands of Elmer Wolf. Because of the nature of the letter we believe he has been blackmailing you.

"The letter, along with a number of other letters came into my brother's possession. He has returned all the other letters to the rightful owners, but he thought it would be more prudent, because of your husband's jealousy, if I brought your letter back to you, and he was right, I can see that now," Effie said.

"You have the letter?" whispered Mrs Warwick in disbelief.

"I do. If Elmer Wolf comes near you again demanding money, you can tell him he no longer has a hold over you. If he threatens to go to your husband, you can tell him it will be his word against yours.

"Edwin has put word out that Elmer Wolf is a blackmailer and is trying to cause trouble between husband and wife, so no doubt your husband will eventually hear about it. I do not think the Wolf, as Clara and I call him, will dare approach, Mr Warwick.

"If, as you say, Mr Warwick is watching us from the upstairs window, how do you want me to pass you the letter?" asked Effie.

"If I can manage it, would you allow me to come to your house and watch it burn? I dare not for the life of me take it into the house with me. Oh, my dears, you don't know how wonderful your visit has been. Elmer Wolf has been bleeding me dry.

"You have seen for yourselves what my husband is like with me; if he were to find out about the letter, he would never let me out of the house again. You have made me feel like a silly teenager instead of a forty-year-old married woman. I will never be able to repay you for this." Mrs Warwick was having difficulty in holding back the tears.

"You owe us no thanks. Giving back the letters to Elmer's victims gives me more pleasure than you are feeling right now, I can assure you of that. We will be happy to receive you at our house to throw the letter on the fire. Be thankful and enjoy the thought that the Wolf cannot threaten you anymore," said Effie, then she asked, "Why do you stand for the way Mr Warwick treats you?"

"It is something that has developed and got worse over the years. Gordon was always a bit jealous when we first met, and I found it flattering, but now it is an obsession with him. He is driving me away. When I had the affair with Gerry, Gerry was so gentle and loving I would have given anything to have been able to run off with him and never have to be suffocated by Gordon, again.

"But the affair did not last very long. Along came somebody single, younger, prettier and richer than me. That was the end of my short-lived affair. I came to realise I could have done much worse than, Gordon," Mrs Warwick said.

"I pity the young girl that married Gerry. She will never have a minute's peace of mind wondering where he is, what he is doing or who he is doing it with. It would not surprise me to learn that Gerry sold the love letter to Elmer Wolf. He would not care a jot what Elmer intended to do with the letter. Gerry would not care if the letter came back to haunt me.

"We do foolish things sometimes, and they come back and bite us on the bottom, this was one of the foolish things I did. I always feel guilty for cheating on Gordon, and that is one of the reasons I let him treat me as he does. I think he has a right to be suspicious of me, or maybe he even learnt about the affair at the time, I just do not know.

"But now, if you have the letter safe, I might try and get Gordon, to let me have a bit of freedom, a bit of life for myself. I would never think about having another affair with anyone ever again, and never in a million years would I put anything in writing if I did. I have learnt my lesson the hard way."

"Do you still see him?" asked Clara. "The man you had an affair with I mean."

"No, he is married and has two children. The affair ended about three years ago. It was not worth the pain and trouble it has caused me, but I can now put it all behind me."

"Elmer Wolf has been blackmailing you for three years?" asked Effie in disbelief.

"He has, but no more, thanks to you, Miss Hunter. Is there anything I can do for you in return?" asked Mrs Warwick.

"I can assure you, Mrs Warwick, we want nothing. I too wrote a stupid letter to someone I should not have, and like your letter, my letter got into the hands of Elmer Wolf. He has been blackmailing me also, but not for three years. Nor for money.

"It is Clara you have to thank though, not me. Clara was the one that came up with the plan to get the letter back, it was just good luck that we found all the letters bundled together and Clara said we should take them all and see if he had been blackmailing anyone else, and believe me, there was more than just you and I that he had been blackmailing.

"Like you, Mrs Warwick, my little indiscretion came back to bite me on the bottom, and I had not even had an affair with anyone. I also learnt my lesson the hard way;

I will never put anything like that down on paper again either. Just knowing that the tables have been turned and, the Wolf is now the one on the run and nasty things, I hope, will happen to him, that is enough thanks for me.

"There was something I was going to ask you though, Mrs Warwick, do you know if any of your acquaintances have someone called Pomroy working for them?" Effie changed the subject.

"Mrs Crowman has a kitchen maid working for her called Dolly Pomroy. I remember that because it is such an unusual name. Mrs Crowman was telling me she has had to have words with the gardener, he was taking too much interest in Dolly Pomroy, and she had to nip it in the bud. Could that be the Pomroy you are seeking?"

"It could indeed, thank you, Mrs Warwick," replied Effie.

"Are you going to tell your husband how he is making you feel now you know your letter can no longer be used against you? If he knows he is making you unhappy, he might back off a bit," said Clara.

"Easier said than done, I have tried on more than one occasion, but nothing seems to get through to him. I shall have to try something else. Seeing the pair of you being able to walk out and go and visit friends whenever you like has shown me what a miserable life I am leading. Will you take another turn around the park with me before I go in?"

Mrs Warwick went in search of her husband. She found him in the spare front bedroom looking out of the window, "There you are Gordon, I thought I would find you here, spying on me as usual."

"My dear, I was doing no such thing, I merely came to the window to see what the weather was doing."

"If you have to lie about something, Gordon, then you are doing something wrong, but I will let it pass. I know you were spying on me, and so do you. I have decided that I do not like living like this; your insane jealousy is driving me away. I have never given you any cause to be so jealous, and if I have, I would like to talk about it, to get it out in the open.

"If it has nothing to do with my behaviour then it must be something to do with yours. You must have something to hide and that is why you are keeping me practically a prisoner in my own home.

"From now on I shall shadow you. I shall go with you to your work and find out what it is you do all day long. I am quite looking forward to it; I am sick of these four walls. The stroll out in the warm sunshine has cheered me up no end. What time will you be leaving for work?"

Mr Warwick began to panic, his wife was right, it was him that had something to hide, and keeping his wife inside their home had been the best way he could think of to keep her from finding out what it was he did.

"My dear, had you told me this before I would have been less protective of you. I am sure you will be even more bored following me around all day."

"What are you hiding, Gordon? Why is it you need me to be cooped up in the house all day? Now you are refusing to let me accompany you to work. I thought it was a good idea then you can spy on me twenty-four hours a day, but at least it will get me out of this house."

"You are taking things to the extreme, Lily. I have never told you to stay within these walls."

"No, not in so many words but you want to know where I have been, what I have been doing and who I have been talking to every minute of the day and it is getting me down. I need to have room to breathe and if going to work with you is the only way to stop you from hounding me, then so be it."

"You will not accompany me to work; I have never heard of such a thing. Do you hear me, Lily?" her husband asked in a threatening tone.

"Very well, I will not accompany you to your work, but I am going out today, and if you dare to question me tonight at supper about where I have been or what I have been doing then I shall hound you like you have been hounding me." Lily turned and walked out of the bedroom slamming the door behind her with such force the window frame rattled.

Having taken their leave of Mrs Warwick, Effie and Clara headed across Frithwood and came to a halt across from a large stone fronted town house.

"This is where Mrs Crowman lives. I thought if we hang around here for a while, we might be lucky enough to see one of the servants and ask them if Dolly Pomroy still works here," Effie told Clara.

After fifteen minutes a footboy come out of the house and headed into the city centre. Clara and Effie set off in pursuit, catching up with him just before he entered the greengrocers.

"Hello," Effie said, "Do you work for Mrs Crowman?"

"I do, but what is it to do with you?" the boy wanted to know.

"Is there a young woman working for Mrs Crowman called Dolly Pomroy?" asked Clara.

"There is. What do you want with Dolly? She will not be there much longer, Mrs Crowman has threatened to dismiss Dolly if she is caught again in the company of the gardener, but she is still seeing him. If old misery guts Crowman finds out, they will both be out on the street."

"If I give you a shilling, will you ask Dolly to come to the corner of Clay Street? Tell her we will be waiting there for her," Effie held out the coin.

"A shilling!" exclaimed the young boy, "I would walk to the South Pole and back for a shilling. Give me the shilling, and when I have got the carrots the cook wants, I am heading back, so I will tell Dolly you want to see her," he held out his hand.

"If I give you the money now, you had better tell Dolly to come and meet us because if you don't, I will go and see Mrs Crowman and tell her you call her old misery guts, then Dolly will not be the only one out on the street. Is that understood?" Effie asked.

"I shall tell her, it is no skin off my nose," he took the coin and went into the shop.

Five minutes later Clara and Effie were following the footboy back towards Mrs Crowman's house. The boy vanished inside the house, and the two ladies carried on to the end of the street and were prepared to wait.

They did not have to wait long, a young woman in a grey dress with white apron and a white mop-cap on her head came hurrying towards them.

"Are you Dolly Pomroy?" asked Clara.

"I am. What do you want to see me about? If Mrs Crowman finds out I have left the house, I will be in even more trouble than I am already."

"To cut a long story short, Dolly, we have been to your mother and father's farm, and they are not doing very well. Your mother told us they had three children, but they had not seen any of you for years. The farm is falling into disrepair. We thought if we could track down at least one of their children, we could let them know what their situation is," Clara said.

"We all left home because our father beat us, all of us, when we were old enough, we all left. Fred went into the army, and I had heard he had been killed, poor sod. Walter, he went to America. Just jumped on a ship and I have not seen or heard of him since."

"I am sorry to hear that," said Effie. "You had better go back now; we do not want you losing your job because of us."

"If I lose my job it will not be because of you. Who are you by the way?"

"Effie Hunter and Clara Lander," replied Clara.

"Thank you for coming to find me and telling me about my parents, but I must be getting back now."

Dolly ran all the way back down the street and was shocked to find the butler waiting for her on her return, "Mrs Crowman wants to see you in the morning room."

With a sinking heart, Dolly knocked on the door and waited to be called in. She found her employer seated on a window seat in the large bay window that looked out over the large rear garden. Dolly could see Henry knelt down tending one of the flowerbeds as she looked past Mrs Crowman into the back garden.

"Where have you been?" asked an enraged Mrs Crowman.

"I was told someone wanted to see me. They came to tell me my mother and father are struggling to cope at the farm, if you please, Mrs Crowman," Dolly gave a small curtsy in the lady's direction.

"In that case, you might as well go and see if there is anything you can do for them; your time here is over. I expect you to be out of this house within the hour. You may go."

Dolly did not bother to curtsy; she turned and left the room. Instead of going to her room to change, she made for the back door and ran across the back lawn to where Henry was tending the flowerbed.

"Henry, I have come to tell you Mrs Crowman has told me to leave, she has dismissed me. I have news that my mother and father need help at the farm. This is a chance for us both to get away from here. I know we have talked about leaving but we had nowhere to go, now we have, I can go home and see my mother, I miss her.

"I am not too keen on seeing my father, but I am a lot older now and know better than to let him bully me. I am more able to take care of myself. Will you come with me, Henry? We can make a go of it at the farm, have our own house to live in and help my mother. What do you want to do, Henry, stop here or come home with me?"

"Go change your clothes and I will meet you out front. You do not have to ask me twice, Dolly. I cannot wait to get out of this place. You told me that your father beat you, well, he will not beat you while I am around," Henry told her.

Mrs Crowman was waiting for Dolly when she returned to the house, "How dare you disobey me and go to see Henry?" she shouted, "Get out of here this instant."

"I intend to, I am going to change my clothes and then you will not see me for dust. You may search me if you wish to, but you will not find anything on me belonging to you. I do not want anything that reminds me of you; I want to forget you as soon as I can. I cannot say it has been a pleasure working for you because it has not." Dolly ran to the back staircase and up to her room.

Henry was waiting for her when she left by the front door, leaving it wide open. Neither of them had any baggage; they were travelling light because neither of them had anything to carry, only the clothes they stood up in.

"We are going to have to walk, Henry, it is about eleven miles, but we should be there by nightfall," Dolly told him.

"What if your parents turn us away when we get there?" he asked.

"They won't. I know my mother won't anyway. She was heartbroken when we all left. If they do turn us away when we get there, something will turn up for us, at least we will be together."

"Like you said, Dolly, it is the best chance we have of getting away. If your mother lets us stay, we will make a go of the farm. We will survive somehow, even if we are turned away; you are right, we will be together. I cannot wait to get the smell of the city out of my nose and never have to do the bidding of that old cow Crowman, ever again. I am in heaven, sheer heaven."

There was a spring in both their steps as they left the city, arms around each other, heading for home.

Chapter Nine

"You were right, Oscar, about the Pomroys," Clara said next morning. "We have found Dolly Pomroy, and she told us the reason they had all left home was because their father used to beat them. She said she had heard the brother who had gone to war had been killed in action, and the other brother had jumped on-board a ship and sailed off to America. Anyway, we told her about her mother and father and left it at that; it is up to her to decide what she wants to do."

"Good, now you have got that off your mind don't be getting into any more adventures. We are heading back home on Friday don't forget," Oscar reminded her.

"Harvey and I are taking Lee and Tom to the zoo this morning; it might be the last opportunity we have. Are you coming with us?" Clara asked.

"No, I have things to do. I hope you have a good time, don't let one of the boys get eaten by a lion," he smiled.

The room door burst open, and Harvey appeared holding up his black jacket, "Look at this," he raged, "There must be ghosts living in this house. I searched my wardrobe high and low for one of my black jackets, and I could not find either of them and now, here they are back in my wardrobe, and look at this," he pointed at the torn lapel. "Someone has been wearing them or its ghosts playing tricks on me."

Clara sat with an air of innocence about her, and Oscar avoided looking at her.

"Never mind, Harvey, you shall have some money to go and buy yourself another jacket while we are in the city. If you go and see Mrs Croft, I am sure she will be able to repair that one for you as well, then you will have an extra jacket in your wardrobe," Oscar tried to soothe the agitated Harvey.

"In that case, I will go and see Mrs Croft, but I am telling you, Oscar, there are ghosts about, can't be anything else."

"I wonder what happened to Harvey's jacket," Clara said when Harvey had gone.

Oscar looked across at his sister and said, "It is not like you to tell lies, Clara."

"What makes you say that?"

"Because I know you know exactly what happened to Harvey's jacket."

"How do you know that?" she wanted to know.

"Edwin told me," he replied candidly.

"What a gabster," said an indignant Clara.

"No such thing, Clara. I went to ask him if he knew what you and Effie were up to. I knew you were up to something; you have only yourself to blame for that. Bringing up a girl is no picnic. I have to look out for you just like Edwin has to look out for Effie. We are comrades in arms he and I.

"If the boot had been on the other foot and he had come to me to ask me about Effie I would have told him, had I known anything that is. We were not telling tales on you and Effie; we both love you and want to keep you both safe.

"You went to Edwin for help, and I am glad you had the sense to do so. I hope Effie knows that she may come to me any time she needs help if, for any reason, she feels she cannot approach her brother. I am willing to do whatever was in my power to help either of you. You do know that, don't you, Clara?" Oscar wanted to know.

"Yes, I do, in fact, I went as far as to tell Lord Hunter exactly that. I told him I could not come to ask you for help because you were not a member of The Ravens Club, that is why I had approached him."

Oscar smiled, "And what was his reply to that?"

"He said he was pleased to know he was second best."

Oscar burst out laughing.

"That is how you knew about the lapel on Harvey's jacket being torn, and why you told him you would buy him a new one?"

"That is correct," he smiled.

"I had to help Effie. Would you rather I had left her to try and find a way to get the letter back on her own?"

"No, of course, I wouldn't. I think it was very brave of you both to do what you did, but you should have come to either Edwin or me for help. You were both lucky nothing untoward befell you."

"Anyway, there's not much time left to get into any more trouble before we leave for home, is there?" she said changing the subject.

"I sincerely hope not."

Elmer Wolf was up at the crack of dawn that morning, he still had a problem getting to sleep, and when he did, the nightmares woke him up. He was pacing the floor thinking of the best way to get Effie alone. Elmer decided to put in place the idea that had come, unbidden, into his head whilst he tossed and turned, trying to get some sleep.

He had decided to drop a note through the Hunters' letterbox asking Effie to meet him in the park at 10 o'clock that morning. He wrote the note using his left hand and signed it 'Mrs Warwick'. One of the men in the inn last night had told Elmer he had seen Mrs Warwick, walking in the park with Effie and that other woman, the one that has not been in Frithwood very long.

He went on to tell Elmer he had thought it was funny, seeing all three of them deep in conversation, taking a turn around the park when everybody knows how jealous Gordon Warwick is, and how he keeps his wife on a very tight rein.

He would use Mrs Warwick's name to get Effie into the park. He knew if he signed the note himself, she would never come to meet him. So, he had risen very early, wrote the note and went to post it through the Hunters' letterbox before most people were up and about. He did not want to be seen posting the letter.

When Wilson handed Effie a letter, she was having breakfast with Edwin. She read it and said to Edwin, "It is from Mrs Warwick, she wants to meet me in the park at 10 o'clock. I wonder what she wants."

Edwin asked Wilson how the letter had been delivered, "It was on the doormat when I went to unlock the door this morning, my lord,"

"Did you see who delivered it?"

"There was nobody to be seen when I looked out, my lord, the street was empty."

"Thank you, Wilson. That will be all."

When Wilson had left the room, Edwin said, "I do not think you should go on your own, Effie."

"Why ever not?" she wanted to know.

"You don't know who actually sent the letter; it could have been anybody."

"Nothing is going to happen to me at 10 o'clock in the morning in broad daylight in a busy park. Anyway, it might be the only way Mrs Warwick can get in touch with me. You know what her husband is like."

"Yes, I do, and that is precisely why I am not convinced it is from Mrs Warwick. If her husband is so jealous, why is she arranging to meet you in the park right outside her home where she could be seen by Gordon Warwick?"

"I should think he will be at work by 10 o'clock, don't you?"

"Precisely my point, why the park, why not invite you into her home? If her husband is at work, she will have the house to herself. I know it will be pointless to try and persuade you not to go alone for I can see you are determined to go whatever I say."

"Yes, I am, I feel sorry for her, not only because of the way her husband treats her but because I know exactly how it feels to be blackmailed. She said she was going to try and get her husband to let her start going out; she might be testing him."

Edwin left the house early and went down the road to the Landers house, "Good morning, Trueman. Is Mr Lander in?"

"He is, my lord, in the library."

"Thank you, I know where it is, no need for you to trouble yourself."

Oscar looked up to see Lord Hunter approaching him across the carpet.

"I have to go and see the bank manager at 9:30 and I do not want to miss the appointment. I want to know what the money situation is if I am going to buy that estate we were talking about. Effie had a letter this morning asking her to meet Mrs Warwick in the park at 10 o'clock, and I do not think it was from Mrs Warwick.

"It might be me being paranoid, but I cannot imagine Elmer Wolf will let the matter of the missing letters drop so easily. If I did not have this appointment to keep, I would have followed her to make sure she is safe. Would you take a wander around the park and keep an eye on Effie for me? You don't have to let her know you are following her and if it is Mrs Warwick she meets, then no harm is done."

"I will be there, Edwin, it is better to be safe than sorry, and it would surprise me too, if Elmer Wolf let the matter of the missing letters drop."

"I might be out of the bank in time to get there before 10, but just in case I am not, I thought I would request your help. I have to go now; let me know the outcome."

"Of course," Oscar replied.

At the library door, Lord Hunter turned and asked Oscar, "Clara not up yet?"

Oscar smiled and told him, "You have just missed her by five minutes. She and Harvey have taken the twins to the zoo. They might be back for lunchtime."

"I just thought I would ask." He closed the door on his way out.

Oscar made his way to the park and positioned himself on a wooden bench placed under some rhododendron trees, but off the well-trodden path. He had a good view of the gate entrance to the park where Effie would enter. He could also see anyone approaching from the other direction. Mrs Warwick's residence was facing the park, and the most obvious entrance into the park from her house was the same entrance that Effie would use.

Oscar must have left the house much earlier than he thought because he seemed to have been sitting there for ages before he spotted Effie entering the park gates. Oscar watched her approaching the bandstand. When she reached it, she went up the wooden steps and sat down on the wooden bench that ran the full circumference with the exception of the open doorway.

Almost immediately after Effie had sat down, Oscar saw Elmer Wolf appear from the rear of the bandstand and sidle along the side, then run up the steps and stand in front of Effie.

"We need to set a date for our wedding. I am not pampering to you any longer, set a date now or the letter goes public," Elmer scowled at Effie.

Effie stood up, and her face was inches from his, she could smell his stale breath, "Get out of my way. How dare you threaten me? You can no longer use the letter to control me. The letter is burnt, and all the other letters you had stashed away with it have been delivered back to their rightful owners. Your days as a blackmailer are over. Word has been put out about your blackmailing, and if you approach anyone demanding money from now on, you had better watch out."

"You are a snooty little madam!" Elmer exclaimed and made a grab for Effie's wrist and twisted it behind her back.

Neither of them heard or saw Oscar appear and Effie was startled to feel a strong arm around her waist as Elmer, unexpectedly, let go of her wrist.

Effie turned to see Oscar standing at her side. She was so relieved she turned into him and buried her face in his chest at the same time throwing her arms around his waist and clinging on for dear life.

Oscar's free hand was round Elmer's throat, and he had him pinned down on the bench.

"If you ever lay a finger on Effie again, you will have to answer to me. Do you hear me? If I hear you have been within fifty feet of her, I will seek you out and break every bone in your miserable little body. Is that understood?"

Elmer could only nod his head; his face was beginning to turn red, and he was gasping for breath under the steel grip of Oscar's hand.

"You seem to have your hand's full, Oscar. I shall be pleased to take this snivelling excuse for a man off your hands."

Lord Hunter appeared at Oscar's side, "I think you had better let him go now, Oscar, his face is beginning to explode."

Oscar let him go, and Elmer fell forward, coughing and choking only to find his nose at the end of Lord Hunter's fist. Then, when he was recovering from the shock of the burst nose Lord Hunter sent another crushing blow to his left eye knocking his head back onto the wooden bandstand.

"I hope you have got the message, Elmer, because if you have not, we can always repeat what we are trying to get through to you now. Get out of our sight and out of our lives, this had better be the last time any of us set eyes on you," Lord Hunter said.

Elmer made a quick escape pleased to be out of the bandstand and heading for home.

"Are you alright, Effie?" asked her brother watching Elmer running for his life out of the park.

She looked up at Oscar and replied, "Never felt better."

"I will leave you to take Effie home, Oscar. I am going to Highbrough Street. I had word yesterday that Fred Pomroy has been seen begging there. He has a hand missing by all accounts," Lord Hunter told them.

"Fred Pomroy is alive? I do hope you are right, Edwin. Dolly Pomroy told us she had been told her brother had been killed in action," Effie informed him.

"It is not unusual for old soldiers who came back from the front with parts of their body missing, to spread it around that they were dead because the last thing they want is sympathy. I am on my way to see if I can find him."

Effie and Oscar made their way out of the park, and to Oscar's delight, she walked by his side and had no objection to his hand still resting on her waist where it remained until they parted at her door.

"Thank you, Oscar, it was very foolish of me. I should have listened to Edwin. I suppose it was he that told you to come and keep an eye on me?" she asked him before they parted.

"It was, and I am glad he did," Oscar smiled down at her. "You had better go inside now. Looking up at me with those smiling grey eyes and tasty looking lips are doing funny things to me that should not be happening in the middle of the morning on a busy street," he gave her a final squeeze of the waist and let her go.

Effie, with a sigh of contentment, watched Oscar until he disappeared, then she ran up the steps and into the house, a smile still playing on her lips.

Lord Hunter walked the length of Highbrough Street but saw no evidence of a man with one hand begging.

On impulse, he stopped at a flower seller and asked if she knew of a Fred Pomroy.

The flower seller informed Edwin that Fred Pomroy was sleeping rough under the Arches and did not appear until around midday.

Edwin headed in the direction of the Arches and eventually came to a very rundown part of the city. He continued on his way passing cardboard boxes with feet sticking out and threadbare blankets covering inert bodies until he came to a crowd of shabbily dressed men and women, all huddled around a big steel drum in which someone had set a fire going. They all eyed Edwin with suspicion.

"Can anyone tell me where I can find Fred Pomroy?" Edwin asked.

"Who wants to know?" one of the tramps demanded.

"I have word for him, about his family," he told them.

"See that blanket over there, that is where you will find him," one of the women told him, and she gave him a black-toothed grin.

All the tramps huddled around the fire watched Edwin walk over to the blanket and were expecting good sport, Fred Pomroy was not known for his friendliness since he had been living there.

Edwin balanced equally on both feet bent down and pulled the blanket away and was ready for any unfriendly greeting that might come his way.

The motionless figure sprung to life and tried to catch Edwin by his throat with his one good hand, but Edwin was too quick for him. He caught Fred by the wrist and brought it down by his side.

"Steady there, Fred. I am not here to do you any harm. I have word of your mother and father."

"What if I don't want word of my mother and father?"

"I am going to tell you anyway. Your mother and father are not in good health; they need you at the farm. Now you have the information; you must do with it what you wish, it is of little consequence to me.

"Your parents did my family a good turn, although they did not know it at the time. So, I thought I would do them a favour and try and find you for them. Your parents are not aware that I have come to see you, if that is what you are afraid of. I shall not inform them of your whereabouts; it is your decision whether you return or not." Edwin told him.

"Much use I would be with only one hand," Fred said bitterly.

"One hand is better than no hands, Fred. You can still milk a cow, can't you? I know what I would prefer, milking a cow with one hand and a roof over my head or feeling sorry for myself and living rough under a rotting blanket." Edwin turned and started walking back the way he had come.

Fred started following Edwin, and he asked, "You think they would want me back?"

"There is only one way to find out. You can always come back to your rotting blanket if they don't. I am not saying it is going to be easy for you, but it has got to be better than this, anything is better than this."

Fred watched Lord Hunter's back until it disappeared around the corner then turned and looked back towards the Arches.

Yes, he thought, *anything has got to be better than this,* and began to follow in Edwin's footsteps.

Fred stood for a long time looking towards the farm. He had not been home for eight years or more. His father had been a hard, cruel man and he did not relish meeting him again. Fred knew his father would ridicule him and tell him he was just as useless now as he had been all those years ago.

Fred would dearly love to see his mother again. He knew she would welcome him back with open arms. He could remember her crying into her apron when he had left to join the army.

Hearing the sound of approaching horses' hoofs, Fred stepped into the side onto the grass verge to let it pass.

The horse was pulled to a standstill at his side, and Fred looked up into the face of a complete stranger.

"Hello," the stranger said, "Can I help you?"

"Who are you?" Fred asked.

"Henry Swift is the name, I am engaged to Dolly Pomroy," the stranger told him.

"Is Dolly here?"

"She is. Do you know her?"

"Yes, she is my sister."

"She will be pleased, shocked and surprised to see you. You must be Walter because we heard Fred had been killed in action."

"Well, you heard wrong," Fred said, holding up his handless arm.

"Hard lines," Henry replied, "Come on up to the house; I will walk with you."

"I do not think that is such a good idea. I thought I would be able to go and see my mother, but it turns out I am not as brave as I thought I was. Please don't tell them you have seen me; I guess it is best to let them think I am dead."

"Don't talk ridiculous, man. Why wouldn't they be pleased to see you? They will be over the moon, and I can tell you I could do with some help on the farm, it is in hell of a state. Dolly and I have only been here ourselves for two days.

"I know Dolly and your mother will be glad to see you; they were both crying when Dolly told your mother she had heard you were dead. Is all this nonsense because of your hand? It could happen to any of us, a slip with the plough or a fall from the barn roof. You have lost a hand, so what? You still have another one, haven't you? You will learn to adapt in time."

"That is easy for you to say."

"Look, Fred, I am a gardener, not a farmer. To be honest, I know nothing about farming, but I am willing to have a go. Your help and experience on the farm would be more than appreciated, one hand or two. Come on up to the house, and don't be daft."

"What about my father?"

"Your father is not much use around the farm now. He did not even recognise Dolly. He seems to be going downhill fast; we have only been here two days and one minute he knows Dolly, the next he doesn't. Your mother says some days are better than others. He sits in a chair by the fire mostly and watches the flames all day long. He does not even know I am here if I have to be honest.

"Your mother says he deserves all he gets because he drove you all away. She has got Dolly back and now you. Your mother will be glad to see you I can guarantee it. Your father could not care less. Your mother has to feed him sometimes. She says he is worse than any baby.

"Your mother needs to see you, Fred, even if you do not stay, come up to the house and let them see you. And to be truthful, you need to see your father. I think you need to see him more than you do your mother and Dolly. You need to see what he has become. You will never have to be afraid of him again, and I mean that in the nicest possible way. The things that happen to you when you are a child seem to linger with you in adulthood. This is the best way to lay that ghost.

"It worked for Dolly; I have never seen her so happy. Your mother says if I am to be living there, Dolly and I have to get married. I have just been to see the parson to make arrangements for the wedding. We are getting married a week on Thursday; you must stay at least until the wedding is over. It has been such a rush. In fact, I need a best man, how are you fixed, Fred, fancy being my best man?"

"If you don't mind having a man with only one hand for best man, I would be delighted, lead on brave knight. Anyone taking Dolly on must have nerves of steel," Fred told him while they were walking home.

Henry walked into the farmhouse kitchen and found all three of them there. Dolly was washing clothes in the sink, Mrs Pomroy was baking a cake and Mr Pomroy was in his favourite chair in front of the fire.

"Mrs Pomroy, Dolly, I want you to meet my best man. I have just found him at the gate and roped him in." He held the door open, and Fred stood in the doorway.

Mrs Pomroy put her hands to her mouth and stared at the figure that was waiting to be invited in. She was unable to speak, and tears started to roll down her face.

Dolly, on the other hand, ran across the room and threw herself at him, wet hands and all. Then she started to pummel him on the chest and said, "Don't you ever do that again, Fred Pomroy, don't you ever die and come back to us. It is enough to give our poor mother a heart attack."

Fred held her close then let her go and went over and put his arms around his mother, and she cried and cried into his chest.

Dolly said to Fred while they ate supper, "Where have you been, Fred, and how is it that you came back home? I thought we had all agreed never to return."

"I was stationed in Africa and had my hand chopped off during a battle, and the army sent me home. I have been living rough under the Arches in Frithwood for the past eighteen months. It was the closest I dare come to home. I wanted to come home more than anything, but I thought you would reject me because of my hand, or lack of it, like the army did.

"This toff came to see me this morning and told me about the situation here at the farm and said I should come home. So, I did. That was about it really, apart from standing like an idiot at the gate to the farm not daring to come up. That is where Henry found me, and he said I was being ridiculous, that you would welcome me back with open arms. What about you, Dolly, how come you are back? Henry tells me you have only been back two days yourselves."

"Similar thing happened to me. Two ladies of quality asked the footboy at Mrs Crowman's to tell me they wanted to talk to me, that I had to go to the end of the street and meet them. I was curious about why two ladies of quality wanted to see me, so I nipped out to see them, they told me much the same as your toff told you. Mrs Crowman was waiting for me when I got back, and she dismissed me. I went to see Henry because we had been stepping out and told him I was going home. I asked him to come with me, so here we are. We are getting married, and we are going to try and sort the farm out. Are you going to stay and help us?" Dolly asked.

"I would love to stay and help if no one has any objection." Fred waited with bated breath.

"Why would we have any objections? This is your home and always will be," his mother told him.

"I think," said Dolly, "That toff of yours, Fred, has something to do with my two ladies of quality. I knew one of them; I had seen her at Mrs Crowman's when she had attended a dinner party once. Her name is Effie Hunter. I noticed her particularly because she was so pretty, and she wore a beautiful scarlet gown. If I could write, I would write her a letter and thank her for what she and her friend have done for us."

"I can write, Dolly, I learnt to read and write in the army. Long days and nights with nothing to do, we all taught each other, the ones that could read and write would teach the ones that could not. The ones wanted to learn, of course, some of the older soldiers said it was a waste of time.

"It is the best thing the army did for me. It has turned out to be one of my pleasures, reading. Whilst I was laid up in the hospital camp, reading kept me sane. If you tell me what you want to say, I will write it down for you. This toff I spoke of, Mother, he told me you had done his family a good turn. What did you do?" Fred wanted to know.

"Nothing really, we didn't know anything about it until they turned up at our door one day and said they owed us some money for some eggs their brothers had borrowed. Stolen really, it was a couple of young lads who took them from the hen coop for breakfast because they had no money on them to pay for them. Their brothers and sisters turned up with the money; if they hadn't, we would not have known the eggs had gone. Good of them to come back, don't you think?"

"Yes, I do, for if the young boys had not stolen the eggs, Fred, Henry and I would not be home right now. I for one will be eternally grateful," Dolly said. "Will you teach me to read and write, Fred?"

"If you wish, of course, I will," her brother told her.

"And me, will you teach me to read and write too?" asked Henry.

"It looks like I am going to be kept busy," said Fred well satisfied.

Chapter Ten

Elmer made his way home with a grubby handkerchief held to his nose. Once inside the safety of his home, he splashed some cold water on his face and looked at his reflection in the cracked mirror which was standing on a lopsided shelf above the sink.

He had two ways to go now. He could think of some way to get back at Lord Hunter and the Landers or, he could cut his losses and leave Frithwood. He decided on the latter.

Taking a battered carpetbag from under the bed, Elmer began to fill it with all his worldly goods. He was surprised to find he had more than he thought. His clothes took up most of the room in the carpetbag, leaving no room for any bedding and he was not going to leave that behind.

Elmer would have to find digs in the next town or city he landed in, and he was going to need his bedding. Taking one of the woollen blankets, he spread it out on the bed, then folding up the sheets and two other woollen blankets he placed them on top of the woollen blanket spread out on the bed. He folded the bottom blanket over the others and rolled them up. Using his leather belt, he fastened them together, realising one belt was not enough to secure the bedding, he found some rope and bound that round as well.

The next thing he had to do was find all his money. Elmer had stashed it all over the house just in case anyone broke in, hoping that way the thieves would not find it all. He had made a small fortune over the past five years or so and he had been very frugal with the money, just in case a day like today happened.

He wished he had done the same with his letters. Leaving them all tied together in one place was a stupid thing to have done. He would know better next time, although he had known better this time, he never believed anybody would break into his house, *Stupid, stupid idiot,* he thought.

Frustrated, he kicked the nearest object, angry with himself for being so stupid for leaving the letters where they could easily be found, and angry with the thief. In fact, he was more than angry with the thief; he felt murderous towards him, if only he could get his hands on him.

It had to be a man that had taken his letters; no thought entered Elmer's head that it could have been a woman. Women are incapable of doing such things.

He was no fool, he knew his easy life would have to end one day and that day had arrived. He thought he was lucky to get away with just a bust nose and a black eye. It could well have been the lockup, or worse.

Now the decision had been made Elmer could not wait to get out of Frithwood in case some other unfortunate person he had bled money out of came looking for him.

Each time Elmer found a wad of notes he put them in different pockets or inside his carpetbag or tucked it in between his folded blanket.

Without a backward glance, Elmer closed the door behind him and made good his escape.

Clara headed for home, leaving Harvey in charge of the twins. They had seen a poster outside of the zoo advertising a boxing match, and of course, the boys just had to go.

The house was empty when Clara arrived home. There was no sign of Oscar, so she went in search of her friend Effie.

Effie was reading in the morning room when Clara walked in.

"Clara, how nice to see you, come and sit down and let me tell you of the little adventure I had this morning."

Effie held out her hand to Clara who took it and they sat on the sofa and got comfortable.

"How did Oscar come to be in the park at just the right time?" Clara asked when she had heard the story.

"Edwin went to see him and asked him if he would keep an eye on me because he thought it was strange that Mrs Warwick, would be dropping letters through the letter box so early in the morning. It turned out he was right. Edwin had to go to the bank and he did not think he would be through with his business in time to get to the park by 10 o'clock.

"As it happened, he would have been, but it all turned out well in the end. The Wolf got a bust nose and black eye, and I doubt I will be seeing him again. But, Clara, Edwin also told us he had been told that Fred Pomroy might still be alive. Edwin has gone to see if he can find him."

"That is excellent news, that Fred Pomroy might be alive, I mean. I wonder what Dolly decided to do," Clara mused.

At that moment Edwin appeared in the doorway, "I came to tell you Fred Pomroy is found. Whether or not he chooses to go back home is anybody's guess."

"Well done, Lord Hunter, I am impressed. I thought you weren't having anything to do with finding the Pomroy children?" Clara's eyes sparkled.

"I did it for the simple reason I wanted to impress you, Miss Lander, and it seems to have worked," he held her gaze.

Clara was the first to cast her eyes down, and she was nettled into saying, "I am sure you did it because you knew it was the right thing to do."

"Are you sure about that?" he counted.

Clara was spared an answer when Wilson appeared behind his lordship and announced, "Mrs Warwick has called to see you, Miss Hunter. She requests a few minutes of your time."

"I will leave you then. Show Mrs Warwick in, Wilson, would you?" Edwin held the door and Mrs Warwick passed through.

"Good afternoon, Mrs Warwick, I was just on my way out."

"Good afternoon, Lord Hunter, I hope I am not intruding?" Mrs Warwick said pulling off her gloves.

"Not in the least." He bowed and shut the door.

Both Effie and Clara stood up as Mrs Warwick came towards them.

"My dear, I hope you don't mind me calling on you at such short notice. I am pleased to see you here as well, Miss Lander."

"No, of course not, you are most welcome. Are you on your own? Have you managed to get out without your husband following you?"

"Shall we sit down and I will tell you all about it. I have a favour to ask of you both."

Effie called for tea to be brought in and Mrs Warwick, once the tray had been delivered and each held a cup of steaming tea, began to explain her predicament.

"After I left you the other day, I went to see Gordon, Mr Warwick that is, and tell him that I was no longer going to stay at home day in, day out and that I was going to go with him to work if he did not trust me. He totally rejected the idea, and he said if I wanted to go out then I could. He would not have me going to work with him.

"When I still insisted on accompanying him to work, he became frantic and insisted that I did no such thing. I think something is going on and he does not want me to know about it. I was wondering if you two ladies would help me by following him to find out where he works.

"I have no idea what he does or where he does it. If I have to be honest, I did not want to know. I am pleased when he leaves the house on a morning for it gives me a bit of breathing space. But the way he changed within minutes of my challenging him has made me suspicious of him. Now I want to know what he does for a living.

"I had thought he worked in a bank, that is where he worked when I met him. There always seems to be plenty of cash around the house. Not that I object to that, but something is not quite right, that is why I have decided to follow him, to set my mind at rest.

"I have been restricted in my movements for so long I would feel much safer if I had the company of friends. You two have turned out to be people I can trust, there are not many people of my acquaintance I can say that about. Most of the people I know are of Gordon's choosing. I know it is an imposition of such a short acquaintance, but I have nobody else to turn to," Mrs Warwick concluded.

"Of course, we will come with you, but it will have to be tomorrow for we leave for home on Friday," Clara informed her.

"Tomorrow will be fine. Most mornings Gordon sets off for work around 8 o'clock. Will you be able to meet me in the park around that time?" Mrs Warwick asked.

"I think it would be best if Clara and I followed him on our own first. Then we will come back to your house and let you know what we had found out, and where he went. If he was to turn around and see you following him, my guess is, he would not go to wherever it is he was going.

"Having three women following behind him, one his wife, I do not think that would be a good idea. He would recognise you straightaway, whereas it would never enter his head that he was being followed if he were to see two women walking down the street behind him," Effie said, "We will keep well back so if he does turn around, he might not recognise us."

"I cannot ask you to do such a thing on your own; it is up to me to find out what is going on," objected Mrs Warwick.

"Nonsense," Clara said, "I think Effie's suggestion is perfectly plausible. We will hide in the park in the morning, and when Mr Warwick leaves for work, we will follow him then come back and report. We shall not be on our own; we will be together."

"If you are sure you don't mind, I would appreciate it very much," Mrs Warwick said.

"Leave it with us, and we will see what we can find out," confirmed Effie. "But first, I shall go and get your letter so you can watch it burn."

Eight o'clock the following morning found Effie and Clara watching the Warwick's house from behind a hedge.

They saw Mr Warwick close the front door and head down the street in the opposite direction of the city. Effie and Clara waited until he was a few yards in front of them, then they set off walking in the same direction but on the opposite side of the street.

Mr Warwick took a left turn into Clark Street, so the two young ladies walked straight on past the end of Clark Street, crossed over the road then peeked back around the corner, up Clark Street and were just in time to see their quarry turn left onto Hope Street.

Effie and Clara followed the retreating figure of Mr Warwick up Clark Street until they came to Hope Street. Glancing up Hope Street they saw him turn right onto Ample Avenue.

The two detectives ran down Hope Street and peered up Ample Avenue. Mr Warwick was still on the move, heading further down the Avenue, heading towards the outskirts of Frithwood.

"I wonder where he is going," Clara whispered.

"I don't know, but we are heading in the opposite direction of the city centre. I know nothing about this area, I have not been this way before," Effie whispered back.

The two ladies continued watching Mr Warwick. He opened a wooden gate of the end house in Ample Avenue, and then he walked up the garden path, opened the front door and disappeared inside.

"Let us go back and tell Mrs Warwick what we have seen," Clara said.

Setting off at a brisk pace they retraced their steps and were shown into Mrs Warwick's sitting room. Effie told Mrs Warwick what they had found out.

"Ample Avenue, I have heard about Ample Avenue, it has a reputation, or at least it had many years ago. I think gambling goes on in Ample Avenue if I am not mistaken," Mrs Warwick told them.

"I have never been there before, in fact, I did not even know it existed," Effie admitted.

"I am going to go to that house, and I am going to find out what is going on." Mrs Warwick stood up.

"We will come with you," Effie told her.

"You will do no such thing," Mrs Warwick said. "You have both been so very kind to me; I will always be grateful to you both. I would never for the life of me put you in harm's way. I would never forgive myself if anything happened to you or you lost your reputation because of a silly whim of mine."

"And if we let you go on your own and something happened to you, Effie and I would never forgive ourselves for not supporting you in your hour of need," Clara counted.

"Very well, I admit I would appreciate the company. I will get my coat."

Mrs Warwick with Effie and Clara standing behind her used the metal doorknocker and banged on the door of an impressive stone fronted, double bay windowed, detached house located at the end of Ample Avenue.

The door was opened by a woman in her late twenties. She was clad in a tight-fitting scarlet and maroon gown with a plunging neckline displaying an ample bosom for all to see.

Her face was made up, but the makeup was tastefully done, and her hair was neatly tied up away from her face with ringlets hanging down her left shoulder, they were blonde and shinning.

The woman at the door lifted her eyebrows at the sight of the three elegantly dressed ladies standing on her porch.

"What can I do for you?" she asked them.

Mrs Warwick pushed the door open and stepped inside, Effie and Clara followed.

"What do you think you are doing pushing your way in here?" demanded the woman in red.

"I have come to see my husband," said Mrs Warwick.

"Have you indeed? What makes you think your husband is here?" asked the woman.

"He was seen entering this, shall I say, establishment. I insist on seeing him," Mrs Warwick told her. "I will not move until he is brought here or I am directed to him."

"There are no men here," she was told.

Looking around the hallway, Mrs Warwick took in the red carpet on the hall floor that continued up the staircase and, she guessed, along the top of the landing. Three girls stood midway on the stairs wearing only tight girdles, fishnet stocking and high-heeled shoes. Makeup was caked on their haggard faces, and their hair could have done with a good brushing.

"Had a rough night, have they?" Mrs Warwick wanted to know pointedly looking at the barely covered breasts of the women standing on the stairs. "Very apt address I think for this place, Ample Avenue."

"It is none of your damn business. Get out of my house, or I will have you thrown out," the woman in red threatened.

"As I have already told you, I shall not leave until I see my husband," Mrs Warwick stood her ground.

"Better go and fetch Gordy," the woman said to one of the girls on the stairs.

No one spoke while they waited for the arrival of Gordy.

When at last Gordy appeared, his mouth dropped open at the sight of his wife.

"What the devil are you doing here?" he raged.

"I could ask you the same thing," replied his wife adding, "'Gordy'."

"You," he pointed to his wife, "had better come with me. You two," he pointed at Effie and Clara, "had better go."

Effie and Clara looked at Mrs Warwick, "Yes, you had better go. I am so sorry for bringing you here to this humiliation. I had no idea," Mrs Warwick whispered.

"You know where we are if you need us. Are you sure you will be all right?" Clara asked.

"Of course, she will be all right. What do you think I am going to do to her?" Gordy wanted to know.

"Thank you for all you have done," Mrs Warwick spread out her hands, a look of helplessness on her face. "I did not know anything about all this, really I didn't. Yes, thank you, I will be perfectly all right, you two go home, and I shall be in touch."

"I am sure you did not know anything about this," Effie said. "I am so sorry, Mrs Warwick." She gave Mrs Warwick a quick hug then taking Clara's hand Effie pulled Clara outside and hurried back up the street at a fast pace dragging Clara with her.

Mr Warwick indicated with his head to his wife, along the corridor from which he had appeared. Head held high Mrs Warwick walked past her husband without giving him a glance. She headed in the direction he had indicated.

"This room, Lily," her husband said.

Mrs Warwick turned and went into the room expecting a grubby, seedy little room, but she found herself in a room filled with expensive furniture, thick carpet under her feet and heavy curtains tied stylishly back at the windows.

A big double desk and a plush leather sofa with two matching winged armchairs. Chinese porcelain adorned the marble mantelpiece and a glass display cabinet was filled with exotic knick-knacks.

Mrs Warwick was pressed to say, "Business must be good, 'Gordy', you seem to have a better lifestyle at work than you do at home. There is no wonder you keep me locked up and short of money."

"I won this establishment in a card game, many years ago. It has kept a roof over your head and fine clothes on your back and I have never kept you locked up or short of money, so don't you dare look down your nose at me.

"While you are here, I might as well show you the rest of the business and be done with it. Come with me."

Mrs Warwick followed her husband to the back of the house, further along the corridor that housed Gordy's office. They came to a set of heavy double doors which he opened, and she found herself in a huge spotlessly clean, gambling room with roulette wheels and card tables spread around.

"You have been running this place all these years and I never knew?" she gasped.

"There was no need for you to know. It was a rundown and anything-goes business when I took over. I cleaned it up. I have a doctor to check out the girls and muscle on hand in case any of the punters get too enthusiastic.

"Lords and Ladies frequent the place. They come for a bit of light entertainment, entertainment that their respective partners look down their noses at. On the third floor, the rooms are kept for anyone that wants to book a room for a couple of hours with someone they are not supposed to be with.

"There are a lot of unhappy people, Lily, all living a lie. Unhappy with their lot, pretending to be the cream of society and in the end, all they want is a bit of rough and tumble, a bit of respite from the onslaught of life.

"They come for a bit of love and tenderness that they cannot find at home. You would be surprised at the people we get in here."

"What about you, Gordy. Is this where you get your bit of rough and tumble?"

"I know you are not going to believe this, Lily, but I love you, always have. I kept you locked away as much as I could because I did not want to lose you. If you ever found out about this establishment, I knew what would happen, you would leave me and that is the last thing I want.

"Now you have found out about it; I will sell up. I could get a small fortune for it, and we can go away somewhere where nobody knows us. There will be enough money for us to live on in comfort for the rest of our lives."

Lily went for a walk around the gambling tables, looking at all the expensive Chinese silk curtains and vases. They alone must be worth a small fortune.

"I want to see the rest of the place," Lily told him.

"I do not think that is a good idea, Lily, the rest of the establishment is for pleasures of the other kind. I have tried so hard to protect you from all this."

"What if I don't want protecting from it all, Gordy?"

"Please do not call me Gordy; it makes me feel cheap."

"They, the ladies of pleasure, do not make you feel cheap when they call you Gordy?" his wife asked him with a raise of the eyebrow.

"No, it is a term of endearment from them. They all respect me. When I first came here, they were living in squalor. Nobody gave a damn about them so long as they were making money for the owner, but I did.

"I was shocked at the way they had to live to stay alive. I turned things around for the girls. I gave them a little kitchen of their own where they can get something to eat. One of the rooms is closed off, so they can get a bath and keep themselves clean.

140

"There are not many violent incidents these days because the clients who frequent this establishment know if they are thrown out, they will not be allowed back in. The girls respect me, Lily, for what I have done for them and for what I still do.

"Bertha, the girl you met at the front door, has been with me since this establishment came into my possession. Bertha looks after the other girls and lives in the basement with her husband. His name is Andy. He is one of the men I employ to keep the peace here. They have a little boy called John."

Gordon Warwick paused and waited for any comment from his wife, when none came, he carried on, "Now I would like you to come with me, there is somewhere else I want to show you."

Gordon held the door open for his wife, and they both walked out into the warm morning sunshine.

Lily and Gordon walked back to their house in silence, and once inside Mr Warwick asked the butler to have the curricle brought round.

Sitting next to her husband, Lily was at a loss for something to say so she sat and watched the city begin to be less and less built-up, as they made their way out of Frithwood. Not long after the city was behind them, Mr Warwick turned left up a dirt cart track and followed it for about two miles.

They came to a large, wooden gate affixed to a stone boundary wall about six feet in height and attached to that gate was a wrought iron plaque saying Orphanage in big black letters.

Mr Warwick handed the reins to his wife, jumped down and opened the gate. Mrs Warwick gave a flick of the reins, and the horse trotted neatly through. Mr Warwick closed the gate after her, jumped up on to the driving seat, took possession of the reins and carried on

141

until they reached a large stone fronted three storey building, with small mullioned windows.

Jumping down, Mr Warwick went around to the other side of the curricle and held out his hand to his wife.

Lily hesitated then she placed her hand in his and he helped her alight. She stood looking at her surroundings, at rolling lawns and neat flowerbeds. She liked what she saw.

"This is an extension from the 'businesses', shall we call it. I am not a monster, Lily. When I won the business in a game of cards all those years ago, I did not know what I was getting myself into.

"There was nobody more shocked than me when I found out what I had won. The ladies who worked there then were dirty and used in the most appalling ways imaginable. Every dropout, gambling addict and troublemaker frequented the place.

"I could find nobody who was prepared to buy it from me, or even to take it off my hands for nothing. I could not give the business away. I think the reason I won the establishment in the first place, for as you know I am no dab hand at playing cards, was the previous owner could not get anyone to purchase it either, or take it off his hands so he unloaded his debt onto me.

"There was a huge mortgage on it, and once that was known, nobody wanted to know. If I had not done something to turn things around, we would have lost everything we had, so I set about cleaning things up.

"Word soon got around that the gambling house could now be relied on to be discreet. I started making good money, and after a couple of years, I had the mortgage paid off and money in the bank. We have girls knocking on the door every night wanting employment. I have to turn them away.

"Out of the six girls that were here when I first came, five still remain, one got married and left. Not only did things look up for the working girls, the neighbouring houses became more desirable and now instead of trying to get the place closed down, ninety-nine per cent of the people in the avenue accept the situation, and they leave us well alone.

"If I do not run the 'business', someone else would, and the neighbouring houses prefer to have what they have since I took over to what they had before.

"Not only do young ladies come knocking on the door, so do children. I found it hard to turn these children away so I looked around for a suitable property I could buy to turn it into an orphanage. It may not be the best place in the world to live but at least the children living here are not having to go scavenging for food in the gutters, and they have a warm bed to go to at night. Let me show you around. As you will see, all our beds are full."

There were children of all ages staying at the orphanage, boys and girls. The boys were bedded down on the second floor in a long dormitory with twelve single beds. Each bed was occupied. A large sparse room with two tin baths and wooden rails with towels hanging from them was across the landing from the dormitory.

The first floor was exactly the same as the top floor, but this housed the girls.

The large kitchen was located on the ground floor at the back of the house. A huge woman in a grey dress, white apron and mop-cap was standing at the sink. Two boys of around seven or eight years old were sitting at the table peeling potatoes. Two young girls sat opposite them, peeling carrots.

When Lily and Mr Warwick entered the kitchen, the four children looked up and smiled at Mr Warwick.

"Hello, you lot, behaving yourselves I hope?" he asked them.

"Jerry has been on the naughty step, Mr Warwick, he pinched Jean's picture book, so Mrs Dobson made him sit on the naughty step," the smallest girl volunteered.

"Shush, Jane, I have told you before, no telling tales," said the young girl next to her.

"Has he now," said Mr Warwick.

The huge woman turned and said, "Nothing to worry your head over, Mr Warwick, just one of those things that children do."

"I am sure it is, Mrs Bellamy. May I introduce you to my wife, Lily. Lily, this is Mrs Bellamy, the cook. She teaches the children how to look after themselves and makes them take turns in helping in the kitchen," Mr Warwick said.

Lily held out her hand to the cook, "I am very pleased to meet you, Mrs Bellamy,"

Mrs Bellamy gave a small curtsey then shook hands, "Likewise, Mrs Warwick. They are good kids for the most, some are livelier than the others, but we manage."

"I am sure you do. How many children do you have living here?" Lily asked.

"There are twelve boys and fourteen girls."

"It must take some managing."

"Not really, the children help me out in the kitchen. It helps to teach them how to cook and how to keep the place clean. They help keep all the other rooms clean and tidy too. It is a good way for them to learn and it helps with the running cost of the orphanage, no cleaners required you see.

"The money can then be spent on more important things. There is Mrs Dobson, of course, she is a nurse and she also helps me keep house. It works out very well for us all," Mrs Bellamy told Lily.

"Where are all the other children?" Lily wanted to know.

"Some of them are out keeping the vegetable plot going, and some of them are in the laundry, others are doing the cleaning. They all have to pitch in to keep the orphanage going, and the children all do it willingly, it is a better place than the one they all came from.

"The girls are taught to sew, to make their own clothes and the boys to look after the land. We also have Mr Fletcher, he is the handyman, and the boys help him to keep the grounds and house in good repair.

"It all helps to provide food and clothing for them all, and at the same time, they are learning skills they might never have learnt had the poor little mites been left to fend for themselves. Mr Warwick provides us with money, of course, for the upkeep of the place. I have been here four years and it is the best job I have ever had."

"Thank you, Mrs Bellamy, it has been very interesting meeting you."

In the curricle heading back home, Gordon said to his wife, "Where to now?"

"How do you keep the orphanage going?" Lily asked.

"The gambling side of the business tends to make a lot of money, never mind the prostitution. You and I have more than enough money in the bank to see us out, Lily. Enough for me to retire now, so from time to time I go to see the kids in the orphanage and make sure they have most of the things they want. The mortgage on the orphanage has been paid off, so the home is safe for the next few years. I will sell up if that is what you want, Lily, I would rather lose the 'business' than you."

"Let us go back to Ample Avenue and talk about it. I have a mind to work alongside you and help all these children that you have saved from a life on the street.

When I woke up this morning, I did not expect to be going to bed tonight knowing I owned a brothel. I have been so bored, Gordon, looking at those same four walls day in, day out. If I can help make a difference to those children, then I shall be willing to work at your side."

"Are you sure, Lily? You will lose all the elite friends you have now. They will all snub you when they find out about the gaming house."

"I do not have any friends, no, that is not true. I have just met two of the most charming young ladies you could wish to meet, and do you know what, Gordon? I do not think they would snub me, they already know about the brothel, and anyway, it would not matter if they did, for they leave for the country on Friday."

"You are willing to come and join me at the brothel?" Gordon asked in amazement.

"I am impressed with the orphanage, and if it means using funds gained via the brothel to keep the orphanage going, then I am all for it. It is about time I had a bit of excitement in my life. Yes, Gordon, I will come and work at your side and I shall go to the orphanage and set up a school to educate all the young children that live there, so when they leave the orphanage, they will be able to read and write and that should help them to find worthwhile employment," Lily told him. "Now I want to meet all the working girls and see what I can do to help."

On arrival at the gaming house, Gordon and Lily found all the working girls gathered at the bottom of the stairs.

"What is going on here?" Gordon wanted to know.

"It's Cora, Gordy; she has gone into labour. We had to send for Dr Robinson because she was losing a lot of blood," Bertha informed him.

"Who is Cora?" asked Lily.

"One of the working girls, she did not tell us she was pregnant until it was too late for us to see to her. She said she wanted to keep her baby. Some men like it, having sex with a pregnant woman, so she has been working right up to the last minute," Bertha replied.

"I am going to go and see how she is," Lily said walking up the stairs.

"You will find her second door on the right," Bertha shouted up to her.

Silence returned to the hall while all the girls waited to see the outcome of Cora's labour.

An hour later a baby's cry reached the little group gathered at the bottom of the stairs. A few minutes passed, and Lily appeared at the top of the stairs holding a tiny bundle wrapped in a soft white blanket, "It is a little girl," she told them all.

"And Cora?" asked Bertha.

"I am afraid she did not make it. She had lost too much blood the doctor said. I am so sorry."

A couple of the girls began to cry, and Bertha asked, looking at the tiny bundle in Lily's arms, "What is going to happen to this poor little sod now?"

"I am, or should I say we, Gordon and I, are going to adopt her. The last thing Cora said was, 'Will you take care of my baby?' and I said yes. So, Gordon and I will give her a home, bring her up as our own."

"It would seem it was a good day when you turned up on our doorstep, Mrs Warwick, if you don't mind me saying so," Bertha told her.

"Thank you, Bertha, let us hope you still think so in six months' time."

Effie called to see Clara. Edwin, having told her they were travelling to Styleham with the Landers on Friday and were to stay at Badger Manor with them for a few days to take a look at an empty estate next door to theirs, had left her wanting to know more. She was as excited as could be, and she wanted to know as much about the estate as Clara could tell her.

Clara and Effie were interrupted with a knock on the morning room door, and Mrs Warwick was shown in carrying a baby in her arms.

"Mrs Warwick, please come in and have a seat. Who does the baby belong to?" Clara wanted to know.

"Me," was the reply.

"Yours, surely not?" said Clara in disbelief.

"Gordon and I are going to adopt her. I hope you don't mind me calling on you here, Miss Lander, but I called at Miss Hunter's house, and I was informed she had called to see you, so here I am. I have come to let you know what I have decided to do. I want you both to know what happened after you left yesterday."

"Of course, I don't mind; it is nice to see you and the baby and to know you are alright," Clara smiled at her.

Making themselves comfortable, Mrs Warwick told them what had happened after they had left.

"It is because of your kindness that little Cora will have a better life than what she would have had if we three had not become involved with Gordon's gaming house. So, on her behalf, I thank you both most sincerely," Mrs Warwick finished.

"We could write to each other, Mrs Warwick. Keep in touch; keep us up to date with all you are doing and let us know how little Cora is getting on. You never know, there might be something else we can do to help one day," Effie said.

"Good idea, Effie," Clara agreed, "we will look forward to hearing from you."

Mrs Warwick stood up and took baby Cora from Effie's arms but made no comment, she just gave them both a gentle smile saying on her way out, "Thank you from the bottom of my heart," and then she was gone.

Chapter Eleven

Friday morning found them all heading north. Effie and Clara were installed inside the carriage, the twins sat up front with the driver, and Lord Hunter, Oscar and Harvey were riding their horses. The luggage had been piled onto a separate wagon.

The weather was warm and the ground firm, so they made good progress as they rattled along.

"I can't wait to see Davey Grange, tell me more about it," Effie said to Clara.

"Lord Wellford lived there with his wife, they had no children of their own, and they did not take to us running riot on their land. When our parents died and poor Oscar was left in charge of us, we all had to learn to keep to the rules Oscar set out for us.

"Lord Wellford threatened to have us sent to the workhouse if he found us on his land, so we kept well away from him. Apart from sneaking into his orchard and pinching his apples and pears before our parents died, there is not much more I can tell you. It is a large abode, though.

"We never went inside, and when his wife died, Lord Wellford became a recluse. We had not seen him for years. But I can tell you it is a beautiful looking building from the outside. Large stone columns on either side of the main entrance with a canopy to shield you from the weather," Clara told her.

"When Edwin and I go to have a look around the estate, will you come along with us?" Effie wanted to know.

"I most certainly will. I am looking forward to it. It will be nice to finally see what the interior looks like."

"Edwin knows the nephew, Lord Wellford's nephew that is. Apparently, he is also a member of The Ravens Club, and Edwin has had a word with him. His name is Wilbert Wellford, and he has given Edwin the keys to Davey Grange.

"Wilbert did not want to come down with us to show us around the Grange, so we have free access to it. We can wander about to our heart's content without anyone looking over our shoulder. Edwin says this nephew of Lord Wellford's is a gambler and he owes a lot of people a lot of money. Wilbert is desperate to sell the estate and get his hands on the proceeds. He cannot afford the upkeep of it. Edwin has told him, if we like it, we shall buy it," Effie said.

"Will you miss living in Frithwood?" Clara wanted to know.

"To be honest, Clara, I can't wait to get away. If all the people in the countryside are as nice as your family, then there will not be much to complain about," Effie smiled at her companion.

It was turned 9 o'clock in the evening and getting dark by the time the travellers arrived at their destination. It was too dark to see anything, and they were too weary to care. They had a bite of supper, and all retired to bed.

Elmer Wolf was unsure of his next move. After leaving his lodging in Frithwood, he had wandered into the city and called into the bank. He had decided, against his better judgement, to place some of his money in the bank even though he did not trust them. He had too much to carry about his person, and it was on impulse that he had walked into the bank, and when he walked out, he had become the owner of a bank book.

He saw the mail stagecoach was getting ready to leave. *Why not,* Elmer thought, so he called into the sorting office and purchased a ticket to the first destination stop. It was to a town called Meeks.

This was the first time Elmer had travelled outside Frithwood. He had never felt the need to go anywhere else; he had all he needed in Frithwood. Now that had changed, things had started getting ugly for him. All he had to do was look in the mirror for proof of that.

Elmer sat hunched in a corner of the coach. He had his head down and his face covered by his hat hiding his black eye as best he could. Elmer had his carpetbag clutched on his knee and his feet firmly resting on his rolled-up blankets. He had refused to let the driver place either of them on top of the coach with the other luggage. No one was going to get their hands on his money.

He wanted his letters back. He missed them like any other man would miss his wife. In fact, Elmer missed them more than some of the men he knew would miss their wives if they were to suddenly disappear like his beloved letters had.

When the mail coach arrived at his destination and he alighted, Elmer found Meeks to be on the small side compared to Frithwood. He soon discovered that if he wanted a bed for the night, he had to walk about a mile to an inn called The Monks Den.

Following the instructions to the letter, Elmer had no trouble in coming across this off the beaten track hostelry. It was situated in a little hamlet called Brodley, two miles from Styleham, and unbeknown to him, two miles from the Landers estate.

Elmer decided he needed to get to another big town or city, this one was far too small for him, but a couple of weeks in this quiet little backwater inn suited him down to the ground. It would give his black eye time to disappear and his cut lip to heal, let the dust settle then start again.

Blackmailing was easy money if he played his cards right. But, two days at The Monks Den and Elmer was bored, he was in two minds whether to go back to Frithwood. Leaving the life, he had always known, had not been such a good idea after all.

He could get a job he supposed, but he had enough money to live on for at least a couple of years, and in that time, he hoped to be able to go back to doing what he knew best. *Money for old rope, until you get caught,* he thought, but he had managed to get away with it so far, and he counted himself lucky not to have ended up behind bars.

There was never going to be a chance of getting his hands on any letters the writers preferred not to go public, in a place like this. No, he needed to be in the middle of a town, a big town or city, where he could keep his eye on members of the gentry.

Elmer, never having ventured out of Frithwood before, had no idea of the location of the next big town or city. He would have to make enquires, get a plan in place and head for greener pastures. Watch and see who was having an affair with whom—watch the filthy rich lose money hand over fist at the gambling tables, he should then be able to acquire some I.O.Us. He had been lucky enough to come across a few in Frithwood, and the love letters had also been easily come by. He had acquired more than one of his precious letters by buying them off the idiots who had no respect for money and found themselves heading for the debtor's prison.

Elmer, on the other hand, had a great deal of respect for money. You would never find him throwing it away on the gambling tables or in the whorehouses. He did not trust the banks either, but he was now homeless, and he had to have somewhere to keep some of his money safe just in case he was set upon by highwaymen, or he became the victim of pickpockets.

Elmer was acquainted with a few pickpockets, but they knew better than to target him. Now he was going into the unknown, so he had decided it was better to be safe than sorry. His lost letters had taught him that.

Not all of his ill-gotten gains had been deposited in the bank. In fact, only a quarter of it, but at least if some mishap occurred and he found himself lacking money, he would still have some money to fall back on. He would keep his fingers crossed that the bank would not take his money and leave him with nothing. He trusted nobody. There weren't many people that he liked either. He was a loner. He did not intend to share his money with anybody.

Since having his precious letters stolen Elmer was loath to leave anything of value in his room, but he was also afraid to go out with it all on his person. He had met footpads; in fact, two or three of them were the closest he got to having friends. He had listened to them boasting about how easy it was to hide in isolated places and jump out on an unsuspecting traveller and relieve them of their valuables.

That's it, he decided, he would try his hand at being a highwayman, see what treasures he could come by, by holding up travellers at gunpoint. First though, he had to get a gun and Elmer did not like guns, and anyway, he did not know of anyone around here that had a gun for sale, and secondly, his horsemanship was practically none existent. He had tried riding a horse once, and he decided it wasn't for him, so maybe that wasn't such a good idea after all.

Elmer was sitting at a table near the window in the taproom of The Monks Den, planning his next move when he heard, "I never thought I would see you down here, Elmer old mate."

Elmer looked up to see Mick, one of his footpad friends he had just been thinking about.

"Mick, what the devil are you doing in this God-forsaken place?" Elmer wanted to know.

"Shush, not so loud. This is my patch. I hope you haven't come to muscle in on my territory. That is not a good idea, old boy," the newcomer Mick threatened.

"I came to get away from Frithwood for a while, a bit too hot for me there at the moment. I was just wondering if I should go back to Frithwood or move on to a bigger town, only I do not know a bigger town or where to find one," Elmer told him.

"I can see from the state of your face you have been in some sort of trouble," Mick told him.

"A bit of woman trouble that is all," Elmer lied. "You know how it is."

"Yes, I know how it is, only I have had the sense not to get caught," Mick replied.

"Well, this country life is not for me, it is too quiet, and there is not enough happening," confessed Elmer. "When my face gets back to normal, I shall move on, one way or another."

"That is because you do not know the right people. A job has cropped up that might be right up your street. Would you be interested?" Mick wanted to know.

"It depends on what it is," Elmer replied.

"Let us just say there are some people who need a driver to take a wagon load of brandy to be stored in a vacant cellar until it is safe to move it on. The regular driver partook too much of the merchandise and making his way home, he took a tumble and broke his leg. Hence the shortage of a driver," Elmer was informed.

"Where does this wagon load of brandy come from? Who wants it hiding until it is safe to move on? Sounds a bit dodgy to me," Elmer wanted to know.

"Ask no questions, and you will be told no lies, or to be more precise, you will save yourself a bullet in the back. You do not need to know about any of that. All you will be needed to do is drive the wagon, help get the barrels off the wagon and down to the cellar, and bring the wagon back. But most of all you keep your mouth shut.

"Since when has it bothered you whether or not it is legal? Not for very long by the state of your face. You don't think for a minute I believe it had anything to do with a woman, do you? You never were a lady's man. Are you interested in this little venture or not?" Mick wanted to know.

"I might be. What does it pay and when?" he asked.

"Dawn tomorrow, we find it best to go just before dawn. If we go during the night, we will need lanterns to light the way and lanterns can be seen from miles away. The property is empty, so there will be nobody around to see us, up early, finished early. Well, Elmer, I am waiting for your reply? Are you interested or not? If not, I will have to get somebody else."

"What is your part in all this?" Elmer wanted to know.

"Same as yours, driver, but like I said, we are one short. We have to move it all altogether; it is safer that way. Can I count you in?"

"You still haven't said how much it pays," Elmer replied.

"Two hours' work for five pounds. You would be a fool to turn it down."

"I did not know you were in this kind of business," Elmer told him.

"It supplements my other pastime. It is getting harder and harder to hold anybody up these days, and when I do, they have left most of their valuables at home. But it still beats working for a living."

"Alright, I'm in. Where and when?"

"Not far to go, Elmer old boy, at the back of The Monks Den at four o'clock in the morning, and wear black. I shall see you then. I am off to let the others know I have found a driver. My advice to you is to go to bed and be ready to be off in the morning."

"There is one slight problem, Mick, I am not very keen on horses. Would I have to hitch it up to the wagon and things like that?"

"Leave that with me; I will see to it that your wagon is hitched up. All you will have to do is help load the barrels and sit up on the driver's seat holding the reins. I will be bringing up the rear, so if you go in front of me, I can keep an eye on you. The horse will follow the one in front. It is not going to be very difficult. I would not have asked you if I thought you were not capable." Mick headed out.

Tom woke early and punched Lee in the ribs, "What do you say to us going over to Lord Wellford's and having a scout around? There is nobody to see us now and anyway, Edwin has the keys to the estate so we will not be doing anything wrong."

"Sounds good to me, let's get dressed and go before anyone else is up. We could take Chester and our two for company." Lee was up and pulling up his trousers.

"Do you think that is a good idea? They might start barking. They usually do when they are first let out, and they might wake the whole house up."

Lee thought about it and said, "Yes, you are right, we had better leave them at home."

Up in the loft in a barn, to the rear of Davey Grange, the sound of wagon wheels alerted Tom and Lee to the fact that they were not alone. Rushing over to the window to see who the new arrivals were, they watched five wagons, piled high with round barrels, slowly heading for the rear of the house.

The two boys held their breath as the wagons lumbered along below them, coming to a halt in the courtyard across from where they were hidden.

Lee and Tom watched as the first driver jumped down from his wagon and he went over to the back door where he took a while to pick the lock. When this was accomplished, the other drivers unloaded the barrels and took them inside.

With the wagon drivers and barrels of brandy safely inside the house, Lee felt it safe to whisper to Tom, "Wasn't one of those drivers that horrible bloke Effie was engaged to?"

"That is where I had seen him before at Effie's house in Frithwood. You are right, Lee, it was him. We had better wait until they have gone before we go back home, I don't want to be caught by him or any of the others, they look a rum lot," Tom whispered back.

It took longer than the boys expected for the men to come back out of the house, get on their wagons and disappear down the drive.

It was still only around 6 o'clock in the morning. Tom and Lee waited until they could no longer hear the rumble of the wagon wheels, then climbed down from the barn loft and ran home.

Everyone was still abed when the twins arrived home so they decided it could wait until breakfast was over before they told their story. Oscar might make them miss breakfast for sneaking out and onto Lord Wellford's land.

Tom and Lee decided to descend on Mrs Ericson, their cook, who was busy preparing breakfast.

"What, may I ask, do you two scamps want? Be off with you; I am too busy to have you two under my feet."

"But we are hungry," wailed Tom.

"Breakfast will be ready shortly," she told them, "Be off with you."

"But we have not had any of your home-baked bread for the past month. Mrs Saxon, the cook in Frithwood could not bake bread like you bake it, Mrs Ericson," Lee told her.

So, Mrs Ericson compromised and sent them off with an apple and a mug of milk each saying that would have to put them on until breakfast was ready.

It was a late breakfast as more than one overslept that morning. The last one to appear at the breakfast table was Harvey.

"Sorry if I held you all up; that was the best night's sleep I have had this last month."

"You have not held us up, Harvey, we started without you," Oscar informed him. "You had better hurry up and get something to eat before the table is cleared."

Lee elbowed Tom in the ribs, "Stop it," whispered Tom.

Lee elbowed Tom in the ribs again and whispered, "You tell them."

"No, you tell them," whispered Tom back.

"No, you tell them," Lee whispered.

"Tell us what?" asked Harvey.

Lee and Tom exchanged glances, neither said anything.

"What mischief have you two been up to now?" Harvey wanted to know between mouthfuls of breakfast.

The silence could be cut with a knife.

All eyes were on the twins, neither spoke.

"You might as well tell us, you are going to get into trouble anyway if you have done something you should not have, so you might as well get on with it," Harvey much experienced in such things wisely advised them.

"You should not have sent us to bed early," Lee looked over at Oscar.

"I do not think 10 o'clock in the evening was all that early," Oscar told them.

"Well, we went straight off to sleep, so we woke up early this morning before anyone else was up," Tom informed them.

No one spoke.

Lee elbowed Tom in the ribs.

Tom elbowed Lee in the ribs.

No one spoke.

"Do you want Edwin and me to leave the room?" asked Effie, thinking it might be because of their presence the boys were reluctant to speak.

"No, it is because of you that we do not want to say what we have to say, but you have to hear it," Lee told her.

"That makes everything extremely clear," remarked Oscar.

"Because of me?" asked Effie ignoring Oscar's outburst.

"Yes, we went out early this morning before any of you woke up, and we saw something. We don't want to upset you," Lee replied.

"Well, whatever it is you saw, it has nothing to do with me, I have only just got up. I have not been outside yet," Effie denied all knowledge.

No one spoke.

"Lee, Tom, you had better tell us what you saw before I get cross with you both," Oscar warned.

Lee elbowed Tom in the ribs.

Tom elbowed Lee back.

No one spoke.

"I tell you what," said Edwin, "The best way I have found for you two to make a decision is to toss a coin, that way no one is taking sides, and whoever loses the toss must tell us what you both saw. Agreed?"

Tom looked at Lee.

Lee looked at Tom.

They both nodded.

Edwin tossed the coin and asked Lee to call heads or tails.

"Heads," said Lee.

"Heads it is," confirmed Edwin.

Lee elbowed Tom in the ribs.

Tom elbowed Lee back then said, "Alright, we saw Elmer Wolf."

No one spoke.

"Elmer Wolf," gasped Effie, her face turning white.

"Yes, Elmer Wolf," replied Lee.

"Where did you see him?" Oscar wanted to know.

No one spoke.

Lee elbowed Tom in the ribs.

Tom elbowed Lee back then continued, "We know we should not have, but we went to have a look around Davey Grange. We knew Edwin had the keys to the estate, so we did not think we were doing anything wrong. We were only going to look around the outside.

We were not going to try to get inside or anything like that.

"Nobody lives there now, so nobody would be around to see us. We climbed over the wall. We got as far as one of the barns to the rear of the house and went up into the loft to have a scout around. The barn door was already open, and we did not have to break in or anything like that, the door was open; honestly, it was. It was a right let-down anyway; there was nothing up there but old bales of hay.

"Whilst Lee and I were up in the loft we heard the sound of wagons approaching so we went to the window and looked out. We saw five wagons piled high with barrels heading our way. Elmer Wolf was driving one of them. One of the other men picked the lock to the back door of Davey Grange, and they took all the barrels inside. Lee and I waited until they all came back out and drove off, and then we ran all the way home."

"It sounds like contraband to me," said Oscar.

"Contraband, you mean smugglers?" asked a shocked Effie.

"Yes, we are only about fifteen miles from the sea here, and it has been rumoured that contraband is smuggled in and brought inland. I have never had any trouble with the smugglers myself but that does not mean it does not go on.

"I have even found the odd barrel of brandy left in one or other of the barns. They do that if they have used your property to cut across as a short cut to their destination. Even if you have not seen or heard them, you might find a barrel left as a thank you. I think that is why nobody ever tells the revenue men about the smuggling that goes on," Oscar told them.

"How can Elmer Wolf be involved with smugglers?" Effie wanted to know.

"Do you think it is something he would do?" asked Oscar.

"I think it is more than likely he is the head of it," she replied. "But as far as I know Elmer Wolf has never been outside of Frithwood. Do you think he has followed me here?"

"I doubt it, we did not know we were coming here ourselves until two days ago, and as far as I can remember, I did not tell anyone we were coming. Did you?" asked her brother.

"No, no, I didn't," she replied.

"Then I do not think it has anything to do with us," her brother reassured her.

"Did he see you?" Oscar asked the twins.

"No, we stayed in the barn until they left. The smugglers never even looked around to see if the coast was clear, which surprised me. But I will tell you this, Elmer's face was in a right state, black and blue all over as though somebody had used it as a punchbag." replied Tom.

"Good, I am pleased to hear it. I think Edwin might have had something to do with that. The smugglers will have known that the Grange was empty and thought it was safe to take the contraband there to hide," Oscar remarked.

"Did you recognise any of the other drivers?" asked Harvey.

"There was that fat man who runs The Monks Den," Lee told them.

Tom burst out crying and ran around the table and threw his arms around Oscar's neck.

"What on earth's the matter?" asked Oscar holding him close.

"I'm sorry, Oscar. I know we should not have gone over onto Lord Wellford's land, but we only wanted to have a look. You will not let them take us to the workhouse if they found out, will you?" sobbed Tom.

"Nobody can take you away you goose. It was Lord Wellford that did the threatening to have you taken from me if he caught you on his land. He is dead now, and I am much older than I was when Lord Wellford made all those threats.

"He only did it to keep you off his land, I do not think for one minute he would have carried out the threats, but we were a lot younger with no experience at looking after ourselves. The threats seemed pretty scary at the time I must admit. Who is going to want two rascals like you two anyway? After an hour they would soon send you back," Oscar ruffled Tom's hair.

"On the other hand, I am pleased to hear you do not want to leave here, that means life has not been too bad for you even if you did lose your mother and father at an early age."

"You are the best brother in the world, Oscar," Tom said into his shoulder.

"You had better believe it," agreed his eldest brother.

"I challenge that remark," Lord Hunter said, "I think I am a pretty good brother too."

They all laughed, and Tom wiped his eyes and took his place back at the table.

"I for one am glad you did go off on an adventure. At least we now know Elmer Wolf has raised his ugly head again. I know to be on the lookout for him. Elmer Wolf, of all people," Effie sighed.

"Why are the smugglers moving their cargo early in the morning? I would have thought the dead of night would be a better option for them. There must be a reason for it," Edwin said.

"The reason for that being, they would have to have lanterns to light their way at night, it is pitch black out there in the middle of the night. The last thing the smugglers want is a horse to break a leg during the expedition. Lanterns can be seen for miles around at night, and that would bring the revenue men down on them. The smugglers are less likely to be seen at dawn, no lanterns needed." explained Oscar.

"Having been given the keys to the estate is an added bonus. We can go and have a look around on our own, anytime we want, with nobody to keep a watchful eye on us or see something they should not. I think I shall go over to Davey Grange straight after breakfast and see if there is anything hidden there that shouldn't be. Nothing as exciting as this has ever happened to us in Frithwood. Would anyone else like to join me?" asked Edwin.

"Me," said Lee.

"Me," said Tom over his little outburst.

"Me," said Harvey.

"Me," said Effie.

"Me," said Clara.

"Well, you are not leaving me behind," added Oscar.

"That is all of us then," Edwin smiled.

"I am going to see if I can find a secret passage or a secret tunnel or something. It is such an old rambling house there is bound to be one or the other," Harvey told them.

"And me," said Lee.

"And me," said Tom.

"I think I will pass on that one," said Oscar.

"Me too," agreed Clara, "but if you do come across one, I will come and have a look at it with you."

"That makes two of us," confirmed Effie, "I have never seen a secret passage before, and I would dearly love to investigate one."

"Secret passages are all well and good, but just remember entry can be gained into the house just as well from the outside, as giving exit to the outside from inside, if you follow my reasoning. If you knew where to look for the secret door that is. You never know who could be coming in when you are not looking," Edwin told them.

"If we do find a secret passage you can always lock it from the inside, put a bolt on to stop anyone coming in but I think a secret passage is a good thing, you never know when you might need a secret passage to escape down," argued Harvey.

"What are we going to do about this contraband? If we do find any that is," Edwin wanted to know.

"I think you and I should call at The Monks Den for a mug of ale tonight. If the innkeeper of The Monks Den was one of the smugglers, we need to drop him a hint that they had better remove the barrels to a different location. That's if we find any barrels, we'd look two right idiots if we go barging into the inn ranting about contraband that isn't there. We had better try and make sure Elmer Wolf does not know that he has been seen and recognised. Put a word of warning in Redfern's ear; let him know how dangerous Elmer might turn out to be," replied Oscar.

"Aren't we going to report it to the revenue men if we do find it?" questioned Edwin.

"Smuggling is a part of the coastal way of life. The smugglers bring it in, and the revenue men try to catch them. They will leave the barrels hidden for a couple of weeks, so the revenue men give up looking for it. The smugglers will then move it on. No, you do not tell the revenue men. Smuggling has been going on for as long as I can remember.

"But it is getting harder and harder for the smugglers. More people are coming to live in the country from the towns and cities, and a lot of them do not know the way of life here in the country. The smugglers don't know who they can trust now and who they can't. Look at them using Elmer Wolf. They could not have picked a worse accomplice if they had tried. If Elmer Wolf is staying at The Monks Den, Mr Redfern needs to be warned," explained Oscar.

"Can we come?" asked Lee.

"Yes, we saw them in the first place," agreed Tom.

"No, you can't, but I will tell Redfern you deserve all the credit," promised Oscar.

"Who is Redfern?" Effie wanted to know.

"He is the innkeeper at The Monks Den. He will be grateful for the information, and it will be a chance to introduce Edwin into the community and let them know he is thinking about buying Davey Grange. The locals will then be aware that Edwin knows where the goods are stored, and he can be trusted not to go running to the revenue men. Word will soon get around, and you will both be welcomed with open arms, this could not have dropped neater for us," said Oscar with a satisfied smile.

"Isn't it illegal to smuggle?" asked Effie.

"Of course, it is," replied Harvey, "but it is the way the smugglers earn a living. The revenue has been aware of it going on for years, but they didn't try too hard to catch them, in fact, it would not surprise me if one or two of them are in on it, the smuggling I mean, that is why the smugglers are never caught.

"But this new lot of revenue men are a different breed altogether. They are trained in the city and sent to the coastal areas to try to catch the smugglers. This new lot of revenue men are not local and cannot be trusted like they were before.

"The government is clamping down on it all. They teach us about it at boarding school, how things in society are changing all the time, some of the stuff they tell us about is interesting, most of it is boring though. I will never use half the stuff they cram into us when I leave school. Like Oscar says, it is getting harder and harder for the smugglers to bring the booty onshore and there are less and less places for them to hide it. I do not think it will be long before they pack it in altogether," Harvey told them.

"I am pleased to hear you are at least learning something for the money I am paying out to keep you at boarding school," Oscar said.

"Of course, they teach us things. I like rugby and cricket, and just before I was rusticated, we had a paper chase, damn good fun that. Someone runs in front and throws shredded paper along the floor, and after he has been given a good head start, we all set off and follow the trail. I came in fourth," Harvey said with pride.

"I hope we have a paper chase when we go to boarding school, and I bet Lee and I will come in higher than fourth; you just watch us," Tom said.

"Bet you do not," Harvey replied, "I can't wait to see what grade you two get for maths."

"After that announcement, I can't wait to see what grade you get," Oscar told him.

Harvey had the grace to blush, and he changed the subject by saying, "Come on, if everyone has finished breakfast shall we get going?"

Chapter Twelve

Lord Hunter let them in through the huge front double doors flanked by two stone pillars with covered canopy. They were greeted by silence. The hall consisted of a wide foyer with an elaborate black and white tile designed floor, inset with a royal blue circle and scarlet centrepiece.

It was very striking. It took the eye away from the impressive, curved staircase with wrought iron balustrade to either side of the uncarpeted, highly polished, wooden staircase leading up to the first-floor landing.

There was an old grandfather clock standing in one corner and a huge wooden table nearly the full length of the hall standing under the staircase. Two shabby looking chairs were placed at either end of the table and in the centre of the table stood a large ceramic bowl full of keys and various odds and ends.

If the hallway was anything to go by the whole house must be covered in dust and smell fusty. As they all moved across the hall, their feet made an eerie echoing sound which bounced off the high ceiling.

"I like this floor," Effie said.

"As do I, in fact, I like the feel of this entrance hall altogether," agreed her brother. "Let us hope the other rooms can equal it. Apart from the fusty smell, we can do without that."

The first door they came to opened into a library; bookshelves ran across two of the four walls. Most of the shelves held various sizes of books; there seemed to be hundreds of them. Unfortunately, the titles of the books were unreadable because they were coated with dust.

Faded and rotting red velvet curtains hung in a big bay window, through which, early morning beams of sunlight came to rest upon a huge double desk.

"I shall have to measure those windows before we return to Frithwood, to see if some of the curtains we have at home can be brought down here and put to good use. But, looking at the size of the windows, I do not think any of the curtains we have back in Frithwood will come anywhere near to fitting these windows," Effie remarked.

"Who cares about curtains?" asked Lee.

"Not me," agreed Tom.

"In that case, it is a good job it is not going to be left to you two to sort out," Effie told them.

"Do not get ahead of yourself Effie, we have not seen the rest of the estate yet, we might decide not to buy it," her brother told her.

They continued into each room, finding paintings still hanging on the walls, most of them were dark and moody, old people's faces gazing down at them with none too friendly an eye.

Nearly all the rooms held old and shabby furniture. No dustsheets covered any of it and dust was in every nook and cranny and on every surface of everything, in every room.

It was a huge house, three storeys high, the interior was in desperate need of a bit of loving care, but it was only cosmetic, an army of cleaners could soon put things to rights.

The whole top floor of the property ran the full length of the house. The roof, supported by thick wooden joists, had skylight windows inserted in it at intervals providing plenty of daylight but it was full of old furnishings of any kind.

Outside, the house, for the most part, looked to be in good order, apart from some of the window frames. It looked like Lord Wellford had replaced the frames in the rooms they had lived in but left the others to the elements.

There were three large stables in need of cleaning out, and four barns all these buildings at least, seemed to be in good repair.

There was a wood to the right and an orchard to the left. Blossom was abundant on all the fruit trees giving promise of a good yield.

A fishing lake ran along the bottom of the grounds, and Tom and Lee's eyes lit up at the sight of the trout swimming beneath the murky surface.

"Well," said Clara, "Whoever buys this place will have their work cut out."

"That might well be Effie and me," Edwin smiled, "I like this place, it has a nice feel to it. We can make it right if you are willing to take it on Effie. Once all the dust has been cleaned away and new curtains hung at the windows, I think it will be liveable, don't you?

"We have our own furniture we can bring down from Frithwood of course. I know it will be like a drop in the ocean for a house this size, but the furniture we bring will make some of the rooms comfortable enough to live in while we work on the others. I would not fancy sleeping in one of those beds upstairs."

"We will come over and help you," volunteered Lee.

"Yes, we can try out the fishing for you, catch you some fish for your tea," agreed Tom.

"Much obliged I am sure," Lord Hunter told them trying to keep his voice serious.

"It would mean selling Harrington Court of course, and using the money to get this estate back to its original splendour, but I think it will be worth it. Don't you, Effie?"

"Yes, Edwin, I do, it will clean up a treat. It will give us something to work on instead of just moping around the city from one week to the next. Let us do it; let's buy the estate and turn it back into what it once was."

"What about the contraband?" asked Tom, "I wonder where they hid it?"

"Good question," said Oscar. "There must be a cellar in a house this size, and I know Lord Wellford liked a drink or two. Let's go back in and do another search. You never know there might be a secret passage down in the cellar, if we can find the cellar that is. I did not see any of you looking for a secret passage while we went around the house by the way."

"No, there was too much to look at, but I am game to go back into the house to try to find the cellar," Harvey said.

"Yes, and it would not surprise me if we have missed some rooms out as well. It is a huge house," Oscar commented.

"I think that is more than likely, but let us try to find the cellar first to see if there is contraband stored down there. We would look a couple of fools if we went barging into The Monks Den telling the innkeeper to move his brandy barrels if there is none to move," Lord Hunter remarked.

They made their way back across the overgrown lawn with Ruby and Max, the Landers two sheepdogs, and Chester running ahead, chasing each other.

The echo of their footsteps could be heard once again when they crossed the hall. They made for the rear of the house, heading towards the kitchen area, hoping the cellar door could be located somewhere in that vicinity and indeed it was.

Lee found it on opening the second door he came to. Stone steps leading down into a dark hole.

"Harvey, go into the kitchen and see if there are any lanterns knocking about, we can use," Oscar said.

Harvey returned from the kitchen holding two lanterns and after passing one to Oscar, he held the other high.

The lanterns pale light helped to give them at least some vision although, even with two lanterns, the cellar was so huge that the sides of the cellar walls were still in darkness.

"Here, take this, Edwin, I will go and get some more lanterns, and I also saw some candlesticks we could use," said Harvey passing his lantern to Lord Hunter.

"Lee, Tom," Harvey shouted from above. "Come up to the kitchen I need a hand."

The twins scurried after their brother. Returning down the stone steps, they both held a lantern in each hand while Harvey brought up the rear bearing two candlesticks. He passed one to Clara, and the cellar was flooded with more light.

Cobwebs were everywhere, but the floor was clear of debris. Empty wine racks stood tall and silent in rows like soldiers on parade.

"I am not coming down here on my own looking for secret passages," Lee whispered to his twin.

"Nor me, it's spooky," agreed his brother.

"I am pleased to hear it," said Oscar. "It is not a place to get locked in especially if the smugglers return or the revenue men. Keep out of here, or there will be trouble if I find out you have disobeyed me. That goes for you too, Clara."

"Why bring me into this?" his sister wanted to know indignantly.

"Because I have lived with you for the past nineteen years, that is why," answered her brother.

This brought an amused smile to Lord Hunter's lips, and his eyes met Clara's.

Clara decided to ignore the remark, and she turned away from the direction they were all following and made her way between two rows of wine racks, and it was there that she came across the contraband.

"Here," she shouted. "Here, I have found them, I have found the barrels. Lord, there must be fifty at least," she added.

The rest of them turned and followed the sound of her voice and found her holding up her candlestick to display the neatly stacked barrels.

"Right, time to make a retreat now we know the barrels are definitely here. Let's lock up. Edwin and I will have a ride over to The Monks Den after tea and have a word with Redfern, tell him to move the stuff to a better location," Oscar said turning towards the stairs.

When Oscar reached home, he went around the side of the house and into the stable. He looked around and found Jack, his stable hand, putting clean straw in one of the stalls. "There you are, Jack. I have an errand for you. After tea I want you to go to The Monks Den and buy yourself a mug of ale. Sit in the bar and watch out for a scruffy little man with a bruised face. You will recognise him if he is there.

"If he is, come outside and wait until Lord Hunter and I arrive. If this man is in the pub, I want to know about it before we go in. If he is not, please stay seated in the pub whilst Lord Hunter and I are talking to the landlord. If you see this man come down the stairs or enter the pub while we are there you must try to let us know because I do not want him to see us," Oscar handed some change over to Jack and added, "For a couple of beers."

After tea, Lord Hunter and Oscar collected their horses from the stables and set off for Brodley. They rode across uninhabited pastures and passed through a small wood. Half an hour later they were tethering their horses up outside The Monks Den. There was no sign of Jack, so it was safe to enter.

On entering The Monks Den the murmur of voices died, and silence filled the small, cosy room, all eyes of the fellow drinkers were focused on the two new arrivals.

"Good evening, Redfern, pleasant evening," Oscar greeted the innkeeper.

"Ay, it is that, all the better for seeing you, Mr Oscar," replied the innkeeper.

"Two of your best beers would be very welcome," Oscar told him.

"Take a seat, and I will bring them over. All your family are well I hope?"

"They are all in fine form, thank you, Mr Redfern."

When the ale was brought over to their table, Oscar said, "Why don't you pour yourself a drink and come and join us."

"That is very kind of you, Mr Oscar, I don't mind if I do." Mr Redfern went to get himself a mug.

"I would like to introduce you to Lord Hunter. He is here to look around Davey Grange with a view to purchasing it. He holds the keys to it, and we had a stroll around the estate this morning. If there is anything you need to see to, then it might be a good idea to get it sorted tonight," Oscar told him.

"Pleased to meet you, my lord," Mr Redfern held out his hand.

"Now if, when you leave, there happened to be a set of keys left on the table, I would know who they belonged to and whom to return them to. I know there is a locked room down in the cellar, carved into the rock, but you can only access it by a special key, the lock cannot be picked.

"When Lord Wellford was alive, we did not have such a problem; we always found the door to the room in the rock had been left open. If any business needs attending to, it will take a couple of days maybe weeks to sort out another destination for it, but in the meantime, there might be a need to, shall I say, hide a certain merchandise just in case the revenue happen to get wind of it," Mr Redfern told them.

"The revenue will not hear of it from us, I can assure you of that. You have a greater problem in your midst. I believe you have a new employee who helped you in your business early this morning. He is bad news, very bad news," Lord Hunter informed Mr Redfern.

"What name would this new employee be going by?" Mr Redfern wanted to know.

"Elmer Wolf," Oscar supplied.

"In what way is Elmer Wolf not to be trusted?" Mr Redfern asked.

"He is very adept at blackmail," Lord Hunter said with venom.

"Is he now, I had it from a very good source he was alright," Mr Redfern stroked his chin.

"If you want anything doing that might not be lawful, he is your man, but it comes with a price. You had better get your business sorted out tonight and without your new driver knowing anything about it or you might find yourself accompanying the revenue men. Just a friendly word of advice," Oscar added.

They spent another half hour talking to Mr Redfern then, taking some change out of his pocket Oscar left it on the table at the side of the keys.

"We will be on our way, thank you for the drink it was very welcome," said Oscar making for the door.

Mr Redfern sat where he was with a scowl on his face. He looked down at the table and scooped up the set of keys and pushed them in his pocket; he left the change where it was.

Mr Redfern finished off his ale then, after scooping up the change, he went into the back of The Monks Den where his wife was working in the kitchen.

"Aggie, I have to go out, and I do not know how long I will be. Will you send young Jo to fetch Mick, and bring him back here? Ask Mick to keep his friend Elmer Wolf occupied and not to let him out of his sight until I return?"

"Trouble?" she asked.

"We could have. I am informed that Elmer Wolf is not to be trusted, so tell Mick not to tell him anything about me going out or about anything else. If you saw me talking to Oscar Lander and his friend, keep your tongue between your teeth. We could have a blackmailer in our midst," he turned and left through the back door.

Up in his room, Elmer was lying on his bed with his hands behind his head. Things had taken an unexpected turn for the better. He had been let into a smuggling ring. There must be money in that. He had to be careful though.

Which way to go, that was the question? He could try and get money out of the innkeeper, tell him if he did not pay up, he was going to the revenue men. But if he did go to the revenue men, they might want to know how he knew about the brandy, and how he knew where it was stored. He might end up being locked up as well, seeing as he had helped transport the barrels and unload them into that empty old house.

Elmer decided it was not an ideal plan to try and extort money from the innkeeper and his friends with the threat of the revenue. Elmer had known Mick for about six years, and Mick had a reputation. You did not cross Mick, word was Mick had his own way of dealing with people he had cause to be angry with, and he could no longer trust. Elmer knew of at least two people who had crossed Mick, they had suddenly vanished, and nobody had seen either of them again.

Elmer decided to go down into the parlour and have a mug of ale and a chat with the innkeeper and try and find out how things stood.

Mick entered The Monks Den via the back door and asked of Mrs Redfern, "Do we have trouble?"

"It seems like it. Doug's gone out; he wants you to keep an eye on that Elmer Wolf until he gets back, make sure he stays here. Doug left just after sitting down to a mug of ale with Oscar Lander and another gentleman I did not recognise.

"Doug looked pretty worried. It is not like Doug to be worried. He said he had been told that Elmer Wolf was a blackmailer and that you were not to say anything about anything to him but to keep him occupied until Doug returns. He particularly requested me to tell you not to mention to Elmer that Oscar Lander has been in to see him.

"Doug has been given some keys and has gone to move the brandy out of sight. Elmer must not know about this. I hope everything is going to be all right," Mrs Redfern told Mick.

Mick Porter was a tall, slim, young man, living off his wits for most of his life. He'd had more than one close shave with the revenue men, but to those he worked with he was a man to be relied upon and trusted. His dress was immaculate, and he had most of the young girls in the village under his spell, but he was ruthless. To cross Mick Porter was a very dangerous thing to do.

"Where is Elmer now?" he asked.

"He is in the snug; he has just come down. Elmer missed seeing Oscar Lander and his friend for they had gone by the time he appeared. That was a stroke of good luck because it was after they left that Doug made the quick exit. That Elmer sits by himself most of the time, he is not one for making friends with the natives," Mrs Redfern told him.

Finding Elmer sitting alone by the fire, Mick went to join him and asked, "How are you settling in, in our neck of the woods?"

"Quiet, very quiet except for the damn cockerels crowing at God knows what hour every morning," grumbled Elmer.

"Didn't you find the bit of business we did this morning entertaining?" Mick asked innocently.

"Throwing heavy barrels up and down isn't my idea of entertainment. Do you get much contraband coming your way?" Elmer asked.

"Keep your voice down, man, I have told you before not to speak so loudly. We do not want the whole inn to hear you. Some, the last lot we dealt with, went like a dream, the revenue men never had a sniff that it was coming in. That is the way we like it. The revenue men have put out a reward for anyone that informs them of the next shipment, but they never heard a thing about this last cargo, nobody tells the revenue men anything around here, it was a piece of cake," Mick informed him.

Elmer, on the other hand, soaked up this information and asked innocently, "When is the next shipment due?"

"I do not know that. Doug lets me know when I am needed, but I know there has been a hold up in moving this last lot on. Thank goodness, the revenue never got wind about the merchandise coming in because they would have been on the lookout for it. It is also a good job too that the revenue does not know where the brandy is stored. I don't think they will search Davey Grange. They have done so a few times in the past, but their search has always been fruitless," Mick confided in him.

Mick was pleased that when they had stored the barrels down in the cellar, they did not possess the key to the hole in the wall, so the barrels had been stacked up to one side of the darkened cellar. Elmer had no way of knowing the brandy was being moved elsewhere, so it could not be seen down in that vast dark cellar.

Elmer was not aware of the hole in the wall, and Mick gave a silent prayer of thanks for that at least. If he had no knowledge of the hiding place, then he could not inform the revenue of it.

Two hours later Doug arrived back at the inn. He met Mick's eyes over the top of the heads of other drinkers and then carried on, into the back to the kitchen.

Mick waited a couple of minutes, drank off his ale and said goodnight to Elmer. He went out of the front door and around the side of the inn and back into the kitchen where he found Doug and his wife in quiet conversation.

"How long have you known Elmer Wolf?" Doug asked.

"A few years on and off, I know he lives in the rundown part of Frithwood, and he is known to the Peelers. Have you seen his face? Something went terribly wrong back in Frithwood for him. That is why he is down here. He has left Frithwood until things calm down. Because of that, I thought he would be a good replacement for Harry when he broke his leg. What is going on?" Mick wanted to know.

"I had a visit from Oscar Lander tonight. He brought with him a toff from Frithwood. He turns out to be a decent sort. He left me the keys to Davey Grange so I could go and store the barrels in the secret room we usually use until we can move the brandy on.

"They said they knew Elmer Wolf was with us. Said the twins had been up early and were up in the loft of one of the stables at the rear of Davey Grange. Apparently, they have met Elmer, and they are not very impressed with him. They came to warn me he is a bad lot. Into blackmailing and they say he has been found out and he had to leave Frithwood, that is why he is down here. If he is into blackmail we might be in a bit of trouble," explained Doug.

"I bet that is what happened to his face. I have fed him a bit of bait. I told him there was a reward for information about the smugglers. I know you said not to say anything to him but if he is a blackmailer we need to know. Let us sit back and see what happens. Shall I go and move the barrels to a different location just in case he does go for the reward and tells the revenue men where to look?" Mick asked.

"No need to do that, the shipment is safe for now. Even if the revenue does get the tip off, they will never find it. I think it is about time we packed in this smuggling lark Mick, don't you? There are so many new faces coming to live here; we do not know who we can trust these days. Let this be our last job. I am getting too old for all this anyway," Doug told him.

"I have been thinking about jumping on a boat and going over to Ireland to try my luck over there. As you say, our luck has nearly run out on us. I might just do that, go and make a new life for myself over the water. This is just what I needed to make me push the boat out.

"But I would like to see the outcome of this little enterprise. If our friend Elmer does try for the reward, there will be a bit of business I would have to finish here first before I set off for new shores. I brought him into this, and I will see him out if I have to, I will see it through to the end. I will not leave my friends at the mercy of a blackmailer.

"What a rogue he has turned out to be. I am sorry to have put you in this position, Doug, I never would have done it if I had known," Mick told his friend.

"Don't you think I know that lad? Let us cross our bridges when we get to them. Everything is safely tucked away. No need to worry about the revenue, they will find nothing," Doug slapped Mick on the back and added, "Off you go home lad and get some sleep, we will see how things stand in the morning."

Instead of going straight home Mick ventured back into the snug to have another word with Elmer, but there was no sign of him, so Mick went home.

Elmer Wolf was heading for the centre of Meeks, it was pitch black outside, but he could see lights flickering in the distance so he headed straight for them. He had seen where the revenue men's office was when he had walked into Meeks two days previously.

Elmer was going to find out about the reward. It was dark and late, but he knew the revenue office never closed its doors. Nobody would see him entering the office at that time of night, so nobody would be able to tell Mick that they had seen him where he should not have been. Mick would never know it was him that had told the revenue the smugglers secret.

There was a lone revenue man sitting behind a desk when Elmer reached the station.

"Good evening," the revenue man said.

"Good evening to you too. I was passing and I thought I would call in and ask if there is a reward for information about smugglers?"

"There is. Do you have information to give us?"

"How much is the reward?" Elmer wanted to know, "In case I hear anything."

"The reward is fifty pounds."

"Fifty pounds!" gasped Elmer.

"We have been after these smugglers for a long time now. It is costing a fortune to run this operation, so any information that leads to the recovery of the smuggled contraband and the arrest of the smugglers is worth a great deal of money. The trouble is, nobody around here is willing to inform on the smugglers, so the money is irrelevant," the officer told him.

The temptation was too great for Elmer. How long would it take him to get that sort of money? He had to do it.

"I was in The Monks Den earlier this evening, and I overheard a conversation about a delivery of brandy. The smugglers took it to a place called Davey Grange and stored it down in the cellar. Two of the smugglers are Doug Redfern, innkeeper of The Monks Den and a man called Mick Porter, one of his customers," Elmer informed the revenue officer.

"You think this is sound information?" asked the officer.

"I do. I am new to these parts, I have no loyalty issues towards the smugglers and if there are fifty pounds in it and you are going to arrest them both, Doug Redfern and Mick Porter, I am willing to take a chance," said Elmer.

"I will need to take your details, and if we find the contraband and make the arrests, you will be the first to know," said the officer dipping his quill in the ink.

Chapter Thirteen

Doug was woken from his sleep around 4:30 next morning. The revenue men pushed their way into The Monks Den ignoring Doug's protests. They found nothing; they even interrogated Mrs Redfern leaving her crying at the kitchen table. It took Doug nearly thirty minutes to get Aggie to stop crying.

Word from miles around soon reached The Monks Den that lights could be seen moving on the moors.

Doug knew it would be the revenue men searching Davey Grange for the brandy, it had to be; nobody else would be at Davey Grange that early in the morning with lights, advertising their presence.

Mick had been right. Elmer Wolf had gone for the reward. Mick had primed him, and he had taken the bait. Doug realised all too late that it had been a big mistake to put his trust in someone he barely knew.

He still possessed Lord Hunter's keys, and he knew he had to get them back to him, so he set off for Badger Manor.

Doug entered the wood belonging to The Manor but had difficulty in finding his way through, it was dark in the wood, and it took longer than he had intended. He approached the Manor from the side, keeping well hidden from any prying eyes.

As he neared the edge of the wood, Doug was glad he had. There were revenue men standing outside

Badger Manor's front door. How was he going to get the keys back to their owner? Doug tested his alert mind to try and come up with a solution. He could not.

"Hello," said a soft voice to his left.

Looking down Doug saw the twins looking up at him.

"Hello to you two, too," he whispered back. "What are you two doing out at this time of the morning?"

"We were going fishing in Lord Wellford's lake, but when we got there the revenue men were all over the grounds, so we came home, and now there are the revenue men at our door too," Lee told him.

"What are you doing in our wood?" Tom wanted to know.

"Well, it's like this. I found a set of keys last night at the table where your brother and his friend were sitting. I told the wife about the keys, and she has told the revenue about them. She did not mean to let it slip, they came and woke us up early this morning, and the poor old girl was so frightened she blurted it out about the keys being left on the table last night. Then to try and cover up her mistake she told the revenue men I had taken the keys back and handed them over to Mr Lander, for poor old Aggie did not know the name of the toff.

"I told the revenue men that Aggie was so frightened of them, she didn't know what she was saying, and the keys she was talking about belonged to another customer.

"I think that is why the revenue men are at your door, asking about the keys. I have to get these keys back to your toff without the revenue knowing anything about it. Like you two, my plan seems to have backfired, I also find the revenue men blocking my way. I did not expect to find them standing on your doorstep.

"Word reached my ears that lights could be seen at Davey Grange. These keys need to be returned to that toff, and pretty soon by the looks of things. I have also to get back to The Monks Den, the revenue said they would be back, and poor old Aggie is in such a state. Someone has told the revenue I am involved with this smuggling lark. They have searched The Monks Den from top to bottom. Aggie's that upset she is fit to drop, she is," the portly gentleman told them.

Oscar and Lord Hunter were woken from their sleep by Trueman, informing them that a revenue man, a Captain Bottomly, was waiting in the sitting room desiring a word with them as soon as possible.

Both Oscar and Lord Hunter were stood facing Captain Bottomly, wearing their dressing gowns.

Oscar was the first to make a move. He held out his hand to the captain and said, "Oscar Lander at your service, and this gentleman is Lord Hunter."

"I was told you have a friend, Mr Lander, that holds the keys to Davey Grange. Would that gentleman, be you?" Captain Bottomly addressed Lord Hunter.

Lord Hunter replied, "And if it is, who told you about the keys to Davey Grange?"

"I cannot divulge that information, but I do need those keys, my lord, to get into the Grange. We have been informed that there is contraband stored there. My men are there now, searching the grounds. Do you know anything about any contraband?" the captain wanted to know.

"How would I know anything about contraband? I had never heard of Davey Grange up to a few days ago, and I am here to go and have a look at the estate with the intention of purchasing it if I like it. I hold the keys, yes, because I am acquainted with the present owner and he gave me them in good faith. Once I have made my decision, I am to return the keys.

"The property does not belong to me. I am reluctant to hand the keys out without the owner's permission. I don't think the owner would take very kindly to me handing over the keys for a troop of revenue men to go trampling all over the house. Mr Lander kindly offered to put my sister and I up for a week or two while I make up my mind whether I want to purchase or not.

"All the Landers, my sister and I have been residing in Frithwood for the past month. We arrived here two nights ago, so how can we have anything to do with any contraband or smugglers?" Lord Hunter wanted to know.

Lord Hunter was racking his brain for a good excuse to tell the captain why he did not have the keys in his possession at that precise moment. He glanced across at Oscar but was rewarded with only the slightest shrug of the shoulder.

"Begging your pardon, my lord, I do not need the owner's permission or your permission to enter the property. We have it on good authority that there is contraband on the premises. I can go and break the door down if I chose, but I would prefer it if we had the keys then there will be no damage done to the property. The decision is yours, my lord," the officer stood waiting.

Before Lord Hunter could answer, the door it was opened by Trueman and a second officer stood on the threshold holding two young boys by the scruff of their collar. "I am sorry, Mr Lander, but this officer insisted on being shown in," Trueman said.

Before Oscar could reply the second officer said, "These two boys say they live here, captain."

"We do live here," shouted Tom trying to escape the Revenue man's grip.

"Take your hands off my brothers this instant," Oscar rushed over to the door and taking command of the twins, he said, "Release them this instant. How dare you put hands on my brothers?"

"What are you doing out this early in the morning?" the captain asked the twins.

"I do not think that is any of your business, Captain Bottomly. My brothers live here; they are not prisoners in their own home. If they want to wander about their own home, they are at liberty to do so no matter what the time of day or night it is," Oscar told the captain.

Lee looked at Tom and Tom looked at Lee.

Lee elbowed Tom in the ribs.

Tom elbowed Lee back.

Tom took a deep breath, "We were only going to go and try to find a secret passage in the Grange, honestly, we were, Oscar. We saw Edwin had left the keys to the Grange on the hall table, we only borrowed them, really, we did, we didn't steal them. We thought it would be a good laugh if we hid in the secret passage and made noises then Edwin would think there were ghosts living there."

They both looked up at their older brother, "So that is where you have been, did you find a secret passage?"

"We did not get into the house, when we got there, we saw hundreds of revenue men hanging around outside, so we came straight home to tell you, but when we got here, we were pounced on by some more revenue men. We did not do anything wrong, Oscar, truly we didn't," Lee told him.

"It's all right, Lee. You have no need to get yourself in such a tuck over it. The revenue man was out of order manhandling you in the first place. I think an apology is in order," Oscar held the gaze of the offending revenue man.

"I beg your pardon, young sirs, my mistake. I hope I have not hurt you?" the officer mumbled, "I did not mean to frighten you."

"Apology accepted, but think twice before you lay a hand on any of my brothers or sister in future or I will not be so understanding next time," Oscar steered the twins to the sofa and made them sit down.

"Which one of you has the keys?" his lordship asked.

Tom took them out of his pocket and held them up.

"Please give them to this revenue man, he also wants to go on a secret passage hunt," Lord Hunter said, "I hope they will be returned once you have done what you have to do, and I trust we will find everything as we left it yesterday, when next we visit the house."

Tom held out the keys, and Captain Bottomly went over and took possession of them.

"You were there yesterday? Did you see anything out of the ordinary?" the captain asked.

"We saw a lot of spiders, dust and dark, spooky paintings," offered Lee.

"Yes, and there were mice in the kitchen too," added Tom.

"I was talking to the gentlemen if you don't mind," the captain gave the twins a cutting glance.

"I think Lee summed it up in a nutshell. We did see all those things. At the moment it is a very dark and depressing place," Lord Hunter confirmed.

"What about the cellar?" the revenue man insisted.

"What about the cellar?" Oscar asked.

"What did you see in the cellar?" the revenue man was not about to let go.

"The same as in the rest of the house spiders, dust and darkness, there were also rows and rows of empty wine racks. Pity that, I thought Lord Wellford kept a good cellar. Maybe the nephew took it all away," replied Oscar.

"Maybe, we might be back to talk to you both again." The revenue man turned and walked out.

"I will expect the return of the keys by lunchtime; it will not take you long to do your search; most of the rooms are empty apart from some old, dusty furniture." Lord Hunter said to Captain Bottomly's retreating back.

"That was a close shave," remarked Oscar.

"Too close for comfort. Quick thinking you two," Lord Hunter said to Tom and Lee when the revenue man had gone. "How did you come by the keys?"

"We were going to do some fishing in the lake, but when we got there, we saw the revenue men searching the grounds, so we came back home through the wood and came across the innkeeper of The Monks Den hiding in there.

"He told us he needed to get the keys back to the toff, which is you, Edwin, without the revenue knowing anything about it, so we took them off him. We changed our story; we had to change our story because we were going fishing really and we would not have needed the keys to do that. We have had to leave our fishing rods in the wood," explained Lee.

"Well done, I am impressed," Lord Hunter smiled at them. "You have certainly rescued me out of a very tight corner."

"I think we got away with that very nicely. Let us hope Mr Redfern managed to hide the goods in time," Oscar said. "Have you made up your mind for certain, whether or not to invest in Davey Grange?"

"I have, and yes, we are going to buy Davey Grange. Effie likes it and is looking forward to doing the house up. I want to go back to Frithwood as soon as I can and sort out the legal stuff before someone else jumps in and snatches it from under my nose. I think we will head back to Frithwood tomorrow morning if that is all right with you Oscar," Edwin wanted to know.

"Whatever you feel the need to do, Edwin, of course, you must do it. While we are on the subject of buying property, I have something to tell you two," Oscar said looking at the twins.

"Mrs Hawkshaw came to see me before we went on our little trip to Frithwood and asked me if I would like to purchase Bluebell House. I told her I did. I had a word with Harvey and Clara, and they both agreed that it would be a good idea if we bought it for you two, for when you leave school.

"I am going to see Mrs Hawkshaw today and tell her that our lawyer will be calling to see her to seal the deal. I wanted to buy it so the two of you can run it together. The house is big enough for you to split it into two, later on, then you will both have your own home when the time comes. It will give you some independence, and it should provide you both with a good living if you work hard."

"You mean you are going to buy Bluebell House for us, Tom and me?" asked Lee.

"I do indeed, but it is not just me, it is Harvey and Clara too, and you two of course. This estate belongs to all of us, not just me. I know there was a will and the deeds came to me, but this is your home as well as mine. So, some of the money we have made from this estate is going to provide you both with a living, I hope. Harvey has his own place, and you will have yours."

"We will do what I did with Harvey; school holidays will be taken up learning how to run the estate then you will know what to do when you leave school. There will be time for play too; I would not expect you to work the land all your school holidays. Harvey did not have any

192

trouble in having fun and making mischief, but he also took on board farm management, and he seems to have turned out all right. Don't you think?" asked Oscar.

"Can we come with you when you go and see Mrs Hawkshaw, so we can have a look around?" asked Tom eagerly.

"If you wish," agreed his eldest brother. "What about you, Edwin, would you like to come and have a look around too? It is not as big or as grand as Davey Grange by any means, but I think you will like it."

"I would love to come and have a look. I have no keys at the moment to go and have another look around the Grange so yes, of course, I would love to come," Edwin told him.

Clara walked into the breakfast room and saw her brother and Lord Hunter still in their dressing gowns.

"What is going on here?" she asked.

Tom and Lee rushed up to Clara, and they were both gabbling on about Bluebell House until she called a halt.

"For heaven's sake, one at a time please, I cannot understand a word either of you is saying," Clara smiled.

Lord Hunter's eyes lingered on Clara. Her jet-black hair hanging in ringlets was shining in the light coming from the window behind her. Her bright blue eyes were brimming with amusement, and she glanced up and caught Lord Hunter watching her. She rather liked it.

"We are going to Bluebell House today, and Oscar is going to buy it for Tom and me for when we leave school, and you have missed the revenue men," Lee told her.

"Effie and I seem to have missed a lot. Where are the revenue men now and what is this about Bluebell House?" Clara wanted to know.

"We know you know all about Bluebell House," Lee said, "because Oscar has told us you and Harvey said it was all right to buy it for us. We love you, Clara."

"And I love you too, especially now I know you are going to be landowners," she teased.

Then, looking over at Oscar, Clara asked, "Is the contraband out of sight?"

"We have no idea, but we think so. Doug Redfern has been smuggling for quite a few years now; he knows what he is about," Oscar told them.

"I am going to get dressed and have some breakfast then we will head next door and see Mrs Hawkshaw," Oscar said heading for the door. "I bet she cannot wait to start making arrangements to go and live with her daughter."

Captain Bottomly and his team rode up the long drive of Davey Grange and joined their colleagues waiting for them at the front door.

"Have you seen anything of interest?" asked the captain still clutching the keys.

"Nothing, Captain, we have seen no movement of any kind. I have sent Scott and Johnson around to the back to make sure there is nobody going out of the back door while we are coming in at the front door. It is as quiet as a graveyard," replied the young guard.

"Good, let's go in then and see what we can find." Captain Bottomly tried three keys before he found the right one; he opened the door and they all trouped in.

Two hours later a frustrated captain and his men were making their way back down the long drive. Having to agree with Lord Hunter and the twins, nothing but dust and gloom. The cellar was exactly as they described it, dusty and empty. He had not given in altogether, though, he was determined to go back and see the innkeeper of The Monks Den.

Doug Redfern's name had been mentioned in connection with the smuggling. It was the first time they had been given a name, and Captain Bottomly was not going to let it go without a fight.

Doug Redfern was stacking empty barrels behind the inn when the revenue men returned.

"Mr Redfern," the captain said, "We have come to resume our search."

"Be my guest," the innkeeper said.

"I have been informed that you know something about the smuggling that goes on in these parts. I know you know something about it because your name tripped off the informant's tongue too easily. Your name and someone called Mick Porter, do you know Mick Porter?" the captain asked.

"Of course, I know him. I know nearly all the people that live around here. A poor innkeeper I would be if I ran the inn from behind closed doors. You have been misinformed. The only thing I know about smuggling is that the revenue men have not had much success in catching anyone in connection with it, or even found any of the contraband you are so determined to place at my door," Mr Redfern said.

"I was led to understand that you are the main man, the one who organises the distribution of the contraband," the captain ignored Doug's last remark.

"I am the innkeeper of The Monks Den, not a smuggler. Again, you must have been misinformed," replied Doug.

"I would like to search your premises, with or without your permission," the captain told him.

"Like I said before, be my guest, you will find no contraband here," Mr Redfern continued rolling his barrels and stacking them.

"Would you like to start with these empty barrels?" Mr Redfern asked.

The captain was about to say no when he thought it might just be a bluff and some of the barrels might be full, "That is an excellent idea, thank you for suggesting it."

Three hours had passed, and the captain was sitting at his desk filling out his report. It did not take him long, nothing to report. Half a day wasted and they had found nothing.

Mick Porter was sitting in the kitchen with Doug and his wife, none of them speaking.

Mick eventually said, "It has to be him; it could not be anyone else. It is most fortunate that we were seen by the Landers twins and Elmer was recognised, or we would all be sitting behind bars now. We have a lot to thank Oscar Lander for. It will not be forgotten."

"What are we going to do?" asked Mrs Redfern.

"Nothing, Mrs Redfern, the revenue cannot tie us to anything so don't you worry your pretty little head over anything. Like Doug said, it has got to be our last time. I am heading for Ireland when we have got rid of the brandy. Then, you and Doug can take it easy and just run your inn and keep out of trouble. It is all over now, but it has been a pleasure working with you Doug, a real pleasure. I am going to miss you, and you too, Mrs Redfern, especially your cooking," he sent her a fond but sad smile.

"Well, I cannot lie I am also glad it is all over," Mrs Redfern sighed.

"Now the revenue has gone will you give me a hand with those empty barrels? They have left them scattered all over the back yard," Doug stood up, and Mick followed him outside.

"Now Aggie cannot hear us; what are we going to do about Elmer Wolf?" Doug asked his friend.

"Don't you worry about that, Doug, Elmer will be dealt with, and there is nothing for you to be concerned about. Everything will be dealt with satisfactorily, and no come back on either of us, the less you know, the better. It is my mistake for letting Elmer Wolf know about us in the first place, and I am well able to rectify my mistake. He will not bother either you or Mrs Redfern again so let us forget about that worthless piece of cargo and get these barrels restacked."

Once the barrels were stacked, Mick said, "I am going to pack my bags and make for the sea, but before I leave there is that bit of unfinished business to attend to. Will you be able to get rid of the brandy without my help? Once the unfinished business is sorted, I don't think it would be a good idea for me to hang around here."

"Don't worry about me or the brandy, lad, I will give it a couple of weeks then deliver the barrels of brandy for the last time."

"I will write to you and let you know where I have landed. You and Mrs Redfern are the nearest thing I have to family. I like the thought of Ireland. I would also like to keep in touch with you, Doug," Mick told him.

"You do that, lad. I will tell Mrs Redfern, and it will make losing you that little bit easier for her if she knows you will be in touch. I have a mind to follow you, Mick, I'll give it a couple of months here to find someone to take over The Monks Den, then we will come and join you. There is nothing here for us now, and I know Mrs Redfern will be glad to see the back of this place, and that will be that, over and done with," Doug told him.

"I would be glad to see you both if you do decide to follow me, true friends are hard to come by, and I think we have proved to each other we are friends. Don't you, Doug?" Mick asked.

"Aye, lad, we have done that alright," Mr Redfern agreed.

Chapter Fourteen

Elmer made his way downstairs to the snug later that morning. He had slept in longer than he had intended, so he was ignorant of the turn of events involving the revenue men and was surprised to see his old friend Mick Porter, sitting near the door, with a mug of ale in front of him, "Mick, you are making an early start with the ale, aren't you?"

"I need it to take the bad taste out of my mouth," Mick informed him.

"Good night last night was it?" Elmer grinned, completely misinterpreting Mick's inference.

"You could say that. We have another job; can you ride a horse?" Mick asked.

"I can but not very well, you will have to go slow," Elmer warned.

"I can ride slowly," Mick said, "Let's go."

"Not before my breakfast, I will not miss one of Mrs Redfern's breakfasts. You want to try one," Elmer told him calling through the kitchen door that he was ready to eat.

"I have had one or two of Mrs Redfern's breakfasts. I will not begrudge you your breakfast." Mick sat back down and was prepared to wait.

Breakfast was over, and Elmer, happily satisfied with a full stomach, wiped his mouth on the napkin and said, "Right. Mick, where to now?"

"I will let you know when we get there." Mick stood up and walked out of the front door with Elmer following.

Elmer saw two horses tethered up outside of the inn. One had a carpetbag fastened to the back of one of the saddles, and a pick and shovel was tied to the back of the other. Mick mounted the horse with the carpetbag and waited patiently while Elmer ungainly mounted the second.

For what seemed an eternity to Elmer, they made their way across flat green pastureland until eventually rolling hills and thick forests began to appear in the distance.

"How much longer are we going to be? I am not used to riding horseback, and my arse is beginning to go numb, and I'm hungry." Elmer grumbled.

"Not much further," replied Mick. It was the first time he had spoken to Elmer since they set off on their journey, words stuck in Mick's throat; it was all he could do to keep his hands off him.

It was getting late in the afternoon by the time they hit the first forest, "I hope you know where you're going," Elmer complained. "I'm hungry. We have not eaten since this morning."

"I think this will do very nicely. We will camp here for the night and set off first thing in the morning." Mick dismounted.

Elmer followed suit and was grateful to feel the ground beneath his feet.

"Where are we going? What are we doing?" Elmer asked. "How much further is it? If I had known it was going to be this far, I would not have come."

"I know if you had known where you were going, you would not have come, that is why I did not tell you.

Go and collect some dry twigs for a fire and then we will have something to eat.

"There is a stream over there. I shall let the horses have a drink then tether them up and leave them to graze. I will get us some fresh water too while you are collecting the twigs for a fire," Mick said unfastening the pick and shovel.

Elmer turned and set off into the undergrowth, Mick followed. Elmer Wolf never knew what hit him.

Mick, taking the shovel and pick, began to dig a hole. He worked away at the undergrowth and found it was not as hard as he had expected it to be.

Dead leaves, earth and rotting wood began to pile up at the side of the grave and soon, the hole was shoulder deep. Once satisfied with the grave, Mick pulled himself up and out of the hole and going over to the inert body of Elmer Wolf, he turned him over just to make sure he was dead.

Elmer's shirt had come out of his trousers and Mick could see what looked like a leather pouch strapped around Elmer's body. Mick yanked the shirt open, ripping off the buttons and there was indeed, a leather pouch hidden under Elmer's shirt.

Without hesitation, Mick opened the pouch and found four rolled up wads of money. Mick soon had the money out of the pouch and into his own pockets, he felt no guilt. Elmer Wolf had taken away his livelihood, and he had to leave the only family he had ever known.

Doug and Aggie had taken him under their wing and given him a place he could go to and feel safe, and Aggie was the best cook in the world, Mick was going to miss his Sunday dinners.

Before Mick tossed Elmer into his grave, he went through Elmer's pockets and transferred whatever else he found there into his own pockets.

Payback time for you, Elmer Wolf, payback time, Mick thought as he dragged the body over to the hole and kicked it in.

The hole was not quite long enough, so Elmer's legs were bent backwards. Mick shrugged. After all, Elmer was not going to need them again. He covered the hole back in, stamping it down as best he could in the disappearing light. Then he dragged dead branches and leaves across the surface hoping it would keep out scavenging animals.

It was pitch black by the time Mick was satisfied with the grave. He was tired and weary, but he intended to go back to The Monks Den and leave the spare horse that belonged to Doug.

The pick and shovel were tied back onto the saddle of the spare horse, and without a further glance in the grave's direction, Mick led both horses back out of the forest, took a chunk of bread and a bottle of water out of his bag and he walked along for a while, drinking his water and eating his bread.

The exercise helped clear his head and it did wonders for his aching body. It had taken much longer than Mick had intended it to take.

Ideally, he should have been on his way by now, but because of Elmer's lack of horsemanship, he was hours behind his planned schedule.

Mick was not all that worried about his lack of progress. Things had gone smoothly enough, and now there was no more threat of being double-crossed by Elmer, no more threat of blackmail from now on. He was the only one who knew where Elmer was buried—the only one who knew what had happened to him, and that was how it was going to stay. Let the maggots enjoy their meal.

After a while Mick mounted the spare horse, hoping to give his own horse a bit of a rest from carrying him, before he headed for Ireland. Retracing his steps, an exhausted Mick headed back to The Monks Den.

Next morning Doug found two horses tethered up at the front of the inn. He went into the kitchen, but it was empty. He went back upstairs and into Elmer's room; there was no sign of Elmer Wolf either. Going back downstairs the first thing Doug saw when he entered the snug was Mick lying fast asleep across one of the benches.

Doug gently shook Mick by the shoulder, and Mick woke up with a start, sitting up immediately before realising where he was.

Mick remembered being so tired when he arrived back at the inn it was all he could do to dismount and make his way to the rear of The Monks Den and let himself in.

The last thing he could remember was lying down across one of the benches in the snug to have a few minutes rest. Intending to rest for just a little while and give his horse a break then get as far away from Brodley as he possibly could.

"What time is it?" he asked running his hand through his untidy hair.

"About five," he was told.

"Damn, I only intended to have a short rest. Never mind it will have given the horse a rest too. Will you clear out Elmer's room and make sure there is no sign of him anywhere?" Mick asked.

"It will be done. I shall go and see to it now, the sooner the better, just in case we have another visit from you know who.

"Take some bread and a few apples with you to eat while you ride. You will make up good time if you eat while on the move. I know Aggie will be pleased to know that you have food with you. You go into the kitchen and fill a bag, and I'll go and clear out upstairs and good luck, Mick. Let me know when you have arrived at your destination, and Mrs Redfern and I will come and join you. Do you have enough money to see you right?" Mr Redfern held out his hand to Mick.

Mick hesitated then ignoring Doug's outstretched hand, he embraced Mr Redfern in a bear hug.

"I have money, Doug. You wouldn't believe how much. You do not have to worry your head over me. In fact, I have more money now than I had when I set out yesterday morning, thanks to Elmer. Let's just leave it at that, shall we? I can take care of myself. I will leave the key you gave me to The Monks Den on the kitchen table." Mick walked into the kitchen to pack some food.

It was a happy little group that walked to the neighbouring property. Instead of cutting across their own land and over the boundary wall they went the long way around. Down their own drive, along the uneven dirt road and up the drive to Bluebell House.

The property was accessed via a wooden gate which was beginning to hang off its hinges and come away from the retaining wall. The drive was neither narrow nor wide but able to accommodate a coach comfortably, and it led up to the house in a straight line.

The name of the house had been devised by the presence of a small wood off to the right. In April it was awash with bluebells. It had been one of the reasons Mr and Mrs Hawkshaw had purchased the property. The bluebells had died off now, but they would be back again next April in all their glory.

Mrs Hawkshaw saw them coming up the drive and was waiting at the open door greet them.

"Come in, all of you, I will put the kettle on. This is a nice surprise. I don't get many visitors. It can be quite lonely you know, living on your own."

"Thank you, Mrs Hawkshaw, I have come to tell you that my lawyer has been in contact with your lawyer and he should be calling to see you sometime today to complete the sale. All my paperwork is signed and ready to be exchanged. All you will have to do is to sign your paperwork then you can go and live with your daughter. There will be no need for you to move out straightaway, whenever you are ready will be fine by us," Oscar smiled down at her.

"Bless you, but I can't wait to leave and go and see my grandchildren and have a bit of time with all of them before I am too old to enjoy them. I will ask Mr Bellaby from the village if he will come and start removing the things I am taking with me to my daughter's. Mr Bellaby has told me he will take me and my belongings to my daughter's so it will not be long before I move out. I am not going to need much, anything that is left in the house I would like to leave for the twins, if that is all right with you and them of course," she told them as she poured out tea.

"Whatever makes you happy Mrs Hawkshaw, I am sure the twins will appreciate anything you leave behind," Oscar replied.

"You bet we will," agreed Tom and Lee together.

"Where are my manners? Mrs Hawkshaw, I would like to introduce you to Lord Hunter and his sister Effie, they are going to buy Davey Grange," Oscar informed her.

"You are going to buy Lord Wellford's estate, are you? I hope you make it a happier place to live in than he did, miserable old coot. Made his wife's life a misery he did. We were good friends, Lady Wellford and I. She used to come down and visit me. I missed her when she passed on.

"Lady Wellford told me all sorts of tales about Davey Grange. She said it was written in an old history book they had, that there was a secret room holding the former owner's treasures. Not Wellford's family treasure, of course, I don't think he had any, but the original owners of the Grange." She passed cups of tea to her visitors.

Continuing Mrs Hawkshaw said, "Lady Wellford told me Lord Wellford was obsessed with finding the secret room and all its hidden treasures. He would not have anyone visit the house because he was frightened of them stumbling across this secret room. He never did find it, not while Lady Wellford was still alive anyway, or she would have told me.

"Mary, that being Lady Wellford, did not believe there was any such room. There were also tales of smugglers hiding their contraband there too, but Mary saw nothing of that myth either," putting some homemade buns on a plate Mrs Hawkshaw placed them on the table.

"It is an interesting house to look at," continued Mrs Hawkshaw, "All it needs is a bit of tidying up, like this place. I am afraid I have let it slide since my Bert died. It is too big for me to look after. Our Gillian married a farmer from up north, bigger place than this, so she doesn't want it. The money will come in handy, help them to improve their estate, get some new livestock and make it a bigger and better home.

"I am glad you are buying Bluebell House; I know you will bring it back up to what it was when my Bert was still on this earth. The twins will be happy here, it is a happy house to live in, but it's time for me to go," concluded Mrs Hawkshaw.

"Do we have a secret room here?" asked Lee munching on a bun.

"No such luck, I'm afraid. We never found one anyway, but you never know, all these old houses hold hidden secrets, so there might be. We never looked for one, so, you keep looking, and you might get lucky.

"But I do know there are smugglers about because my Bert came across them one night when he heard the hens making a commotion, and he went out to see if there were foxes about. He didn't find any foxes; he found smugglers instead. Next day Bert found a barrel of brandy in the barn, best brandy he had ever tasted he said," Mrs Hawkshaw confided.

"Well, Tom and I will have a search for a secret room when you have left. If the smugglers have left another barrel of brandy in the barn, we will give it to Oscar," Lee told her then added, "and we will help Edwin and Effie to find their secret room too."

Mrs Hawkshaw gave a delighted laugh, "You just do that young man. Go and have a look around now if you want to, see what you are getting for your money."

Tom and Lee looked at each other, grabbed another bun each and shot off.

While Tom and Lee made a search of the house, the grown-ups made a tour of the outside. The grounds were extensive but neglected, the herd of cows that once roamed the pastures were long gone and so were the sheep. The only living things that Mrs Hawkshaw had retained were her hens.

As luck would have it, her lawyer came to see her while they were all there and Oscar was relieved to know that the sale had gone through.

On their way home Tom said, "While we were having a look round upstairs, Lee and I thought we might ask you if we could change the name of the house. Bluebell House, it's a girl's name," he said with disgust.

"There is nothing wrong with girl's names," Effie countered, "After all, I am a girl."

"You are not a girl! Lee and I have decided to adopt you as our sister. Most of the lads we know are always complaining about their sisters, but not us, we like our sister and we like you too, Effie, so we decided to adopt you. If you are our sister, then you are not a girl," Tom said logically.

"That is the nicest thing anyone has ever said to me, thank you. I will look upon you two as my brothers from now on," said a smug Effie.

"I say, that is a good idea. I will adopt you too," said Harvey with enthusiasm. "If you are my sister then Lord Hunter will be my brother, what a lark. Just you watch the faces of my friends at boarding school turn green with envy when I tell them."

Clara's eyes danced as she looked over at Lord Hunter and their eyes met, but there was something in his eyes that made Clara's stomach turn over and the colour rush to her cheeks, and she looked away.

Effie said, "Thank you, Harvey, this is a day of surprises," and there was only the smallest tremor in her voice.

Lord Hunter asked, "What about you Oscar, do you want Effie for a sister too?"

"Good God, no, Effie as my sister, that is the last thing I want," Oscar replied much to the indignation of the twins.

Tom said, "Poor Effie. Take no notice of him, Effie, we still love you."

"Thank you, Tom, but please do not take on so on my account because having Oscar as a brother is the last thing I want too," Effie said, not in the least offended, and put her arm across Tom's shoulder.

Lee, observing this, ran to the other side of Effie and he took her free hand, placed it across his shoulder making them all laugh.

Oscar looked Effie in the eye and said, "Lucky twins."

Effie looked Oscar in the eye and replied, "Their reward for being nice."

"I will remember your method of reward," he told her.

"What's he on about?" asked Lee.

"Beats me," replied Tom.

To change the subject, Oscar said, "I don't see why you can't change the name of your house if you don't like the one it's got. What do you want to change it to?"

"After Harvey took us to have a look around the boarding school last week, we were in the stagecoach, on our way home, and the stagecoach had to pull up sharp. We looked out of the window to see why we had stopped so suddenly, and we saw some ducks crossing the road," answered Tom.

"They waddled straight across the road taking no notice of the huge horse having to wait for them to pass and it made us laugh. It made us feel happy, so that is what we want to call our house Ducks Crossing. If it made us feel happy seeing such a sight, we think having our house called Ducks Crossing will make it a happy place to live. We also decided we were going to buy some ducks, make a little duck pond for them," Lee explained.

"When did you see that?" asked Harvey, "I did not see any ducks crossing the road, and I was on the same coach."

"You were sitting in the corner of the coach fast asleep, snoring your head off, and you missed them," Tom told him.

"I was not though, I do not snore," said the indignant brother.

"Do too," said the twins in unison.

"I think that is a delightful name for your house," agreed Clara, "And a delightful reason too, it makes me smile just thinking about it."

"I can't argue with that," agreed Oscar.

Without the keys to Davey Grange, there was not much Edwin and Effie could do, and Edwin wanted to get back home as soon as he could. He wanted to be in residence at Davey Grange before Christmas.

Lord Hunter had these thoughts in his head while they were approaching Badger Manor. He was much relieved to find Captain Bottomly waiting in the hallway.

"Good afternoon," said Captain Bottomly, "I am here to return the keys to Davey Grange."

Captain Bottomly was talking to Lord Hunter, but his eyes never left Clara.

"Thank you," said Edwin taking possession of the keys, "Did you find anything of interest?"

There was a short silence before Captain Bottomly's eyes moved from Clara to Lord Hunter, he coughed and said, "No, my lord, we did not. It looks like we were fed false information. We tried to find the man who told us there was contraband stored at Davey Grange, but when we got to The Monks Den, my men found his room empty and his clothes gone.

"He must have gone in the middle of the night, owing the innkeeper two weeks' rent. We think he was after the reward money and he must have heard we found no contraband where he told us to look, so he took off. Sorry, we troubled you, but I hope you will understand,"

and Captain Bottomly's eyes wandered over to where Clara was standing, and their eyes met.

Lord Hunter did not miss this exchange, and for the first time in his life, he felt a pang of jealousy which was fuelled even further when the captain, taking his leave, raised Clara's hand to his lips and kissed it.

"Now why would the captain kiss the back of your hand and not mine?" Effie wanted to know with a twinkle in her eye.

"He obviously likes me better than he likes you," her friend replied, and she twinkled back.

"I must admit he looked very dashing in his uniform and a captain to boot," Effie added.

Lord Hunter was listening to this conversation, and it did nothing to dispel his fears.

To change the subject of the captain, Edwin asked, "I wonder what happened to Elmer Wolf?"

"I think it would be best if nobody asked that question again. You do not cross the smugglers and get away with it. The smugglers have their own set of rules, they have too much to lose and there are too many of them for you to escape punishment if you do cross them.

"I don't think Elmer would have known what he was getting himself into. Blackmailing vulnerable women is one thing, but informing on the smugglers is an entirely different and dangerous thing to do. I think it will be best if we do not enquire after him," Oscar told him.

"Well, I for one hope he has got his just deserts," said Clara with feeling.

"Me too," agreed Effie. "Shall we go and have a final look around the Grange before we leave for home tomorrow?"

"Yes, and let's try to find that book Mrs Hawkshaw was talking about. The one that mentioned the secret room," Lee said.

"I don't think finding the book would serve any purpose, even if we did find it. It must have been read and reread umpteen times, and obviously, the secret room was never found. If there is a secret room that is, which I doubt. Any clue to a secret room in the book must have been found by Lord Wellford long ago surely. If what Mrs Hawkshaw said is true, that is all he did, search for the elusive room," argued Edwin.

"I bet we can figure the secret out if we can find that book," said Tom.

Lee digested this information and although he would dearly love to find the secret room he was beginning to get to that age where secret rooms were a thing of childhood. Boarding School loomed ever closer, and a new adventure was about to begin.

When the revenue men had disappeared down the drive, Trueman entered with a note addressed to Lee and Tom. Opening it Lee read:

Many thanks for your help over the keys lads.
You have to find a door that is hidden behind
the fourth wine rack in the cellar. To move the
wine rack there is a handle under the third shelf,
pull it out and twist it to the left. The wine rack
can then be pulled out and the door to the secret
room will be revealed. You will have to use the
largest key on the set of keys to open the door
and you will have found what you are searching for.
I trust you to leave things as you find them.
Redfern.

"Why is he telling us?" Tom wanted to know.

"He knows boys like finding hidden rooms. This is his way of saying thank you for helping him deliver the keys and keeping your mouth shut," their eldest brother told them.

After lunch they all entered Davey Grange to find that Captain Bottomly had been true to his word, nothing had been disturbed or broken. Even down in the cellar, everything was as they had left it, with the exception of the brandy barrels, these were nowhere to be seen. Only the empty wine racks remained.

Tom and Lee were in their element. They took out their little note and read it out loud again.

Unfortunately, there were wine racks on all four walls and the information they had was the door was behind the fourth wine rack.

The grown-ups watched and waited while Tom and Lee started counting the wine racks until the rack with the handle under the third shelf was found.

Tom pulled on the handle and twisted it. It gave way with a satisfactory click. The wine rack sprung slightly away from the wall. Pulling the wine rack further out, they found a thick wooden door.

A chalk mark encircled a loose piece of wood. Oscar ventured to put his fingernail between a crack and it swung down, revealing a strong steel lock.

Lord Hunter took the keys out of his pocket and finding the largest key on the ring he inserted it in the lock. The door opened inwards.

What they saw when they entered the room left Tom and Lee disgusted. It was not a very big room, hardly big enough to hold the barrels of brandy, and all seven of them.

The cave was constructed out of solid stone, ideal for storing barrels of brandy, but not much good for anything else. The contraband barrels were stacked one on top of the other waiting to be removed at a later date.

"What a let-down," moaned Lee.

"You can say that again. We have dreamed of finding a secret room and what do we get, a hole, not even a secret passage to go with it. It was not worth the effort we put into finding it," complained Tom.

"I think we should close and lock the door and leave the cellar. We do not want to be found down here in case there is another search by Captain Bottomly," Lord Hunter said.

"Yes, I think you're right, Edwin," agreed Oscar. "I think the next time you look in here it will be empty except for one barrel, for services rendered."

They closed and locked the door then pulled the wine rack in place and made sure it had locked back into place before they all tramped up the stone steps again and out of the cellar.

Before they left, Effie said to Tom and Lee, "Before we blow out these candles, I think you should burn that note, don't you? You don't want the revenue getting their hands on it." Effie had learnt her lesson about putting things down in writing.

"Yes, it needs to be burned," agreed her brother. "Let's burn it while we are in the kitchen then hopefully that will be the end of our smuggling involvement."

When the rest of them had retired for the night, Lord Hunter and Oscar were sitting in the library drinking a glass of brandy.

"Is this brandy some of the you-know-what?" asked Edwin.

"Might be," conceded Oscar.

"Nice," said Edwin.

"Very nice," agreed Oscar, "Not much left now though, nearly at the bottom of the barrel. I hope when the smugglers move the brandy, I find another barrel in the barn."

"You will keep an eye on Clara for me, won't you?" Edwin wanted to know.

"Keep an eye on her, what do you mean by that?" asked Oscar.

"You must have seen that scoundrel kiss her hand?" asked an indignant Edwin.

"You mean the captain?" laughed Oscar.

"Damn right I mean the captain," Edwin said.

"Are you jealous of Captain Bottomly? You a lord and you are jealous of a captain," Oscar's eyes twinkled.

"It is no laughing matter," scowled his lordship.

Oscar's enjoyment at the situation bubbled over into heartfelt laughter, and his lordship took up a cushion and threw it at his laughing friend.

Oscar caught the cushion without difficulty and had to try very hard to control himself again.

Edwin asked, "Is this what you call a quiet country life?"

Oscar burst out laughing again, and this time it was infectious, Edwin joined him.

Next morning, Lord Hunter and Effie had said their goodbyes and made an early start back to Frithwood. Oscar and Clara were sitting in the dining room when later that morning, Trueman knocked on the door and said, "There is a revenue man at the front door, Miss Clara, by the name of Captain Bottomly, he asked if you could spare him a few minutes."

"Captain Bottomly," said Clara, "What on earth does he want to see me for? Alright, Trueman, tell him I will be with him directly."

"Very good, Miss Clara," Trueman replied, closing the sitting room door and making his way across the hall to the front door.

Trueman opened the door and passed the message on to Captain Bottomly, then closed the door firmly in the

215

captain's face. Trueman had no love for the revenue men, so he had left him standing on the doorstep.

Clara put on her bonnet and went out to see what the captain wanted, "Good morning, Captain Bottomly."

"Good morning, Miss Lander, thank you for seeing me. Could we take a walk?" he asked.

"We can take a walk to the bench over there, so long as I can be seen from the house. Rules were made many years ago when our parents died. We have all followed the rules to the letter, and they have served us very well," Clara smiled at him as they walked across the lawn towards the wooden bench.

Captain Bottomly waited until Clara sat down then sat next to her, but not too close.

"Do you know anything about smugglers?" he asked.

"I know when I was younger, I used to lie in bed and wish I was a boy so I could run away from home and become a smuggler, also a highwayman, or a pugilist, or a constable of the peace, but I have sadly grown out of all that.

"I shied away from being a princess, or a great lady, or an actress, it comes from living with four men I suppose. Smugglers and highwaymen, they were the most romantic heroes in my dreams," she confessed.

"I have seen you in Styleham many times, Miss Lander, the first time I saw you I thought you were the most beautiful thing I ever laid eyes on. I was captivated. I intended to try and make your acquaintance, but you are such an elegant lady, and I a mere captain, I dare not for the life of me approach you, now it is too late.

"I had a visit from my commanding officer this morning. I was told that having been stationed here for the past two years and never having made a difference to the smuggling, my team and I were being moved further

216

up the coast. Information has been received that smuggling is rife up there.

"We leave tomorrow. We shall probably not see each other again, but I wanted to tell you how much of an impression you have made on me. Like you and your smugglers and highwaymen, I shall look forward to seeing you in my dreams. I knew you had stolen my heart in that very first sighting, but I also know it could never be. I shall treasure these few moments I have with you and move on with my life.

"I would also like to explain to you why I became a revenue man. Like you, most people find smugglers romantic, but I have to disillusion you I'm afraid. I have seen at first hand some of the misery they cause.

"I come from an industrial town, and my father, mother, brothers and sister all worked in the mills, working on looms producing lengths of cloth and it provided them with a living. The mills are closed down now, most of them anyway. There is one or two still operating.

"The cloth that is smuggled in from abroad has closed a lot of our mills down, making our countrymen lose their jobs. It is the same with the breweries, I have two uncles who find themselves out of work, cheap brandy coming in from abroad, and so it goes on," the captain told her.

"I am sorry, Captain Bottomly, that your family is out of work because of what the smugglers do but you have to understand, it is their living too. It might be illegal in the eyes of the law, but the smugglers also have wives and children to feed. There are no mills around here for the menfolk to find employment. I do not think for one minute the smugglers intend to see their fellow countrymen out of work. It is a hard life Captain Bottomly. People do what they have to do to survive."

"I can understand that, Miss Lander, but it is still illegal to smuggle goods into this country. Smugglers might be romantic heroes to some, but to others, they create misery. Lost revenue for our own country and our own people, not just my family but hundreds of other families as well. I decided to do something about it that is why I became a revenue man. I might have lost this battle, but there will be another. I did not want to leave with you thinking ill of me," he concluded.

"Why would you think that, Captain Bottomly? You are an officer of the law, and I am a law-abiding citizen; therefore, I am grateful to you for your dedicated work. I think it is your conscience that is playing tricks on you. I admit I do not think of you on a personal nature but that is not because you are a revenue man. I do not know you, Captain Bottomly. If I go around thinking romantically of every man, I see then life would not be worth living. I would end up in a lunatic asylum," she told him.

He smiled at that and replied, "In that case, Miss Lander, I shall leave contented, if not satisfied. I must take my leave of you now and thank you for your understanding. If I had left without speaking to you, I would have spent the rest of my life wondering if I had spoken out about my feeling then things might have turned out differently. I can now accept that they wouldn't," he stood up and held out his hand.

Clara put her hand into his and he held it for longer than he should but she did not withdraw it.

"Goodbye, Captain Bottomly, I hope you catch your prey next time."

"I shall get lucky one of these days, who knows maybe my luck has changed already," he brought her hand to his lips before he walked away.

Clara watched him until he disappeared then turned and slowly walked back towards the house. Looking up, she saw Oscar watching her from the sitting room window.

When she entered the room, he asked, "Is everything alright, Clara?"

She went and put her arms around him and rested her head on his shoulder and burst into tears.

He let her cry herself out and waited for her to speak.

"Captain Bottomly thinks I am the most beautiful thing he has ever seen," she told him.

"And that is something to make you cry?"

"No, that was not what made me cry; it was something else he said," she replied, blowing her nose on the handkerchief he had given her.

"And what was that?"

"Maybe I will tell you one day, Oscar, but I would like to think about it for a while if you don't mind."

"Very well, but you know I am always here for you, Clara, no matter what, don't you?"

"Yes, Oscar, I know. It was nothing nasty, in fact, it was something very special he said. It struck a chord with me and gave me a bit of a shock. I will tell you; I promise. I do not think there is ever going to be anything I could not tell you. I love you and Harvey and Tom and Lee. We are not unaware of what you have done for us, Oscar, what you have sacrificed for us all, I can assure you of that."

"You are talking rubbish, Clara, I have sacrificed nothing. I could not have better brothers and sister, and I most certainly would not have liked it if I had been left on my own. I love you all as much as you love me. It works both ways, Clara. There is nothing I could not say to you if I needed comfort, or advice or help, so for goodness sake, do not go thinking I have sacrificed myself for you all, I have not.

"If you don't want to tell me what Captain Bottomly said, then that is alright too, we all need a bit of privacy now and again there is nothing wrong with that."

"One thing the captain told me was that the revenue men are leaving. They have had word there is smuggling going on further along the coast, and they have had instruction to transfer. He also told me why he became a revenue man. I never thought of the harm the smugglers are doing to our country.

"His family has been hit because the company they were employed by went out of business because of the contraband cloth being cheaper than the cloth being produced in our mills. I felt guilty for lying to him but on the other hand; there was no way I could tell on Mr Redfern."

"I don't think you will have to worry your little head over Mr Redfern, the smugglers or Elmer Wolf ever again, Clara. I called into The Monks Den yesterday to let Mr Redfern know that Edwin is buying the Grange and it would be advisable not to use it as a storeroom again.

"Mr Redfern informed me there would not be a problem in future because he is thinking about retiring. He said Mrs Redfern had put her foot down and she was standing no more nonsense. The revenue men's visit had upset her. He told me she had received a letter from her family and they were going to visit them.

"He thought it was best, to get as far away from here as soon as possible. The smugglers can no longer trust anybody anymore, so the further away he goes, the better," Oscar told her.

"That is good news. What about Elmer Wolf?" she asked.

"Mr Redfern said Elmer had vanished without a trace, there one minute, gone the next. Elmer left without paying his bill, and the revenue men were after him for supplying them with false information. Mr Redfern said we had no need to give Elmer Wolf another thought. I did not push for more details; I left it at that."

"What do you think happened to him?" she insisted.

"I know what I would like to have happened to him, but knowing and wishing are two different things. Let Elmer Wolf rest in peace from now on, shall we, Clara?" he asked.

"Very well, Oscar, if you think it's for the best."

"I do."

Mr Redfern had cleared out Elmer's room putting all his things in an old canvas sack, making sure there was no sign that he had ever been there.

He took the sack and hid it in a priest hole located behind the china cabinet in their sitting room.

When they had closed up for the night, Mr Redfern locked the door leading into their sitting room.

"Why are you locking us in?" asked his wife.

He put his finger to his lips and whispered, "Keep your voice down, Aggie. I have something to show you."

He pulled the china cabinet away from the wall, revealing the priest hole. He pulled out the old canvas sack.

"What have you got there?" Aggie whispered.

"Elmer Wolf's belongings."

"What are you going to do with them?"

"Burn them, I did think about selling them, but I have decided to burn them, get rid of anything that belongs to Elmer Wolf once and for all. I am going to search his pockets first because he owes us two weeks' lodgings." He proceeded to empty the pockets.

Aggie took up one of the garments and started to help her husband go through the pockets. Not only did they find loose change and folded up paper money, but they also found a gold watch and chain and two gold rings.

The watch and chain had been sewn inside one of the jackets; Aggie had felt it when she was feeling in an inside pocket. This discovery led them to cut open every article of clothing and to hunt inside Elmer's socks and shoes.

At the end of the search, they could not believe the wealth that was piled up on their table.

Doug decided to go and do a further search in the empty room, and he found cash hidden under the carpet, under the mattress and stuffed into a pillowcase.

He also found, tucked under the mattress, a bank savings book. Taking it all back down to their sitting room, he put his treasure on the table with the other loot.

"The revenue men did not do a very good search of Elmer's room. Look what I have found. All this money was hidden under the carpet and stuffed into pillowcases. It's a good job they were looking for Elmer and not his belongings."

"There must be a fortune here," Aggie whispered, "What are we going to do with it? Where is he, Doug, where is Elmer Wolf?"

"We are going to keep it, of course. It is no more than he owes us. He has taken our livelihood away from us and our dear friend Mick has had to flee the country.

"Do not ask questions you would not like the answer to, Aggie. Just be happy Elmer Wolf will never cross our threshold again. Elmer Wolf will have no use for these now, so finders' keepers," he replied.

"There is this though." Doug produced the bank savings book.

Aggie opened the bankbook and gasped at the amount, "Where did he get all this money from?"

"Blackmailing I would guess."

Aggie stood up and went over to the fire and threw the savings book into the flames and watched it burn.

"What did you do that for?"

"A bit of smuggling here and there I have let slip, but I will not let you risk your freedom by trying to get money out of a bank account that belonged to a blackmailer, one that has disappeared at that. There is a line I will not let you cross, Doug, and this is it.

"I have had enough of this life, Doug, dodging the revenue every time there is a shipment. Waiting here not knowing if you are going to come back or whether I will be visiting you in jail or even burying you. It is harder for me to sit and wait than it is for you to know what is going on out there," Aggie said.

"I have been thinking, Aggie, Mick said there is good horse stock over in Ireland. He was thinking of going over there to try his hand at going straight, to try to get into the horse racing business. We have a bit of money saved up, Aggie, and now there is all this." Doug gestured to the table.

"What do you say to us packing our bags and heading off to Ireland to give Mick a hand? That is if he lands up in Ireland. He is going to write and let me know. I told him we might follow him and Mick said he would be delighted to see us," Doug waited for Aggie to say something.

She remained silent.

"We have no children or family to keep us here, Aggie. I know you had a soft spot for Mick. You treated him like you would a son. Why not go and join him? Help Mick set up a stable if that is what he wants.

"We will use these ill-gotten gains to buy some horse stock, after all, Elmer Wolf took Mick's living away from him too. Made him flee the country and leave you and me behind. Mick told me you and I were the nearest thing to family he has ever had.

"You are not the only one that has had enough of this life. We will have to do it right though, we will have to get someone to run The Monks Den and let everyone know we are leaving or else the revenue might think we have something to hide and we do not want that, do we, Aggie?"

"That would be wonderful, yes, let us go and join Mick. As you say, we have enough money put by to see us both put to rest. I feel ten years younger already."

"I just have the contraband to deliver in a couple of days. Now the revenue men are gone, it will be safe enough to move it on. Then off we go as soon as the letter arrives and we know where we are going. It will give us time to think about what we are taking with us and what we are leaving behind. We will not be able to take everything, so you set about thinking of what you want to take, and I will see about getting someone to run The Den," he told her feeling ten years younger himself.

Four weeks later the letter arrived, and Doug stood in the snug reading it while his wife watched him through the connecting doorway.

Doug looked up from reading the letter and caught his wife's eye. Seeing her watching him he mouthed 'Ireland', and she heaved a big sigh then looked down and carried on peeling potatoes, but he did not miss the tear that dropped onto the back of her hand.

It was late one night after the revenue men had departed for pastures new and Clara and Oscar were just about to retire for the night when Trueman announced, "Mr Redfern to see you, Sir."

"Show him in, Trueman, and you may go to bed. I will lock up after Mr Redfern leaves."

"Very good, Sir."

Mr Redfern crossed the carpeted floor with his hand outstretched in Oscar's direction.

"Thank you for seeing me at such short notice, Mr Lander."

"Not at all, Mr Redfern, it is unexpected at this hour but not an unpleasant surprise. I prefer your presence to that of the revenue men."

After shaking hands with Oscar, Mr Redfern walked over to Clara and taking her hand he raised it to his lips, "Good evening, Miss Lander."

"Good evening, Mr Redfern," Clara smiled, but her heart was racing. Was Mr Redfern the bearer of bad news?

"Sit down, please," Oscar indicated a well-used leather armchair.

"Much obliged I'm sure," and Mr Redfern took his seat.

"I wanted you to know everything is neatly sorted out. If the revenue men were to call again, there is nothing for them to find, the merchandise has been removed."

"Good, I am pleased to hear it."

"Really, I came to give you this," Mr Redfern held out a large iron key to Oscar, "I will not need it again. I made a copy of the key to the storeroom down in the cellar over at the Grange before I returned them to your toff. I had to have it to enable me to get the barrels out so I could move them on."

"I will pass it on to Lord Hunter the next time I see him."

"I also wanted to let you know I am aware of the debt we, the smugglers, owe you, if it had not been for you, this outcome might have been quite different. Mind you don't fall over the barrel in the barn the next time you have cause to enter it. The sooner the better if you do not mind my saying so, Mr Lander.

"I also wanted to let you know we are leaving in the morning, Aggie and I. A couple from the village are taking the inn over, and Aggie and I are going to visit family, so I do not suppose we will be seeing each other again."

"You will not be returning to The Monks Den after your family visit?"

"No, nothing to keep us here now, we do not intend to return."

"Your family, do they live close?"

"I would rather not say, Mr Lander, if you don't mind."

"No, in that case, I don't suppose we will be seeing you again. I wish you good luck and hope you and your wife keep well. I know it was a hard job running The Monks Den, but I never heard a bad word said against you, Mr Redfern, I think you will be sadly missed. Don't forget to give Mrs Redfern our blessing, will you?"

"I will that Mr Lander, she will be much obliged. I have not forgotten the part the twins played in this, and I have brought them something that is dear to my heart if you don't mind me passing them on. You told me it was the twins we have to thank in the first place for spotting Elmer Wolf. To show my appreciation, I have come to see if it would be all right for the twins to have my fishing tackle? It was my only passion apart from Aggie of course."

"That is very kind of you, Mr Redfern."

"We cannot take it with us, so I wanted to give it to Tom and Lee. I know they like fishing, they told me so that morning we met in the wood when they brought the keys back. It will be too big for them to use at the moment, but they will grow into it. It is expensive fishing tackle, well worth keeping. I have left it outside on the porch. I did not want to bring it into the house, in case it smells of fish you understand."

"I am sure Tom and Lee will be delighted with it. In fact, as it is so near Christmas, I am sure Clara will wrap it up for a Christmas present from you and Mrs Redfern. They are still at that age where Christmas is a magical time.

"Unfortunately, it might be the last Christmas they see it like that. We all grow up, and they are doing so at a gallop. Thank you, on their behalf. As you say, they like their fishing; you cannot go wrong with anything related to the sport for them." Oscar held out his hand, and Mr Redfern stood up.

"I will not keep you any longer, Sir. Once again, we cannot thank you enough," Mr Redfern shook hands with Oscar and he nodded to Clara.

Oscar escorted him to the door. When the door was closed on Mr Redfern, Oscar locked it and secured it with two bolts.

"Why didn't you ask him about Elmer Wolf?" Clara wanted to know when Oscar re-joined her.

"Because, my sweet, I do not want to know what happened to Elmer Wolf, and neither do you. Just forget about Elmer Wolf. Let that be the last time his name crosses your lips; he will not cause us any more trouble, Clara, enough on the subject, please let it drop," he looked down at her as she gazed up at him from the sofa.

"It is just natural curiosity," Clara told him.

"I am well aware of that, Clara. There is no one better equipped than I to be aware of your curiosity, but for this once, I am asking you not to mention that name again then it cannot bring the wrath of God down on our shoulders.

"Promise me, Clara, no more about you-know-who, there I have already forgotten his name." Oscar stood looking down at the pretty, upturned, little face of his sister.

"Very well, Oscar, I promise," Clara agreed.

Oscar held out his hands to her and pulled her to her feet.

"Good girl, let us go to bed before anyone else comes knocking on our door."

Chapter Fifteen

It was two months since Lord Hunter and Effie had returned to Frithwood, and Effie was bored. She was doing all the usual things she did before she had met Clara, but now Effie could see no point in any of it.

Effie missed them all. Each time she thought of the twins it made her smile. She was thinking of them now, and she suddenly had an idea, it would give her something to do.

She made her way to her bedroom and over to the wardrobe. Effie hunted around at the bottom of the wardrobe until she found her oil paints and brushes.

What Effie needed now was a piece of wood. Putting on her outdoor clothes, she headed for the city centre and the timber merchants.

On Effie's return, she met Edwin in the hall, and he asked what she was carrying.

"I will tell you later, it is going to be a surprise," she said and ran to her bedroom.

Four days later Effie closed her bedroom door and went to find Edwin. First, she went into the library hoping to find him there, no such luck. So, she went in search of Wilson and found him having a cup of tea in the kitchen. Wilson jumped to attention when he saw Effie.

"Sit down, Wilson, and enjoy your tea. I have only come to see if you know where Edwin is?"

"No, Miss Effie, he went out just after lunch, and he has not come back yet," Wilson replied still standing.

"If you see him before I do, will you ask him to come to my room?" Effie asked.

"Very good, Miss Effie," Wilson replied and let out his breath when Miss Effie had left the kitchen. He sat back down and picked up his cup of tea.

Effie was hanging about in the hall when Edwin finally appeared.

"Edwin, where have you been? I have been waiting ages for you," Effie accused.

"I have been to see Wilbert Wellford. He is trying to get more money out of me, and I have told him I have made him an excellent offer for Davey Grange, and I am not paying out any more money.

"Wilbert wants me to buy all that old furniture he has left in the house. I have told him he has to go down and sort everything out for himself. It is up to him to remove everything from off the premises, not me. It will cost a fortune to get rid of all that old furniture. So, at the moment we are at stalemate I am afraid. This is taking a lot longer than I thought it would." he apologised.

"I have full confidence in you to get it sorted out, Edwin. But never mind that now, I have something I would like you to see and get your opinion on it. Come up to my room and have a look."

"What is it you want me to see?" Edwin asked following her across the hall and up the wide staircase.

"Wait and see; I want you to tell me what you think, truthfully, I mean, not just to be kind, I want the honest truth."

"What's all the rush about? Is this surprise going to disappear or something?"

"Don't be silly, Edwin, I just want your honest opinion about this, and I have been waiting hours and hours for you to come home."

Effie led him into her bedroom and stood Edwin in front of an easel where there stood a piece of wood with a painting on it.

"What do you think?" she asked pointing to the painting.

A smile spread across his face, and he said, "They will love it."

"Do you really think so?"

"Effie, there is nothing there to dislike; it is perfect."

"I thought I would give it to them for Christmas, a shared present."

"There is no wonder they decided to adopt you as a sister, very bright boys in hindsight. Effie, it is perfect," Edwin placed his arm across his sister's shoulder, and they both stood looking at the painting with a smile across their face.

The painting consisted of a pale blue sky, a brown road separating a green field running from the bottom left-hand corner to halfway up the right side. A duck pond was located in the bottom right-hand corner with two white ducks swimming in it. Five other white ducks were marching, in a straight line, from left to right across the road, heading for the duck pond. Bright scarlet letters reading 'DUCKS CROSSING' ran across the pale blue sky.

"I don't think you could give the twins a better Christmas present, like they said, the image makes you smile," her brother said giving her shoulder a squeeze.

Oscar and Clara had been kept busy over the last few months. Oscar travelling between Badger Manor and Meadow Lodge making sure the harvest was gathered in.

Clara likewise helped with the harvesting, but she also spent a lot of time at Bluebell House.

Mrs Hawkshaw was happily installed at her daughters, and Clara was sorting things out as best she could at Bluebell House for when the twins and Harvey came home for Christmas.

Most of the furniture had been left and all the curtains and carpets, but the furnishings needed washing, and the furniture required a good polish.

When Clara had finished hanging the last pair of clean curtains, she stood back to survey her handiwork. She hoped the twins would see a big difference in the house when they finally arrived home from their first term at boarding school.

Clara had told Oscar she had not realised how much she would miss the twins and Oscar had to agree with her, he missed them too.

"Any regrets, Effie?" her brother asked as they stood in the hallway of their empty townhouse. Not theirs for much longer, at the end of the week the new owners would take possession.

Effie looked around and shook her head. "No, Edwin, no regrets. I am looking forward to getting settled in at the Grange and seeing Clara again; it is going to be fun."

"Only Clara, Effie?" her brother asked looking down at her.

Effie had the grace to blush and replied, "And the twins of course."

"Oh yes, I had forgotten all about the twins," he teased.

"I hope we haven't made the wrong decision, Effie. If we have it is too late now to change our minds, we have burnt all our bridges, and it is sink or swim from now on. It is going to cost a lot of money to get Davey

Grange back to something like it used to be, but I think with a lot of hard work and a lot of good luck we should be all right.

"We can turn things around and make it into a paying estate once again. One last look around then off we go, Effie, and no looking back."

Before they finally left Frithwood for Styleham, Lord Hunter called at his lawyers and handed over the keys to the house. Then joining Effie inside the coach, the coachman cracked his whip, and there was no looking back.

Lord Hunter and Effie arrived at Badger Manor just minutes before the arrival of Harvey and the twins, and it was chaotic. Chester and the Landers' two dogs pleased to see each other again were running around and barking.

Tom and Lee were both talking at the same time while Harvey was giving Clara and Effie, each, in turn, a warm embrace and a kiss on the cheek.

"**CHESTER**," shouted Edwin, "**QUIET**."

Chester calmed down but went to all the Landers, in turn, to greet them with his wet tongue.

"Sorry, we have descended on you at such short notice Oscar, but we wanted to get here for Christmas and before the snow came. We had problems with the exchange of the Grange. Wellford's nephew would not agree to come and remove all the rubbish that is left in the house, and I would not agree to the completion until he did.

"In the end, I think his gambling debts played a large part in his agreeing to his lawyer's suggestion to put a clause in the deeds, to the effect that everything left in the property or on the land belongs to us, for us to do with as we wish," Edwin told him.

"I did not have a clause put in the deeds when I bought Bluebell House," Oscar told him.

"I think there is a vast difference in what Mrs Hawkshaw left in Bluebell House and what is left in Davey Grange. Anyway, Mrs Hawkshaw is a much nicer person than Wilfred Wellford. I do not think Mrs Hawkshaw will come knocking on the twins' door to take back any of her old furniture. Do you?" Edwin asked.

"No, I don't suppose she will, nothing there of any value," agreed Oscar.

"Wilfred has agreed to the clause, so all the contents belong to Effie and me, we can get rid of any or all of the things left there if we so wish. Our lawyer pointed out to us we were buying the deeds to the property and land, not the contents of the house or any farming implements etcetera that are hanging about," Edwin said.

"Yes, and of course there are all those paintings as well. Are they included in the clause?" Oscar asked.

"Everything, he wanted nothing but the money. Now he can't come demanding any of the things left in the house, especially if we have used them for firewood," Edwin grinned.

"Good job too," agreed Oscar.

"Our servants have been coming down here with our furniture, on and off for the past few days. We decided to leave them to it. Let them get two of the bedrooms cleaned and ready for Effie and I to use. But things have not gone to plan, it has taken more time to clean out the bedrooms than we expected. The bedrooms are not quite ready so here we are, come to descend on you for a couple of nights. I hope you don't mind?" Edwin asked.

"You are welcome any time, you know that you are welcome to stay with us over Christmas if you wish," Oscar told him.

"That is very kind of you but a couple of nights should be sufficient, and both Effie and I want to make a start on things," Edwin replied.

"If there is anything I can do to help, all you need to do is ask," Oscar offered.

"I shall take you up on that offer, have no fear about that, you may regret putting out such an invitation. I will need help and advice on getting the farm started that is for sure. I know nothing whatsoever about farming so don't worry, I shall be constantly at your side," Edwin told him.

"Because you are being kind enough to accommodate us for a couple of nights Clara, Edwin and I would like to invite you all over to the Grange for Christmas day. It will be our first Christmas there, and we would like to share it with our friends," Effie told Clara.

"In that case, we will be delighted to spend the day with you. I will give our servants the day off," Clara decided.

Effie was delighted to be able to show Clara the letter that had arrived at their house in Frithwood. It was from Dolly Pomroy:

Dear Miss Hunter

>*I would like to write and thank you and your friend for letting me know about my mother and father.*
>*I got dismissed by Mrs Crowman so my boyfriend and I went home, and we are now living here.*
>*Also, if you know that toff that went to see our Fred, can you tell him same? Fred came home too and is now living back at home with us.*
>*Thanks,*

Dolly Pomroy.

"Oh, I am so pleased for them all. How nice of her to write and let us know. What does Lord Hunter say to being called a toff?" Clara asked.

"He said, 'Don't show it to Harvey for God's sake, or it will be all around boarding school'," Effie said, and they both laughed.

"Have you heard from Mrs Warwick?" Clara wanted to know.

"No, I haven't, and to be honest, Clara, I don't think we will. Mrs Warwick is fully aware of the position she is in now, and I don't think she would risk associating with us. She knows how easy it is for the loose word to spread like wildfire amongst the tittle tattlers and reputations can be lost overnight."

"Maybe it's for the best then."

"Yes, sadly, maybe it's for the best," agreed her friend.

The following few days sped by. Harvey took the twins over to his estate for a few days, Lord Hunter and Effie moved into the Grange, Oscar and Clara made ready for Christmas.

At the end of the week, Oscar was just about to set off to collect Harvey and the twins and bring them all back to Badger Manor for Christmas when he saw Effie walking up the drive towards him.

"Hello, Effie, this is a nice surprise." Oscar smiled at her from his perch on the coach.

"I have come to see Clara. I am sick of the dust and dirt at our place," she told him.

"I am sorry, Effie; Clara is over at Bluebell House putting the finishing touches to the house. I am on my way to collect the twins and Harvey. If you would care to take a drive with me, I would be delighted to have your company. That should blow the dust and cobwebs away."

Effie hesitated only a second. She held up one hand to Oscar and her skirt up with the other. Oscar reached down taking the proffered hand and Effie, placing her little foot on the footplate, allowed him to pull her up to sit beside him.

"I am glad to see you are warmly dressed, but if you would not mind holding the reins, I will jump down and collect a couple of blankets for our knees or, you may ride inside the coach if you would prefer."

Effie took the reins.

Oscar ran across the hall and into the library, going over to the fireplace he gave the bell-pull a tug, then, taking up his quill he was putting it to paper as Wilson opened the door.

"Ah, Wilson, would you nip upstairs and bring me down a couple of blankets please."

"Yes, Sir."

Oscar scribbled:

Edwin, I have waylaid Effie, and I am taking her to Harvey's with me to bring them all back home for Christmas. Clara is in Bluebell House at the moment but I am expecting her back any minute so I want to be on my way with Effie before Clara arrives back, just in case Effie changes her mind about coming with me, and I don't want that. Clara will be alone when she returns from Bluebell House. If you want to grab the opportunity to have a few hours with her all to yourself, now is the time.
Oscar.

Wilson came back bearing blankets, and Oscar shook the loose sand off his letter, folded it up and slipped it into an envelope.

"Thank you, Wilson," Oscar said taking the blankets. "Would you see that this letter is delivered to Lord Hunter, at the Grange, straight away?"

"Very good, Sir," replied Wilson taking the letter.

"I hope you won't mind if we travel at a fast pace, Effie. The ground is hard but not icy, and I shall not overturn us, time is of the essence. As you know it soon gets dark, and you never know if it will snow at this time of year," he told her whilst tucking one of the blankets over her knees then the other one across his own.

"If I thought you would overturn us, Oscar, I would not have agreed to come with you in the first place," she stated logically.

"I am pleased you have faith in my horsemanship." He set off down the drive at a steady trot.

Once they were out of the gates and heading north, Oscar set the horses into a gallop and travelled at this pace in silence for a couple of miles then he slackened the pace and relaxing, he glanced across at Effie, she turned and caught him looking at her, and she smiled up at him.

"It was good to have you back in my home, Effie."

"It was good to be back."

"Will you miss Frithwood?"

"No, I have no regrets, we can have a ride over to Frithwood any time we like and go to the shops. I have had my fill of balls and tea parties, all the same old gossip, all the dressing up and being ogled by oafish young men trying to make an advantageous marriage with the first woman they meet with money of their own. No, I like it here in the country; the company is so much nicer."

"Do you class me as an oafish young man out to make an advantageous match?"

"There is the occasional oafish young man that I would not mind being courted by."

Silence reigned between them for a few minutes and Oscar, who had never been much of a ladies' man, felt uncomfortable and at a loss for something to say.

"I have to tell you, Effie, the thought of marriage has never crossed my mind. I have never had time for myself like other young men, oafish or not. I am not very experienced in the petticoat line. Marriage had never entered my head until now, and I will be damned if I can rid myself of it. It is all I can think about these days, it will not leave my mind and it will not do. I have too much responsibility at the moment to think about marriage."

Effie did not answer but sat watching the road ahead in silence.

"Are you cold?" he asked.

"No, if there is one thing I am not, it is cold. Disappointed maybe, but definitely not cold."

"Disappointed about what?"

"I think, Oscar, you will have to work that one out for yourself. You strike me as an intelligent young man."

He drove in silence for a while, and Effie sat next to him watching the road ahead also in silence.

So, instead of saying anything and making matters worse, he reached over and took her hand, holding it loosely so she could withdraw it if she wanted to.

She did not. She left it where it was, cradled in his. To add to his confidence, she moved across the seat to sit closer to him.

Silence again, and Oscar racked up the pace a little. He was delighted at the fact she had not objected to him holding her hand, but he knew he had to say something so he cast around in his head hoping she would understand his situation.

"You have thrown my plans into the wind, Effie. I have the responsibility of the twins to consider, there will be about another six or seven years before they will be able to look after themselves, but even then, I shall have to keep an eye out for them." Oscar glanced across at her.

Effie remained silent.

"As you know," he continued, "Lee and Tom are now at boarding school, so they are only home on school holidays but even so, I do not expect any woman to take on responsibility for them. I had not intended to fall in love until I could ask someone to be my wife, but then you came along.

"I told you earlier, I cannot get the thought of marriage out of my mind and I blame you for that. I want to share my home with you, Effie, it felt empty when you left and went back to Frithwood, but it all changed again when you returned to Styleham." He waited for a reply.

None came so he plodded on.

"I know it is asking too much to expect anyone to take on a readymade family. Then there is Clara to consider, of course. Clara has been running our home since she was fifteen years old. I do not think I could tell her she was no longer in charge. If I married, how could I cut her out?"

He waited for her answer.

She made none.

He was confused. Effie was acting like she was offended at what he was saying and yet he was still holding her hand in his. She made no move to either remove her hand from his clutch or to move away from him; he was uncomfortably aware of her thigh still touching his.

"Have you no answer for me?" Oscar finally asked.

"So far, I have heard nothing that merits a reply."

"I have just explained to you why I cannot ask you to marry me for the next five or six years. I thought you would understand."

"You tell me you love me but I have to wait for six years before you can do anything about it and you want a reply. What do you want me to say?"

"That you understand."

"Very well, I understand."

Oscar was not used to dealing with women. Clara was different, she was his sister, but Effie, she made him feel very uncomfortable. Oscar wanted to take her in his arms and make mad, passionate love to her. But he did not have the nerve to do so. He could tell she was displeased by her silence but confused by her closeness.

They drove on in silence holding hands until Oscar pointed out Meadow Lodge and only then did Effie slide her hand out of his and move slightly away from him.

Oscar jumped down and went to the other side of the coach to help Effie down only to find she had jumped nimbly down without any help from him.

Harvey had heard the coach approaching, and he came out to meet them giving Effie a brutal hug in greeting and told her he was extremely surprised but very pleased to see her, and he led her into the house with his arm around her waist.

Much to the annoyance of Harvey's big brother, Effie placed her arm around Harvey's waist and smiled sweetly up at him as he led her indoors.

Lee and Tom came out of the sitting room and threw themselves at Effie and then at Oscar. Harvey ordered tea.

While they waited for the tea to be delivered Harvey insisted on showing Effie around his home and he did so with pride and satisfaction. Effie had to admit it was a pleasant four bedroomed farmhouse with extensive grounds, barns and outhouses.

Once the meal was over, their trunks were fixed to the back of the coach, and the horses changed, they set off back to the Manor with Harvey sitting up top with Oscar and Effie inside the coach with the twins.

Effie found the ride home very amusing. She was kept entertained by the twins telling her of their first term at boarding school. About the friends they had made and the names of their teachers.

The twins told Effie that Harvey was the captain of the senior rugby team and they hoped they would be picked to play for the junior rugby team next term. They were also going to try for the cricket team as well. There was also rowing.

Effie found out that Harvey was a popular young man at school and because of it, Lee and Tom were made to feel welcome. Not like some of the other boys who were bullied by older boys.

By the time next year came around there would be another intake of boys for the bullies to pick on but Lee and Tom, by that time, would be two of the old boys so they would be all right.

Effie listened to the twins chattering away and the time passed most pleasantly.

When Badger Manor was reached, Harvey and the twins alighted, and Oscar turned the coach around and headed back down the drive taking Effie back to Davey Grange.

Oscar did not dare ask Effie if she would like to sit up front with him. She had not said a word to him while they were at Harvey's and what was she doing letting Harvey put his arm around her.

Oscar had started to feel ridiculously embarrassed for declaring himself when it was blatantly obvious Effie was offended by what he had said. Or was she? Why had she held his hand?

Lord Hunter was waiting at the front door when Oscar pulled up. He opened the coach door and held out his hand to assist Effie to alight.

Effie ignored her brother's hand and snapped at him, "Men are imbeciles," and marched straight past him and into the house slamming the door behind her and completely ignoring Oscar.

Lord Hunter looked up at his friend and asked, "What have you done to put Effie in such a puck?"

"I have no idea," Oscar replied.

Lord Hunter's eyes twinkled with merriment, and he burst out laughing.

Oscar looked around for something to throw at his laughing friend but could find nothing, so he took off his hat and threw that at him instead.

Then he set off at a gallop down the drive with Lord Hunter's laughter ringing in his ears.

Lord Hunter went in search of his sister and found her in the sitting room.

"Effie, what has put you in such a puck?"

"Nothing, Edwin, I have never been so happy in my life," his sister told him. "What makes you think I am in a puck?"

Looking at his sister Edwin could well believe it. Effie was glowing with health.

"It might have something to do with you calling us men imbeciles."

Effie gave a delighted laugh, "Yes, that was a touch of genius, don't you think? Oscar told me he loved me but could not marry me," she told him.

"And that makes you happy?" Edwin was astonished.

"Yes, of course, it does. Oscar cannot marry me for all the right reasons," she explained.

"And what would they be?"

"The twins, Harvey and Clara."

"I would appreciate a more detailed explanation," her brother told her.

"Oscar said he had to wait for five or six years before he could think of getting married because of the twins only being eleven and he did not want Clara to think she was being replaced by me," she said happily.

"But that is nonsense."

"Exactly," Effie replied, glad they had now come to an understanding.

"You are not going to leave it at that, are you?"

"Of course not, my plan is set in place."

"What plan?"

"I am not talking to him," he was informed.

Edwin opened his mouth to say something but shut it again; he was left speechless.

Then after a few seconds, he ventured to remark, "You women live in a complex world." He turned and left, with her amused laughter echoing in the hallway.

Chapter Sixteen

Had Oscar known it, his friend had not had much more success with Clara than he'd had with Effie.

On receiving Oscar's letter, Edwin had made straight for Badger Manor.

It was Chester that found Ruby and Max and alerted Clara she had a visitor.

Clara came around the side of the house following her dogs excited barking and found them chasing Chester across the lawn.

Clara smiled at Edwin and informed him, "I am sorry, Oscar is not in. He has gone to pick up the twins and Harvey, to bring them back here for Christmas."

"That leaves just the two of us then for Effie is not at home either. Would you care to come over to Davey Grange and see what progress we have made since you were last there?"

"Alright, I would like that very much. I know I have not seen much of Effie since you came down here, so yes, Lord Hunter, I would love to come and see how things are progressing. I will just leave a note for Oscar then, if they get back before I do, they will know where I am," Clara told him.

Clara turned, and she headed back the way she had come shouting over her shoulder, "When do you expect Effie home?"

"Your guess is as good as mine, you know what you women are, if you drop on someone to talk to, you could be away for a day and a half," replied Edwin. "She went out about an hour ago, and she has not yet returned."

"In my experience, Lord Hunter, men are much worse at gossiping than us women, but that is a topic to discuss at another time and place, I will get my bonnet."

Clara vanished back around the corner of the house, and after leaving a note for Oscar, telling of her whereabouts and grabbing her bonnet, she made her way back to where Lord Hunter was waiting for her.

That was easier than I expected it to be, thought Edwin. They cut across the lawn, taking the short cut across the fields and over the side-dividing wall. This route was beginning to have a clearly trodden path leading from one estate to the other.

By the time they were inside Davey Grange, Clara's cheeks were a healthy red from the exercise and fresh air.

Looking at her Edwin thought how beautiful she was with her jet-black hair, blue eyes and rosy cheeks.

"I would dearly love to find the secret room, Clara, if only to get one over on the twins, I keep trying, but I have not had much success yet."

She threw him a dazzling smile that made his heart knock against his ribs. He was rendered speechless at the emotion that racked through his body. This was something that had never happened to him before.

He had a reputation with the ladies, but it had more often than not been the ladies that had thrown themselves at him. He had enjoyed most of the dalliances he had got through, but at the end of the day, he had known that they were only dalliance.

Clara was something else, she was beautiful, lively and totally innocent and he adored her, but her attitude towards him was that of a brother, and this made him unsure of himself and left him feeling like an inexperienced sixteen-year-old.

Feeling ridiculous and tongue-tied Edwin, for something to say, blurted out, "Do you want to save any of these old portraits or paintings hanging on the walls?"

"Do I want to save any? Why are you asking me? They are not my paintings to save or discard."

He felt colour rise to his cheeks; he had been thinking of her living there in his home, as his wife, putting each room in order.

"They could be if you wanted them to be. Effie and I will more than likely put them out for the gardener to burn. We have brought all our own paintings from Frithwood. I thought you might like to keep one or two or all rather than make a bonfire of them," he replied to cover his confusion and only succeeded in making things worse.

"We could have a look I suppose, but there are a lot of them. I should hate for them all to be burnt, after all, someone lovingly painted all these, and if it comes down to you and Effie burning them, then I would prefer it if you gave them to me. I will put them up in our attic and try and find out about the people who painted them," she told him.

Peering closely at the nearest picture Clara continued, "They could do with a good clean. It does not look as though they have been cleaned since the day they were hung."

"You may well be right. I had thought about putting them all up in our attic, but you have not seen the rubbish that is up there. I doubt there would be enough room for a teacup, let alone all these paintings. That is why I thought a bonfire would be best," he told her with a straight face.

"Well, it would not. You should never destroy anything that is a work of art. What you like might not be to the taste of others and vice versa, but that does not mean it is not a good piece of art," she told him glancing across at him then noting the twinkle in his eye.

"You are teasing me, I should have known better, living with four men," she laughed.

Walking around the room, she looked at each picture or portrait in turn, she remarked, "I don't think I would want to be greeted every morning with such stern arrogant faces that most of these old boys have."

"In that case, it is the attic for the portraits. What about the landscapes?"

"When we were in Frithwood, Effie took me to a street where artists had studios, and she showed me around. I enjoyed doing that; there were corners in some of the studios stacked with old canvases. I asked Effie what they were doing there, and she told me that when people were getting rid of paintings, they would take them to the artists they liked and give them to them.

"The artists would then paint over the old paintings and create their own. Effie said the artists were living on the bread line and being given canvases to reuse saved them a lot of money. Why don't you do that? Give the paintings to the starving artists instead of letting them rot in the attic," she asked.

Before Edwin could reply Clara told him, "Some of the frames are nice though, they may be worth keeping. You can reframe some of the paintings into the nice frames that might improve some of them, if they had a nicer frame."

He stood looking up at a portrait of an old man with a wrinkled face who was looking down at him, "Do you think this painting would improve if it had a better frame? I rather like this old boy he is not as stern as the others. I wonder who he was."

Clara went and stood next to Edwin and looked up at the old man in the picture. His eyes looked down at her, and he made her smile. There was amusement in his eyes and the smile on his old thin lips was a gentle smile.

"No, I think the portrait would improve if it was cleaned, the frame suits it, the dust and grime do not. Remove the build-up of years of dirt, and I bet all the colour would then show through. I would not mind being greeted with this kindly old gentleman each morning."

They both stood and looked at the old man without saying anything.

"You need to find out how to clean them though, don't try to do it yourself if you don't know what you are doing, you might spoil them. I think I shall call him granddad. I never knew either of my grandfathers, but I would like to think they would have looked like this old gentleman, wrinkled face, smiling eyes and lips."

"I knew my grandfather on my father's side, and he looked nothing like this old gentleman. He was a stern, strict, old sod and I was glad when he passed away. When you hear people say there was not a dry eye at his or her funeral, that was not the case at our grandfather's funeral.

"There was plenty of wine handed around, and the party went on until the early hours of next morning, sad to say. I think everyone that knew him was glad he had gone, including my father. Let's have a walk around and see what we want to keep and which we want to get rid of, sorry put up in the attic," he smiled down at her.

Clara noted he had said 'we' again, but she decided not to comment on it and she let it ride. She rather liked being included in the decision-making on what he should keep on show and what was to be relegated to the attic.

She liked the idea of looking at all the paintings in more detail too. She liked art and appreciated the skill of the artists even if she did not care much for the painting itself; she could appreciate the talent.

The third room they had entered was what Edwin called a smoking room. It was wainscoted to all walls. Four dark brown leather chairs were scattered around, a drinks cabinet, a desk, some bookshelves and an old threadbare carpet of indefinable colour. The room smelt strongly of tobacco and Clara curled up her nose.

Edwin went over and opened the window.

"I will just let a bit of fresh air in here. I think Lord Wellford must have been a heavy smoker. I will close it in a few minutes. It is cold outside and not much warmer in here. It is a huge house to heat, so we only have a fire going in the rooms we are using," he explained.

"Have you found the book Mrs Hawkshaw told us about?" she asked.

"No, we have not, but there are lots of books in the library, it might take us a lifetime to go through them all."

"By the smell of this room, I bet Lord Wellford must have spent most of his time in here. Was all this furniture left in the property by Lord Wellford's nephew?"

"All the furniture in here was, but not all the furniture you see will have been left by Wilbert. We brought our furniture and things from Frithwood so all the decent pieces you see will be ours. All he wanted was the money to pay off his gambling debts. It was an easy way out for him. He got the money without any of the work involved in removing anything he did not want to keep," he told her.

"But there must be some value to some of the articles Lord Wellford left surely?"

"When we were down in the autumn and we had a look around the estate I did not take much notice of the contents that were left in the house. I was not expecting to get any of it, so there was no use trying to guess its value.

"I did not want him demanding any of the items back he had left here. If I had got rid of them, he could demand money for them as they are legally his. His lawyer suggested the clause so that any items left in or on the estate on completion of the sale would be legally ours. If I am to do all the hard work, sorting everything out and getting rid of all the rubbish nobody wants; I think it is only fair that Wilfred signed the contents over to us. Don't you?"

"Yes, I do. I think he got the better deal."

He laughed at her and remarked, "There are one or two things left that are going to be worth the effort. To be truthful, Clara, I don't think the nephew did a lot of looking around. Now I have had the time to have a good look at all the items left here and assess the contents, there are some good bits of furniture in some of the rooms.

"Some of the ornaments and tea sets must be worth quite a bit of money. If Wilfred had not been so idle, he could have taken most of the contents and sold them on. It serves him right for not taking the trouble to find out. There is a grand piano for a starter. Do you play?"

"No, I don't. Do you?"

"I have done a bit, I can get a decent tinkle out sometimes." He smiled at her.

"You are full of surprises, Lord Hunter."

"There are plenty more to come."

She asked, "Such as?"

"All in good time, Clara, my darling, all in good time." Their eyes met, and Clara felt herself blushing, and she looked away.

"Do you notice something different about this room?" she changed the subject.

Looking around he asked, "In what way, different?"

"There are no pictures on the walls in here."

Edwin cast his eyes around the room and had to agree.

"What do you think that signifies?"

"I do not know it was just an observation. About that book, have you looked amongst the books in here? If he spent most of his time in this room, then Lord Wellford could have been studying the book, trying to find out its secret.

"Maybe he did not like all the miserable old men in the portraits looking down on him as he searched. It could be he thought they were laughing at him because all the previous owners had tried to find the treasure and they too had failed."

"Maybe you are right. Let's have a quick look through these books, shall we?"

They checked the spines of the books on the bookshelves, flicking off the dust, but came across nothing of import.

"What about the desk?" Clara suggested.

"It's worth a try I suppose."

Their search turned up nothing.

"If there is a secret room, I think it is here, in this room. All this wainscoting, all these panels look the same. What if one of them is a door and all we have to do is find the catch to release it," Clara was now feeling excited.

"Do you really think there is a secret room?"

"Don't you?"

"If I am to be brutally honest, Clara, no, I do not. I have outlived my childhood passion for secret rooms and passages a long time ago. It was Lee and Tom that got my imagination going again, but at seven and twenty, alas, my dreams have been dashed once again."

"Why did you ask me to come and have a look at what progress you have made since you came here when you have not shown me anything you have done yet?" Clara wanted to know. "All you have shown me are one or two rooms I have already seen, and nothing has been done to these. Now you tell me you do not think there is even a secret room to find."

"I thought it was the easiest way to get you here," he confessed.

"Why didn't you just ask me?"

"I didn't think you would come."

"Why did you think that?"

"I thought you had a liking for Captain Bottomly."

"Captain Bottomly!" she exclaimed, "What made you think that?"

"It had something to do with you making sheep's eyes at him when he came to Badger Manor, and he kissed the back of your hand," he remarked.

"I did nothing of the sort," Clara glared at him.

"I beg your pardon, my mistake."

Clara looked across the room at Lord Hunter. If he had thought she had flirted with Captain Bottomly, maybe Captain Bottomly had thought the same, and that is why he had told her he liked her. Lord Hunter made her feel guilty for something she had not been aware of, and she snapped, "I think I had better go."

"I am sorry if I offended you, Clara, it was not intended, I can assure you."

"You have nothing to apologise for, it has nothing to do with you, but I feel I must go home now. Thank you for your hospitality." She turned and left the room.

Lord Hunter ran after her, "I will walk you home."

"There is no need to do that, I shall cut across the lawn and climb over the boundary wall, and I will be home in no time. Good afternoon, Lord Hunter."

Lord Hunter walked into the library, went over to the window and watched Clara's straight back get smaller the further away she went until she disappeared altogether.

Now what did I say to her to make her rush off like that, Lord Hunter thought to himself.

Tears ran down Clara's face as she made her way home. She had liked Captain Bottomly on further acquaintance and hearing Lord Hunter say he had seen her making sheep's eyes at him had upset her. She had not intended to mislead Captain Bottomly in any way; she was not a flirt.

By the time Clara reached home, she had dried her tears and was back in control of herself, or so she thought.

As Clara was making her way back home over the fields, Oscar was heading up the long drive of Davey Grange with Effie still encased inside the carriage.

The house was quiet, and Clara felt alone for the first time in her life. She had been given a note by Trueman from Harvey, saying he and the twins had gone off to Ducks Crossing, and Oscar had taken Effie back home. She could not wait for her brothers to return and fill the house with noise once more.

But when Oscar returned home from dropping Effie off, he did not say anything at all to Clara. He went into the library and shut the door.

After an hour Clara could stand it no longer, so she tapped on the library door and went in. She found Oscar standing at the window with his back towards her. She did not think he had even heard her come in.

Walking over to Oscar she slipped her arms around his waist and held him tight. He, in turn, looked down at his sister's face and saw that she had been crying.

"Something wrong, Clara?" he asked kindly.

She nodded and asked him, "And with you?"

He nodded, "Do you want to talk about it?"

"You know when I had been talking to Captain Bottomly, and I came in crying, and you asked me what was wrong, and I said I would tell you one day?"

"I remember."

"He said the first time he saw me he thought I was the most beautiful thing he had ever seen. I was extremely surprised by this remark for I remember seeing him, but he had not made an impression on me.

"The captain also said, 'I knew the first time I saw you I had lost my heart,' or words to that effect. That was what made me cry. It made me cry because that had also happened to me, but I had not realised it at the time. I knew the first time I saw someone that he was the one for me; it just felt so natural to be in his company." She started to cry again.

Oscar stood and held his sister while she cried herself out, "The special someone wouldn't be Edwin Hunter by any chance, would it?"

Clara nodded and sobbed, "Edwin accused me of making sheep's eyes at Captain Bottomly and he made me feel guilty. Do you think Captain Bottomly thought I was making sheep's eyes at him?"

"No, Clara, I do not think Captain Bottomly thought you were flirting with him, but I do know Edwin was insanely jealous of him, of the way Captain Bottomly looked at you. I thought Edwin was going to punch him."

"I never saw Captain Bottomly looking at me," Clara told him.

"No, my little innocent, I don't suppose you did."

"You think Lord Hunter is jealous of Captain Bottomly?"

"Oh yes, very jealous. You should look at yourself in the mirror sometime, Clara, and see what we men see. You are very beautiful, and I am surprised more men are not knocking on the door."

"What makes you think Lord Hunter is jealous of Captain Bottomly?"

"He told me."

"Lord Hunter told you he was jealous of Captain Bottomly. I find that hard to believe."

"Have you ever known me to lie to you?"

"No."

"Then why should I lie about that?"

"Was he having you on?"

"No."

"I don't know what to make of it; I hope you are right. I like the thought of Lord Hunter being jealous. That is enough about me. What about you, why are you so sad?"

"I told Effie I loved her and it did not go down very well. In fact, she says I am an imbecile, and now she is not talking to me."

Clara burst out laughing, "Effie called you an imbecile. What on earth for?"

"I have just told you, I told her I loved her."

"That cannot be the reason, Oscar."

"It was really confusing, Clara. She let me hold her hand and sat so close to me our thighs were touching, but she ignored me and she would not speak to me. I asked her why she did not have an answer for me, why she was not replying to my confession that I loved her, and do you know what she said? 'You have not said anything yet that deserves an answer.' What sort of reply is that?"

"Did you ask her to marry you?"

"Of course not, how can I? I explained my circumstances and told Effie I would not be able to get married for five, six or even seven years. How could I ask anyone to marry me and take on the twins? And then there was you. I did not want you to think I was replacing you with Effie, Clara. You have run this house more or less since our parents died. But then again, how could I ask Effie to let you keep running the house when she would be mistress here if we married."

"It is no wonder she is not talking to you. Did you ask her if she minded about the twins? After all, they did adopt her, and she was very pleased about that. As for me, Oscar, I would go and live with Harvey, or at Bluebell House, sorry Ducks Crossing, and the twins can come and live there with me until they leave school. Or the twins and I can go and live with Harvey. You no longer have to be the only one to be responsible for all of us Oscar.

"Poor Effie, you do her an injustice, she loves the twins as much as we do. For you to insinuate she would want you to get rid of the twins, or me, is an insult to her intelligence. No wonder she thinks you are an imbecile; I think she is right. Go get her, Oscar, and don't take no for an answer."

"You think so?"

"I think so. If you don't, then you really are an imbecile."

"What you said about Captain Bottomly saying as soon as he saw you, he knew you were the one for him, well as soon as I saw Effie, that first day in Frithwood and she stood up gallantly to Harvey's innuendo about her being loaded. That was my downfall. I thought she was magnificent and Effie had done no flirting with me, it just happened, and I have not been able to get her out of my mind since."

"Why are you telling all this to me? It is Effie that wants to hear it. Not that I don't want to hear it, of course, I do, but I do understand why you said it, and I am sure Effie does too. You are making a huge mistake by not asking Effie to marry you, Oscar. These are poor misguided excuses, and you must go immediately and sort it out.

"That first day at Frithwood was when I knew there was something about Edwin that I liked, but I was too inexperienced to understand what it was. Exactly like you when you looked at Effie when Harvey told her she was loaded and the twins thought he meant she had a big bust and they burst out laughing, I looked across at Lord Hunter.

"He was looking at me and our eyes met. Something happened to me. I did not realise what it was until Captain Bottomly came out with his statement and it upset me because I was like you, Oscar, I thought I could not leave you to look after the twins on your own and to run the house as well.

"We are both being utterly silly. Harvey is quite grown up now, I know he acts silly sometimes, but he is a tower of strength in an emergency, and I know he would want the twins to go and stay with him as well. Here we are, you and I, feeling sorry for ourselves and all the time the twins will end up with more homes to go to than the King," Clara looked up at her brother with shining eyes and a dazzling smile.

"Captain Bottomly was right about one thing, Clara, you are very beautiful and I am very proud of you, I am proud of all of you, and I love you all very, very much. The thought of any of you thinking I wanted to get rid of you was more than I could bear. We have been through some bad times, Clara, but we have come out of it all right, haven't we?"

"Yes, we have, and we could not have done it without you."

"Right, I am off to see Effie."

"I will come with you and get Lord Hunter out of your way."

"Oh really, I do not mind at all you using me as an excuse to go and see him, but I should go and wash your face before we go if I were you," he pointed at his eyes and drew a ring in the air with his finger adding, "Messy."

"I have no need to use you as an excuse, Oscar, Lord Hunter and I are trying to find the secret room or something like that."

"Still harping on about that, are you? I will not ask you what that or something is, better to live in ignorance and let my mind wander."

"Someone has to find the secret room, and I am determined it is going to be me," Clara ignored her brother's last remark, but he did not miss the smile on her face before she turned and went to wash it.

Only three more days to Christmas and I have a feeling it is going to be our best Christmas ever, thought Oscar while he waited for his sister to re-join him.

Chapter Seventeen

Wilson opened the front door and informed Oscar that his lordship and Miss Effie were in the sitting room.

"Thank you, Wilson, we will announce ourselves."

"Very well, sir."

Oscar opened the door without knocking and caught Effie by surprise, and she jumped up quickly. Oscar heard her sharp intake of breath and smiled across at her.

Clara caught Lord Hunter's eye and said, "We have some paintings to sort out I believe."

Lord Hunter was up and leading Clara out of the room before Effie could protest.

When the door had closed behind Edwin and his sister, Oscar walked purposely forward and took Effie in a crushing embrace and kissed her passionately.

Effie did not object but returned his kiss with just as much passion.

Lifting up his head, he asked, "Will you marry me, Effie?"

"Certainly, I will marry you, Oscar, but I am telling you now, I shall not wait six or seven years, or even five," she said with her head resting on his shoulder.

"Good, because I cannot wait six or seven years either. Clara tore a strip off me, told me I had done you an injustice by thinking you wanted me to get rid of the twins. If I offended you, Effie, I apologise. I did it with the best intentions and of course thinking about it now, I was an imbecile. Are you sure you want to be married to an imbecile?"

"Yes, Oscar, I am quite sure. You have done much better second time around," and while her arms were around him, she patted him on the back.

If Effie had looked up, she would have seen a self-satisfied grin as wide as the ocean on Oscar's face, but then again, if Oscar had looked down, he would have seen a knowing smile playing on Effie's lips.

In the hall, Lord Hunter asked Clara, "Which room shall we start on first?"

"Why not start where we left off last time, in the smoking room."

"The smoking room it is, but there are no paintings in the smoking room for us to look at, as well you know."

Once the smoking-room door had been closed behind them, Edwin asked, "Are you feeling alright now, Clara?"

"Perfectly well, thank you."

"What did I say to you that made you turn and run?"

"If you must know, Captain Bottomly told me he liked me, and when you said I had been making sheep's eyes at him, I thought I had given him the wrong impression. I rather liked him when I got to know him better, and I did not want him thinking I had been leading him on. Oscar told me I had not and that you made the remark because you were jealous of the way Captain Bottomly had been looking at me."

"The devil he did."

"Yes, he did. Was Oscar lying to me?"

"No, but Oscar should have kept his big mouth shut."

Clara looked at him and her eyes danced, he was lost.

Edwin let his eyes wander down to her breast and linger there, and then raising his eyes to meet hers, his comment was, "Effie is not the only one who is loaded."

"I didn't think you had noticed."

"I have noticed," his voice was husky.

Clara walked across the carpet to him where he was perched on the edge of the desk and pushed herself between his legs and asked, "What exactly do you mean by me being loaded?"

His eyes wandered down again and came to rest on her breast. They lingered there for a few seconds before coming up to meet her gaze.

"You have bulges where bulges should be and very nice, they are too," his hands now on either side of her hips.

"They might be false."

"They had better not be."

Clara swiftly turned and walked back over to the fireplace out of his reach and said, "I wonder if Captain Bottomly thinks I am loaded."

"Captain Bottomly had better keep his thoughts to himself if he knows what is good for him."

Edwin was just about to follow Clara across the carpet and stand no more nonsense from her when the door burst open and Effie and Oscar walked in, both grinning from ear to ear.

"Damn it, Oscar, your timing is deplorable," snapped his lordship.

"Don't blame me, blame your sister, she could not wait to come and tell you both we are getting married," said Oscar smugly.

Effie ran over to Clara and gave her a big hug then she ran across the room and threw herself at her brother and promptly started to cry.

"What are you crying for now?" asked her dumbfounded brother.

"I am so happy," she sobbed.

"Here, Oscar, take this leaking tap off me and get lost, the pair of you. I was talking to Clara when you so rudely interrupted," a frustrated Edwin told them.

"You can talk to Clara anytime. Oscar and I are going back to the Manor to tell Harvey and the twins our good news. Are you coming with us?" Effie asked dabbing at her eyes and completely ignoring her brother.

"Yes, of course, we are. I can't wait to hear what Harvey has to say about Lord Hunter becoming his brother-in-law," Clara laughed.

Clara and Effie walked along in front of the two men, arms around each other's waist and Effie said, "You know when Harvey said I was loaded, Clara? Well, I am not the only one that is loaded. I have found out that Oscar is loaded too, in that department," and they both started giggling.

Edwin looked at his friend, and his shoulders shook in silent laughter.

Oscar chose to ignore both Effie's comment and Edwin's mirth with poised silence.

"Is he? I never thought about Oscar like that. I have seen the twins and Harvey, of course. I had to bathe them, and I will tell you this, Harvey was a stinker. I had to practically hold him down in the bathtub and make him get washed, and I always ended up wetter than he was, but Oscar, no, I have never seen him without clothes."

"What about Edwin, is he loaded in that department?" Effie wanted to know.

"Effie, I am sorry to have to inform you, your brother, I am afraid, is a very slow worker. I think he is afraid of treading on Captain Bottomly's toes. Edwin has only got as far as telling me he thinks I am also loaded. All in the right places, of course. It might take a while for me to find out about him, but I will let you know when I do. Don't hold your breath though, Effie. I would not want your death on my conscience."

It was Oscar's turn to look across at his friend's embarrassment, and Edwin was pushed into saying, "I think our two sisters need teaching a lesson. Don't you, Oscar?"

"I could not agree with you more. I will leave it up to you to dish out the punishment to my sister, whilst I deal with yours."

"I could not have put it better myself," agreed his lordship.

Effie and Clara looked at each other then broke away, one running to the left and the other to the right.

The two gentlemen watched as the two ladies sped away in opposite directions.

Edwin said with a delighted smile on his face, "I think we have given them enough head start, don't you?"

It was Oscar that caught his wayward bride-to-be first, and they were completely oblivious to Clara's squeals of delight when his lordship caught her around her waist and spun her to face him. The squeals were silenced.

"Will you marry me, my beautiful, innocent, Clara?" Edwin asked after a while.

"Now I have found out that you are indeed loaded, I can hardly refuse can I. Of course, I will marry you, Edwin."

Edwin burst out laughing and added, "You and Effie between you will send me 'round the bend. You do know that, don't you?"

"Yes, dear, but we will come and visit you in the asylum."

When Harvey and the twins were told of the good news, none of them were surprised, but they all agreed it was going to be the best Christmas ever.

They were all sitting around the dining table on Christmas day when Effie suddenly stood up once dinner was over and went behind the sofa. She came back to the table carrying a large brown paper parcel tied up with string with big black letters written across the front that read:

TO TOM AND LEE, MERRY CHRISTMAS
LOVE FROM EFFIE.

Effie handed the parcel over to Tom and said, "Merry Christmas to you both, I hope you like it."

"Hurry up, and open it, Tom," Lee said impatiently.

"It is addressed to both of us so, I think you should help me rip some of the paper off too," Tom told him and that is what they did.

With the paper removed and the painting of Ducks Crossing was revealed to all, Effie was relieved to find it met with approval from everyone, especially, Tom and Lee, who thought it was the best Christmas present they have ever had.

Harvey asked the twins, "Shall we three go and put the board up at Bluebell House? The sooner everyone knows that 'Bluebell House' is now called 'Ducks Crossing' the better?"

"Oh yes, please, Harvey," said Lee and Tom together. The twins ran over to Effie and kissed her on the cheek then shot out of the room with their brother.

When the three young men had left the table, Clara said to Edwin, "What has happened to Granddad, I noticed the other day that he had gone missing."

"I have sent him to be cleaned," he told her, "Shall we go into the smoking room and carry on trying to find that elusive book?"

"I think that is a very good idea," Clara stood up when Edwin moved her chair back for her.

Alone in the dining room Oscar pulled Effie to her feet and kissed her, and there wasn't even any mistletoe over her head.

"Effie, thank you, thank you for doing that sign for Tom and Lee, it means so much to me that you would put yourself to the trouble for the twins like that. It was a lovely thing to do."

"You do not have to thank me for that, Oscar, I did it because I love the twins, they are adorable, and I also enjoyed doing it too. I only hoped you would all think it was good enough to be put outside for everyone to see. I am no artist you know."

"It is perfect, just like you," and he kissed her again.

Lord Hunter and Clara were doing much the same thing in the smoking room. When Edwin released Clara, they proceeded to look for the diary. It was Clara who came across it, sitting on top of the mantelpiece covered in dust.

Knocking before they entered the dining room Clara ran over to show Oscar the book. The four of them spent the next hour reading the diary, trying to make sense of it. The only reference that was made to any treasure in the book was written amongst other entries, and it read:

Anyone interested in the treasure must use their eyes. It is hidden in plain sight for all to see.

"No mention of a secret room or passage or anything. If the treasure is, or was, in plain sight, it must have been found years ago. That is why Lord Wellford never found it. But who knows, there might never have been any treasure in the first place," Clara said.

"The twins will be disappointed, that there is no secret room mentioned," Effie said.

"It might be a good thing for they do tend to rise early. I can just imagine them walking along a secret passage making howling sounds at 6 o'clock in the morning."

They all laughed, and a comfortable silence fell around them until Oscar asked, "Did we tell you about Mr Redfern, the innkeeper of The Monks Den?"

"He went away, didn't he?" said Edwin.

"He did. But you remember me telling you once if you do the smugglers a good turn, they do you one back. Just before they left, Mr Redfern came knocking on our door. He had some really good fishing rods and fishing tackle he could not take with him, so he wanted to ask the twins if they wanted it. He said one good turn deserves another.

"Unfortunately, they were in bed when he called, and he did not see them, needless to say, Tom and Lee did not say no when they saw the fishing tackle. Clara had intended to wrap it all up for them for Christmas, but it was left outside on the porch where Mr Redfern had placed it and, as you say, Edwin, they are early risers. They spotted all the tackle before we could hide it from them.

"Mr Redfern also gave me a key he had made for the secret room in the cellar at Davey Grange. He said, as he had to give the keys back because of the revenue men, and he knew he would need the key to be able to get back into the room to remove the merchandise and finally deliver it, so he had a spare key made. He no longer has need of the key so he asked me to pass it on to you. It is over at Badger Manor. I will give it to you the next time you come over," Oscar told Edwin.

"I suppose I am a few trout short in my lake then if the twins have new fishing rods?" Edwin smiled.

"I am not sure about them using Mr Redfern's rods, they are a bit big for them at the moment, but I am not saying you are not a few trout short in your lake either. Very tasty they were, I must admit. You were in Frithwood at the time, or we would have invited you over to partake," Oscar told him.

Easter came, and the double wedding took place, and Clara found herself mistress of Davey Grange. It was not much different from being mistress at Badger Manor except it was bigger, colder and still full of dust in most of the rooms.

One morning, Edwin said to Clara, "I have had a letter from Smithsons. They are the firm that I sent that portrait of Granddad to, to have it cleaned. Remember?"

"Granddad, oh yes, I remember. I had forgotten about him."

"They write that the portrait is worth a lot of money, by a famous painter, Rubens, and did we want to sell it?"

"Do you think he was trying to tell us something?"

"Who was trying to tell us something?"

"The old man in the painting, of course, the one we called Granddad."

"Tell us something, such as?"

'Anyone interested in the treasure must use their eyes. It is hidden in plain sight,' Clara quoted.

"You think the painting is the treasure?"

"Not just that painting, the house is stuffed with them. What if there is more than one painting worth a lot of money? Hence, treasure in plain sight."

"I hope you are right, Clara. We could use some money to help restore this estate. It is soaking money up like dry sand soaks up water. Do you know anything about paintings?"

"No, do you?"

"No."

"Effie might, she likes painting."

"No harm in asking, shall we go and see her?"

"Missing her already, are you?"

"I would not mind casting my eye over her; I cannot deny it."

"In that case, my darling, Edwin, let us depart for Badger Manor. Will you sell the painting of Granddad?"

"No, that is one painting I will not sell, that is our painting, Clara. I shall always think he approved of us, the way he was smiling down on us, so I intend to keep him."

"Good, I am pleased to hear it; I like the old man, whoever he is."

Edwin and Clara found Effie feeding the hens. Effie's face lit up when she saw them.

"I am so pleased to see you both, come on in out of the cold, and we will have some hot chocolate."

In the sitting room sipping hot chocolate, Effie and Clara brought each other up to date with what had been happening since the last time they had seen each other. Edwin had gone to find Oscar who was in the cowshed overseeing the milking of the cows.

Oscar, observing Edwin bearing down on him, strode over to greet him with an outstretched hand.

"This is a pleasant surprise."

"Actually, Oscar, Clara has come to see Effie. We think we have worked out the puzzle of the treasure that has been vexing past tenants of Davey Grange. To be precise, Clara thinks she has worked it out, and I think she is right.

"I sent one of the portraits to be cleaned, an old man, Clara happened to mention she liked it. I have had a letter from the restorer I sent it to, and he informs me it is worth a lot of money and did I want to sell it. Clara thinks that some of the other paintings could be worth a lot of money too.

"There is one room that has paintings covering every wall. Clara thinks the treasure everyone talks about is the paintings, because they are in full sight, as stated in the diary. It sounds logical to me. Clara has come to ask Effie if she knows of anyone, we can ask to come down to have a look at them. We have nothing to lose and everything to gain. If by any miracle Clara is right, half of what we get for the paintings will go to Effie of course."

"She is pretty smart that sister of mine," Oscar said. "It sounds logical to me too, let us keep our fingers crossed that she is right."

Clara explained about the paintings to Effie and she said she knew a Jack Waverly. He owned an art gallery on Forsythe Street in Frithwood. Effie said he was always looking for new paintings to sell in his gallery so she would write and ask him if he was interested in coming down to have a look at them.

Jack Waverly was a tall thin, man of about fifty years of age his dress was immaculate and his boots shone. Mr Waverly was shown the paintings, and he was extremely excited at what he saw.

He walked around the rooms three times, checking and rechecking, the signatures at the corner or each painting.

"You have a fortune here, some of these are by very famous artists, too expensive for me to buy them all off you, but I think I could manage one or two of them. Then when I sell those, I will be down for more. Had you any in mind that you wanted to sell?" he asked Edwin.

"No, we will have to discuss it and see what we want to keep and what we want to sell. We cannot keep all these, if they are valuable, we would end up being the victim of theft. Would you like to stay the night? We will have a family meeting and discuss the matter. Half of them belong to my sister, of course, so she will have to be consulted," Edwin told him.

And so, the mystery of the treasure was solved. Most of the paintings were sold at intervals, and the money was used to bring Davey Grange back to its former glory.

Effie used her share of the windfall for much the same purpose, putting most of it into Badger Manor, and some of it went to help the twins with the cost of restocking Ducks Crossing but she also put a little away for a rainy day, because you never know what life has in store for you.